jogging

sandra hochman
jogging
a love story

TURNER

Turner Publishing Company
Nashville, Tennessee
New York, New York

www.turnerpublishing.com

Jogging, A Love Story

Copyright © 2017, 1979 by Sandra Hochman. All rights reserved.

This is a work of fiction. All the characters and events portrayed in this book are either products of the author's imagination or are used fictitiously.

Cover design: Maddie Cothren
Book design: Glen M. Edelstein

Library of Congress Cataloging-in-Publication Data

Names: Hochman, Sandra, author.
Title: Jogging : a love story / Sandra Hochman.
Description: Nashville, Tennessee : Turner Publishing Company, 2017.
Identifiers: LCCN 2017002568 | ISBN 9781683365167 (pbk. : alk. paper)
Subjects: LCSH: Love stories.
Classification: LCC PS3558.O34 J64 2017 | DDC 813/.54--dc23
LC record available at https://lccn.loc.gov/2017002568

9781683365167

Printed in the United States of America
15 14 13 12 11 10 9 8 7 6 5 4 3 2 1

for Ariel, my daughter
        Rene Schwartz
        Alexandra Schlessinger,
        good friends

"*The gift of Life is the gift of energy. We live through action, movement, change.*"

Richard Grossman
Choosing and Changing

jogging

1.

In his dreams Jerry was making love to the brown-eyed seaweed goddess, his great love from the past: Ursule. She was incredibly beautiful and he entered her body like a sailor sailing home. In the dream she had no age. Then he awakened and found that he was in bed with Lillian, his wife.

He went to the living room. Looked out the window. It was daybreak. The sun on Central Park West made everything pink. He went back to the bedroom and took his jogging shorts and sweat shirt quietly out of the closet so he wouldn't disturb Lillian. Softly he put on his running shoes.

A few moments later he was out in the park. He was relaxing, running at his own pace, slowly breaking into a long run. He felt the high coming, the erotic high. He thought about Ursule. He thought about his autobiography. He began with the miracle, Ursule. When he lived with Ursule by the sea: that was over twenty years ago, he realized, barely believing. They had rented a house in Atlantic City. And they had lived and loved and left. And the sea went on, the green meadows bloomed, his essays were written, the guests were fed and shown around, the drinks were downed and the old painters came to visit. And they lived and loved and laughed and left. They made love on the sand while the moon shone down. Ursule was his sea goddess. He tasted salt water on her breasts and her belly, her cunt. And the summer went on in the sealike place where things bloomed. And he wrote his words, nestled in the wind. And he dragged his thoughts to shore the way fishermen trap lobsters. And he saw the big red lobster claws and he loved them.

He thought of all this while jogging.

In the high he could return to pleasant things.

Nostalgia? The desire to return to the past?

That was then. This was now.

2.

Once Jerry Hess wrote beautiful prose. Now he was beyond all that, beyond the need, too, for money. He didn't even know what his assets were nor what he owed the government. His wife, Lillian, took care of all that. She was always ahead of *things*. Knew about *things* before anyone else. The one thing Lillian knew nothing about was *motion*. When he discovered that he could imitate the agitation of nature by jogging she told him that he was wasting his time.

"Why jogging? What does it do for you? Is it the pain that appeals to you?" she asked.

"I don't feel pain. I'm in better shape than you think."

"Well, can't you find better things to do with your time?" Her face grew hard and obstinate. A fury was building.

"Lillian, when was the last time you tried something new?"

"Why don't you stop finding fault with me, Jerry?"

"Well, why don't you simply try it? I bought you running shoes."

"They were grotesque. Especially as an anniversary present."

"Didn't you think they were a symbolic present? Wouldn't you like to run away from our marriage?" He was *projecting*.

"Stop questioning and cross-examining me, Jerry. If only you would stop asking me question after question. It's like being in court these days even when I come home from court."

"As you wish," he said.

She walked up and down the hallways of the apartment with an air of concealed anxiety. Suddenly she looked at the man she had lived with for twenty years. She had a soft expression, recognizable as her mixture of remorse and tenderness at inflicting unwitting sorrow upon others. She smiled at him. It was the face of the old Lillian. The Danish girl he had fallen in love with and married. But he knew that face would not last. Once more the peculiar shadow of her discontent would cast itself over the fourteen-room apartment, over the relationship. Another scene would follow. There was a deep ache inside Jerry Hess. But it wasn't sorrow. Rather, it was the ache of a man who publicly has everything. An exhaustion of the spirit took over his body as he sat in a grey velvet chair quietly smoking a Gauloise and looking at his wife.

A forty-two-year-old bounder with large blue eyes and thick blond hair, no wrinkles, small nose, high cheekbones, muscles in shoulders, thick chest hairs, flat stomach, runner's thighs, all the senses sharp—thriving arteries and veins that led him to this question: Who am I? The handsome, urbane art merchant, walking through crowds, surrounding himself with "finished" people who have adapted themselves to who they were, moving through living rooms, dinner parties, restaurants, offices, art galleries, moving over the track of Central Park, the West Park Racquet Club, The Turtle Bay Swimming Club in the United Nations Hotel, the Century for lunch, the discotheque after dinner, Cachaca, Studio 54, eating at Melon's, banking at Morgan Guaranty, shopping at Gucci,

4

walking down Madison Avenue, the word "handsome" shining over him like a cloud ("masculine" might be more the word)—smelling of something hidden which women pick up, the strong smell of a virile man, a man still young and carefree, a man strong in the legs—with a nimble lexicon, a man who punned, who liked good books and good wine—who treasured his desk, his opera tickets, his son, a man who heard voices in shells, who was tough and quick-tempered, a man who liked to run, who knew what to do with himself on Saturdays, stalking under the sun, a man familiar in the boot of Italy, the handprint of France, the dots of Japan, a man who walked down the streets, in the sunlight, smelling of health and good nature, a man laughing at the fables of his life, feeding on sunshine, sadness banished under the mask of suntan, an idle peddler out for a walk.

The eye. The nervous eye. Or was it a "Nervous I" and the body was trying to tell him something? Jerry knew that he should listen to the body. Jerry Hess seldom looked in the mirror. When he did spy on himself he wasn't disappointed in what he saw. His body was strong, the body of an athlete. He had played Shakespearean roles at Harvard before he left and his voice was his outstanding feature. It was a cheerful voice, deep and never unhappy or whining. It was a voice that gave confidence to hesitant clients. It was never hard, or pressured. It was not a voice that betrayed confusion. Once, when a client was accompanying Jerry Hess to the airport, discussing the purchase of a rare Cézanne—a tulip in a vase—the client had been struck with the seeming perfection of Jerry Hess's life. Driving back to the city, the client asked the chauffeur, "What is the secret of Jerry Hess's confidence? Why is he always so happy?" The reply came: "It's because he has no problems, sir."

Jerry's hands were the hands of a peasant, and it was in his hands that his strength showed. They were hands that liked to stroke large dogs, hands that when he had held his baby son were gentle; they were also hands that had plunged through a window

5

and given, on occasion, black eyes and split lips to bums who had tried to rough him up. Wherever he was seen, at art auctions, at gambling casinos in Europe or the Bahamas, at ski resorts, there was a passionate strength about Jerry Hess that attracted both women and men. He had a touch of the brute in his face.

Jerry had gone for a medical checkup. "The best in the city," Dr. Tustmaker was not a man to mince matters.

"Your body's great, Jerry, but there's something that I don't like. You complain about a twitch in your eye. How long has that been going on?"

"I told you. I've been twitching away for about a week."

"It's the classic case of anxiety, Jerry. Stress. I don't like it."

"And you think I like it?"

"You've got to cut out whatever is bothering you."

"OK, first I'll get rid of Lillian. Then I'll put all my art in storage. But suppose after all that I'm still twitching?"

"OK. What's bothering you?"

"I'm thinking of making a lot of changes. They're exciting, but frightening."

"We pay for change just as we pay for material things. If yours is a change with a sense of purpose it can be exhilarating." (God, doctors are often so boring, Jerry thought. So *sure* of everything.)

"But it's not clear to me yet exactly the changes I want to make." Jerry was putting on his clothes. "You see, for me the first gift of life is the gift of energy. We live through movement, action, change. I think that *change* should be sought by everyone in search of self-realization and self-fulfillment. Change is the way we build a future. My problem is I don't know exactly what I want to change yet. I know that change is not turning oneself into someone different, but rather an *expansion* of what one really is." (Was he *boring* too?)

"You're on the right track, Jerry. There's nothing I can do about that nerve in your eye. It's not organic."

The doctor watched Jerry carefully as he left the office. A man of medium height, still with all his hair, a tanned strong body, the walk of an athlete. Was that nervous eye the price he was paying for *insight*?

6

He loved jogging.

Why? Lillian had asked him. It made him feel fresh. Good. Young. It took him away from Lillian and her spoiled executor's personality. She was a good lawyer. A successful one. But she was used to manipulating his time—and that annoyed him. She planned everything. Vacations. Sex. Portfolios. Dinners. His life. Her life. Their son's life. She overplanned. One day the dog chewed up the datebook and she cried. The dog had chewed up her plans. When he had first met her in Copenhagen, she had a mischievous sparkle in her large green eyes. Now they were the hard, green, unsmiling eyes of a lawyer.

That's why he jogged. He knew it. To get away from her. But somewhere in all his running was a new frontier. He felt it when he ran for the first time and now, after running for two years, he still felt it. He felt that underneath his tight skin there was someone else there. The subterranean writer. The marathon runner. The hunter. There was another, younger Jerry with whom he had made friends in order to live. Under the fear of growing old was a person who understood the workings of the body. Good eating habits. Good music. Mobility. It was true that by moving he felt younger. That he might, singularly, defeat death: certainly the aging process. Jogging made him want to be better in everything he dreamed of doing. Made him want to make love. He feared death now too often. He woke now, quite often, sweating. Was this the menopausal trauma he had heard about? Was he to go from infancy to menopause without stopping for maturity?

The inner track around the reservoir is one point five miles. Jerry Hess jogged around this track four times a day. When he jogged his six miles in the morning in Central Park, he was just one of the many runners, all with different costumes and getups. Running at their own speed. He loved

7

watching the women. Some ran without anything under their shirts. He could see their breasts moving up and down. These women seemed ready to make love. They had sweat pouring down their faces and were steamy and sensual. They licked their lips as they ran; they took their bodies seriously. Once he had picked up a heavily breathing Mexican woman who ran so well she could have been a marathon runner. When she noticed him she slowed down.

He jogged with her to her apartment, which was on York Avenue. It was a modern glass cage, but he barely noticed. She took off her jogging shoes, her shorts, her shirt, and threw herself on the bed. "Mi corazón," she said. Her body was covered with sweat and when she was naked the sweat was streaming down her legs. His cock was hard for hours; she told him earnestly that she hadn't felt any cock that hard for years. He remembered how that excited him and he felt he was drowning in the deep of her. He swam there for hours, in that sea of darkness, until it was too much for both of them, and they came. He had a feeling he could go on forever, forever making love. He felt the jogger's power, giving her pleasure again and again, as if there was no end to the motion of love. It was the first time he felt a new poetry in him, a new potency.

"*Mi corazón, mi corazón,*" was all she said.

Jogging made him want to fuck.

It also made him realize that he had his own world. Away from the art world, tycoonery, phonies, problems, the constant distractions of telephones, clients, lunches at Les Pléiades and Le Périgord. It was his release. Running. His own space. His own key to finding his former self. Often he felt like a he-camel in distress, or, worse, a mechanical toy. He was often tired of his sleepwalking life. He felt he was not real. Jogging was where life was better than he could ever imagine. Into himself he ran. He ran smack into who he was.

3.

Running.
  Running.
  Why the hell am I running? It was a question he asked when he first started jogging and he found himself hating to get up in the early morning and move his legs when he would have preferred to sleep. At that time he was aware that his body was aging and had become *alien* to him. The fact that not only Lillian was a stranger, but that he was a stranger to himself began to take hold of him with an annoying, perplexing regularity. His dreams were seldom erotic. His own flesh was becoming distant to him. He was a stranger to his own life. He never could be alone, or free to do as he pleased, except when he was in motion.
  "We don't have a marriage, Lillian. We have projects," he said gently to her one morning as she scribbled down notes on a yellow pad at breakfast. Lillian, not one to waste time, always kept him occupied with her "business propositions."

"That's all part of the operation of being rich," she said cheerfully without looking at him.

They were sitting in the dining room looking out at one of the best views of Central Park in New York. He had read, once, that the earth was most fertile where the most death was. In all his wealth he felt death. It was morning, and Lillian was already giving him *orders.*

"Jerry, for Christ's sake, don't come late to the screening." Lillian was always going to a meeting or a screening. She was fanatic about punctuality.

"What difference does it make?" he asked, passing the white napkin over his lips and wishing she could be quietly erased without anyone tracing the crime to him. How could he *kill* her without anyone knowing? He could *snuggle* her to death. Had snuggling ever been the reason for murder? He thought about it as he ate his rye toast. He didn't see why not. It left no trace. He could pretend to hug her one morning, in bed, just snuggle her and shut that mouth forever. The thought was pleasant to him.

"This screening is important. The producer's my client."

"Why do you need me?"

"I don't *need* you. I want you there."

"I think I've got a late appointment. I know I'm scheduled to meet a collector—"

"Why are you so infantile? Do you have to depend on your secretary to wipe your fucking behind?"

"I just don't happen to recall who or when."

"Well, fuck it. I want you at the screening."

"Why?"

"Because the picture is going to Cannes, darling, and I'd like your opinion."

"I don't know anything about movies. It's a stupid business."

"The picture happens to be about Michelangelo."

"What does that have to do with me?"

"You're supposed to be a fucking expert on the Renaissance."

"Stop saying 'fucking' all the time. It's annoying."

"Well if I were doing it more, I wouldn't be saying it."

10

"We can't do it when you're always at the office or a screening. We never seem to even meet in bed."

"What the hell could you *do* if we were in bed?"

He knew what *that* meant. He hadn't been able to get it really up *for her* in two years. Perhaps she thought, in her vast ignorance, it was his fault.

"I could snuggle you."

"What does that mean?"

"Never mind."

"Well, if at all possible, perhaps you would care to meet me at the screening room. It's at 425 Fifth Avenue."

"You don't need me there."

He wondered why he was behaving like someone mentally ill. Why did he put up with her? Why not just tell her to fuck off?

She softened. "I'm sorry. I'm in a bad mood this morning. You don't know what a struggle it is to be working on this estate case." She got up from the breakfast table and kissed him. He wondered if he should tell her he was leaving her. He wondered if there was anyone running around the reservoir that he could follow home and fuck. He wondered why he lived his life under sedation in the unspeaking peril of being Lillian's husband. Lillian was the sort of woman who brought red, shiny remote telephones to the pool at their house in East Hampton. She listened all summer long to news on her remote radio. She was the remote *woman*. Why didn't he just remove her and have done with it?

"Do you know that almost all crimes that take place in the morning are domestic crimes?" he said.

"You made that up, Jerry."

"I did. But it sounds good."

She sat there eating her toast. He wished she had an ex-husband to go back to. He wished she would run—for the state senate—and he could be left in peace while she lived in Albany.

"I don't know if you've noticed, but I think I look younger since I began running."

"I've noticed. I know it's a national craze. But what do you really get out of it? Why is it so important to you?" (Her eternal question.)

11

"I told you, I look younger. It's fun to run around the park. It's a nice way to experience New York City."

"That makes more sense than any other explanation."

Had he ever really enjoyed making love to her? It seemed beyond his comprehension. Why was he the mammal in captivity? He flapped around in the domestic pool, flapped his wings, barked a little, trained to behave exactly the way a seal behaves in captivity. Everyone thought they were so happy. Jerry and Lillian. So much for public opinion. She was a good zoo keeper. She tossed him his sardines. Kept the pool clean. Polished the equipment. But did he really want to be a seal?

It wasn't just that Lillian had stopped loving him. Or that he had stopped loving her. It was that so many other couples seemed to be *friends*. And Lillian was not his *friend*. She was too busy for that. Then, why was he with her? The old soft shoe. "Because of the *children*." But he didn't really have children. He had one son. Was his nearly grown-up son a reason for his captivity?

4.

His son, Jerry, Jr., had one ambition: to be a ski instructor. He was painfully putting up with Deerfield Academy until the day came when he could escape the trivia of books and actually ski for the rest of his life. He had the golden, tight body of an athlete. Jerry had watched enviously while Jerry, Jr., played football in the fall. How he envied his son who had a career of hotdogging ahead of him. Being rich meant that his son could do anything. Jerry, Jr., had the future. Jerry felt alienated from the future. Just as Prospero had been shipwrecked on an island, he, Jerry Hess, was shipwrecked on his own island of marriage in the Dakota. It wasn't such a terrible fate.

The Dakota, with its thick castle walls and turrets, was one of the three or four truly elegant apartment houses left in New York. It had been built when *nobody* lived that far uptown, which was why it was called the Dakota, the inference being that it was *nowhere*. Lillian, with her lawyer's shrewd sense of money management, had made him buy the apartment for a hundred thousand dollars. Now it was worth almost a million. It was on a list of thirty most desirable co-ops in New York—fourteen rooms of Gothic architecture on the outside, old masters and great modern art on the inside. Being a private art dealer meant keeping all the *good stuff* around the apartment. He had El Grecos under the beds. Cézannes in the closets. The study was filled with Rouault clowns. He often felt like a Rouault clown himself.

5.

"Why do you stay with Lillian?" his psychiatrist asked him.
"If I knew, I wouldn't be here, would I?"
"You might be here. And making progress."
"I used to love her."
"And now?"
"I don't think I love her."
"Who do you love?"
"My son. And Cézanne."
"Is Cézanne your favorite artist?" (The analyst thought he had made a *breakthrough*.)
"No. Cézanne is my dog, a black Labrador."
"You love your dog?"
"Yes. And I love fishing. My paintings. My parents. My house in East Hampton. Muhammed Ali. Jogging. Especially jogging."
"Why jogging? What does it do for you?"

He wanted to snuggle the psychiatrist. After he killed Lillian he would kill his analyst. His problem was he never "identified" with his analyst. His doctor had a body like a shmoo. He needed to jog. Jerry thought, perhaps if I had gone into deep therapy with Anna Freud, I might have truly found the key to my anxieties. Anna Freud was a genius. Who the hell was this shrink? And why was Jerry Hess afraid to change? To leave Lillian? To choose other women? To make a new life? All around him were similar men in midlife crisis who were managing to open up their souls to strange, sexual women, rap, and come through the crisis with dignity and new vitality. Why was he *tense*? Why was he *dissatisfied*?

"I'm looking for a cure for tenseness and anxiety."

"There is no magical cure," the doctor said. (How many *times* had he said that?)

What was the *point* of spending thousands of dollars sitting on that couch to be told always there was no cure for what he had? It was all crap!

"Why don't you buy a Jacuzzi?"

Was he serious? Was that what he was paying for? To hear about mechanical bathtubs? Was that the kind of philosophic question Freud had once asked Fliess? Was a *whirlpool* the answer to all of his deep, soul-searching questions?

"We have to stop in a few minutes."

The analyst was a life-coach. He was always telling him when it was time to start to gather his anxieties and start to leave. Perhaps he would have been better off investing money in a vineyard. Wouldn't it be better to put his fingers in the earth? At the end of a few years he'd at least have wine.

"Mr. Hess, I'm going to be taking a vacation. I will not be able to see you next Monday."

His analyst was always taking vacations. He had a good life. He, Jerry Hess, never took vacations. Only business trips. It was the price of being an art dealer.

"Where are you going?"

"I'm sorry, my next patient is here."

His analyst always kept his vacations mysterious. Life was so

16

mysterious. Jerry realized, sadly, he really needed to spend more time with the old gang. The boys he grew up with in Brooklyn. When they felt *anxious*, they went out and bought clothes. That was what it meant to be poor. You *bought* things. When you were rich, you never shopped. You lamented. Complained. Searched. He was tired of his life. Weary. Even weary of analysis.

"You're not in analysis, Mr. Hess. You're in therapy."

"What's the difference?"

"In analysis, you come five times a week and lie on the couch. In therapy, you come four times a week and sit on the couch."

"Why can't I be in analysis, doctor?"

"You're the one who should answer the question for yourself."

"I guess I'm a sit-downer, not a lie-downer."

"What made you late today?"

"I was jogging."

"You have no sense of time."

"I have a sense of survival."

The analyst studied him for a moment then said, "I'm afraid your time is up. Another patient is waiting."

All the patients he saw in the waiting room looked like pleasantly disturbed people. They all carried books to read while they waited. It was almost like being in college. He was studying himself. It was an interesting subject. He wondered when he would graduate in himself. Who was he? When he was jogging it didn't matter. One thing he knew: he loved jogging. It went beyond analysis.

6.

Some mornings he felt that he, Jerry Hess, reluctantly middle-aged art tycoon, was living a third world war, but he didn't know it. It was as if some invisible revolution were taking place in front of him, that made everyone unable to understand what the meaning, the true meaning, of *relationships* really was. His love life was out of shape. That much was clear. In some way he knew that he had surrendered to Lillian; all of his property and soul.

"When are you leaving for Paris?"

"Tomorrow. Why don't you come?"

"Are you crazy? In the middle of an important trial?"

"Pretend I'm your client."

"I have a hard time pretending."

"It's easy. I pretend all the time."

"What do you pretend?"

"That I'm desirable. That I'm still writing. That I enjoy my profession. That I take camping trips."

"Jerry, you're a flamboyant man. I'm often glad I married you."

"How often?"

"What difference does it make? By the way, have you ever thought of buying an airplane?"

"Why?"

"I think it would be a good investment."

Lillian thought of everything as an investment. It was mystical. Everything existed to thwart the Internal Revenue Service. She was constantly flirting with the IRS. There were no joys in life. Only deductions. No delights. Only tax shelters; and the bottom line. She was condemned, professionally, to being in the purgatory of legal stealing. Her brains were pitted against the entire United States government. He didn't have a home. He had a sixty percent tax deduction. He didn't have a wife. He had an auditor. An advisor. She clocked everything he said with her little clock.

I'm going to leave you, Lillian. Why didn't he say it? "Dearest Lillian. I have run away from home because I am horny and need a fresh piece of really tight ass. You never gave good head, Lillian, so I am now in Australia. Good luck to you." Why didn't he write it? Or write her a marital thank-you note.

"Dear Lillian. Thank you so much for the past twenty years of my life. You have managed my money admirably. And the house has always been so clean. The houses I mean. I long to come back and fuck you. In another incarnation. Meanwhile—thanks for the service, the hospitality." If only he could send her a thank-you note and leave. He had a good case against her. She was no longer supple and sexy. She wore cold cream on her face in the morning. Her left foot had a bunion. Was that a reason to hate her? A bunion. Instead they would discuss, intelligently, their relationship. It was a New York hobby. Similar to Backgammon.

"It isn't as good as it used to be," he finally said.

"Are you tired of me?"

"No. Of myself."

"Did you ever think this would happen?"

"No. Did you?"

"No—and I don't understand what you want, Jerry."

"Peace."

"What else?"

"Isn't that enough?"

"What's wrong with you, Jerry?"

"I'm a loner."

"Who isn't?"

"You're not."

"Why do you hate me? I just can't handle this."

"I hate that word, Lillian. You always use it."

"Which word?"

"Handle. You don't *handle* people."

"What other words do I use that you hate?"

"*Life-style*. That's my least favorite expression of yours."

He struggled to understand the meaning of the conversations. Most of them had no beginning and no end. They were just philosophical.

As he did every morning, Jerry fanned out from the Dakota, and ran through Central Park to the track at the reservoir. Getting his body to glide was what he worked for until under his jogging suit he was sweating and his bones moved by themselves. That's what it meant to really run. Muscles, bones, legs, all moving without his really trying to move. He felt as light as helium. It was painful but once he was out there, he was a running machine. He could float through his luck, his life, his love affairs, his deals, his flops, great thoughts of mankind; he could enter easily into the jogging high. He could literally *sail* into the park. As he thought of how much he loved jogging, he also thought of Lillian, and how he had pretended to love her that morning.

"I'm going to Paris next week. I hope you'll come with me."

"Thank you, I have several important meetings."

Good. Then I don't have to take you, he thought. Perhaps there's a little red-light district I can visit with some of the boys from the Louvre.

"Where are you staying?"

"The Crillon."

Another lie. But he couldn't risk her popping in on him.

21

As he ran, thinking of Lillian, he tried to reverse his feeling of dislike to feelings of friendship. Why *couldn't* they be friends? He had written her countless love letters when she was pregnant. He had truly loved her big stomach which looked like a rising handkerchief with a bunny in it—one of those magical acts he had seen so often as a child.

When Lillian was pregnant with Jerry, Jr., everything seemed possible. Magical. A tightrope dance where neither of them could ever fall down. When they first married, they had lived on Riverside Drive. He was building up his art collection then, buying paintings for hundreds of dollars and selling them for thousands.

"My Jerry could sell cigarettes to a cardiac patient," his mother had always said. It was true. He was a good salesman. He looked honest. And understood painting.

Riverside Drive soon became West End Avenue. Finally they had moved to the Dakota, where Jerry, Jr., was born. Nannies followed. So did butlers. So did Filipino cooks who often cut their fingers. Chauffeurs. Dinner parties. Bills from Venice Market. Success grew like a wheel around his life. But it wasn't Buddha's wheel of life and endless death. It was Lillian's wheel. Her Rolodex, to be exact. Her acquaintances, clients, connections, friends, good friends, and best friends filled the largest Rolodex on Central Park West. And they were coded. The friends. On the wheel the pink cards were for rich friends. The white cards were for everyone else. That way, when she was making out a list for a charity or political benefit, she didn't have to bother with those who couldn't possibly contribute anything but their hungry mouths. Lillian was superorganized. She made sure he had what every self-made prince is supposed to have. A co-op. A house on the ocean in East Hampton. A house in Bedford. A movie projector and a screening room in all three houses. A pied-à-terre on the Costa Brava. He had more than that. He had antiques. Boats. Three cars. Shoes and suits by the hundreds. He had tennis racquets and skis even though he didn't really have time to ski or play tennis. They looked good in the hallways of Lillian's life.

7.

Jerry remembered reading about the King of Thule, who ran away from his city every night to embroider a sail in his tower. The winding spool and thread were his only delight. One day, leaving all the hysterical women of the court behind, the King of Thule set sail into the sun. Saying good-bye to women and wealth, he was never heard from again. Wasn't that what he was doing? Setting sail. As Jerry ran through the park to reach the reservoir on a hot sticky spring morning, he realized that was what he was doing. Setting sail. Gliding away from his home every morning. To the track. He had trailed love down to the end. He had heard what the ear could not hear. Seen what the eye could not see. What the mind takes down at night like embroidery. In a sense, he now had nothing but jogging to give him joy. Jerry Hess. King of the Dakota, king of the art world and private wheeling and dealing. Jerry. Running. He was the King of Thule, sailing his boat slowly into the sun.

"If it's all right with you, darling, tonight we're eating dinner at Tino's," Lillian said.

They were always eating dinner out. Whatever happened to a good meal at home? The only time they ever ate at home was at their dinner parties. Otherwise, there were all these elegant little bistros. Lillian only liked expensive restaurants. She needed friends around her, waiters, menus to stare at, orders to give. Italian atmosphere. Whenever Jerry wanted a bowl of chili, he had to sneak off by himself like a fugitive, poring over his banquet of beans.

He was not a self-destructive man. For the past twenty years with Lillian he had cultivated the *jardin* of a good life. He was a most practical man. That was it! The creative writer in him had never developed. It was a cancer inside of his skin. He had married Lillian, been proud of being a lawyer's husband, been proud of her accomplishment. He was not a male chauvinist pig—not a sexist or a class-conscious snob—not a racist—not even gloatingly smug like the other tanned middle-aged Adonises of the Hamptons. He had just arrived at a place where change was not only desirable, it was biologically necessary.

He kept a log.

The price of change will be hard to pay. But I will pay it gladly. What do I want to change to? When was I happiest?

Memory:

I remember when I was a boy and my parents drove up to Vermont for the summer. I was a city boy who fell madly in love with Earth, with seeds that grew, with grass. I had never seen barns painted red, never smelled apples ripening on trees, never walked through a "carriage barn" or felt the green leaves turning in the sun. That was a world without neurosis, a world of holidays and celebration. Wouldn't it be just like me, Jerry Hess, to give up the city and live somewhere in the woods? To return to earth? To give myself a change of life that would go deep down into the essence of solitude? What would it be like to run in the morning in the fields of grass?

That was it. He was tired of the mediocrity of New York. The sameness of the world that he had shaped. Nature was never boring. He could talk to trees. Would that be so horrible?

"What do you mean, talk to trees?"

"I don't know, Lillian. Natural things seem so much better than the life we've carved out for ourselves. Sometimes, when I'm flying back to New York, driving back in the car, I experience culture shock. A certain *nausea* to be back in this huge cage of buildings, miserable human beings, scratching, stressful, trying to live like humans, but breathing filthy air. This is no home."

"Where would you want a home?"

"Vermont?"

"You have to find it in yourself, Jerry. You have to dig into your suffering, dig into your suffering until you feel at home in *yourself*. Inside of you is the home you're looking for. You think a flight to the *country* will change things?"

"At least nature isn't mediocre."

"Perhaps you should start writing again, Jerry. Try to write each day, write slowly, write patiently, write a monograph on Cézanne."

Lillian tried to be helpful.

Jerry thought with horror how much he *owed* her. Was that what kept them together? Gratitude? Lillian had been *good* to him.

Jerry was realizing, slowly, that the marriage was over. He no longer wanted to be married to her. It was up to him to become capable of living without her. And yet . . .

He remembered Lillian when she was young. She had been one of the only women in Harvard Law School, and when he met her, he found her Danish practicality a welcome release from Ursule's theatrics. Doggedly, Lillian applied herself to making him happy. If he loved the sea—she found a house by the sea. If he wanted a party—she took whatever money they had and made a gracious smorgasbord, serving all the golden herrings and pink beet salads and schnapps that he loved. And now he was caught in that situation so many women and men had faced—he had now to destroy everything he had so patiently built in order to feel *whole* again. Was it possible to live without the friendly routine that marriage provided? He saw Lillian when she was young, sitting on a chair at an open window by the sea. They had gone to the South of France for the month of April, soon after the baby was born. His mother had been "thrilled" to play grandmother and he and Lillian had flown to Cannes, the city he knew so well. They had stayed at the Majestic, in a suite that opened up to the sea. He had surprised her with flowers and for her birthday had bought her a watercolor of her favorite painter, Picabia. Jerry knew that although Picabia was long since dead, his dentist lived in Cannes. Figuring that poor painters pay their dentists with pictures, he had spent an afternoon while Lillian swam and rested, climbing the hills of Cannes until he came to the tiny building where Picabia's dentist had lived. He had paid a hundred dollars for a watercolor that was worth at least three thousand, but the dentist was happy to sell it for a hundred. It was of a pregnant woman in blue, from Picabia's early period, when he was still painting figures. Her red-fingernailed hands, long and slim, resting on her pregnant belly were identical to Lillian's hands. When he woke her and presented her with the watercolor she had wept with joy and grief.

"I have everything a woman could want, Jerry. It frightens me."

"Why should it frighten you, sweetheart?"

"It's too much. A beautiful child. A career that I love and am good at. A husband any woman would want—a husband who is thoughtful, generous, and a great lover. I love you so much, Jerry. Sometimes I think if you were drowned or stolen away from me I couldn't live."

"Don't be silly, Lillian. If anything happened to me you would rise like the phoenix."

"No. There are so many things I have never told you."

"Tell me."

"I'm not like you, Jerry. It's so hard for me to tell you everything I know, everything I think, everything I feel. It is hard for me to begin to tell you everything which delights and hurts and astonishes me. When I was a young girl, fresh from Denmark, I always felt like an outsider. My father worked in the embassy and even though I spoke English I had no friends. I developed a fear of solitude. I would sit in the maid's room and read and remember Denmark. My mother had bought me the Betty Betz career book and as I read through the book I saw all of the opportunities that were open to me in America. I imagined being a doctor, a nurse, a fashion illustrator, and finally settled on a lawyer. When other girls were 'dating' I worked to be the best student at Barnard and later, Harvard. My own rule of law was: be on guard against American men. And when I met you—lost—adrift in Copenhagen, where I spent the summer with my relatives—you seemed to *need* me. I listened to your life, to your love affair with Ursule. I told you what I thought. That you should start a new life."

And as the sea air came into the room he held her in his arms. He had so many tender feelings toward Lillian then.

He had appreciated his home, the smell of floor and furniture wax, the order, the flowers, clean linen, clean windows, the polished silverware, the knowing what he was doing each night. He had appreciated not having to "think" about Lillian. She was independent, self-sufficient as a cat, caused no trouble, made no scenes, and he had an ecstatic awareness of her gifts. She was smart, helpful, tactful; those were the days when Lillian seemed the essence of the *order* that he sought. What had happened? When had he stopped bringing presents? Being thoughtful? When had his life partner become his life enemy? Was it really Lillian he was trying to get rid of? Or the mediocrity of his own life? Sometimes when he went to the ballet with Lillian he would see the dancers on the stage moving with great ease and it was then that he would have a vision of gracefulness. The world they moved in was a world without horror, without fear, a world of energy and value and calm.

Lillian.

The past.

The sea.

How had he become a *practical* man?

Didn't he want to leave his house? His life?

Jerry wrote notes to himself about change, notes about wanting to leave, notes about desperation.

Thoughts about depending on Lillian had led him to desperation. He wrote about it and kept his counsel.

I'm sadly leaving my house. Going on to another house. I'm leaving this living room with painted floors and pink satin couches, pictures that balance on wire, the soft gold umbrella lights. I'm off to the house of my love. The skin of my love is soft. The hair of my love is soft. The lips of my love said, "Leave the city, leave the crowds and the glass and smell the curl of very soft hair." And the more she told me the more I wanted to try my luck. "I want you to know, my love, I am from a distant land where everything is dead as the dead man's bone. I would have you know that my house and my city have burned." That's how I came naked to my love. She said, "Soon you will find out" and I could not tell. But a sign said, "Take her mouth," and I took her mouth. In case you have not seen me walking away from————. In case you did not see me slamming the door on————. In case you did not watch me say good-bye to————. To birthday books, animal trees, shells, the gold frames, the long cigarettes, let me tell you this—I'm off to another house. And going is easy. Easy as walking out into the sunlight. Out of the rooms, to re-invent love.

He wanted, in some deepest sense, to re-invent Jerry Hess. But who was his love? Was it the *dream* of the impossible woman who he would never meet? Was he, Jerry Hess, to behave like some foolish shipping king? Going through the seas of life to find still another mermaid whom he would discard once she turned into flesh?

His anxieties grew. He recognized that things were not as they were, not as they would ever begin to be again. He felt that he was experiencing some terrible experience that would either bring him down, as disasters bring people down, or would strengthen him. "Bend, do not break. Bitter is the bough that breaks. But if you break you will grow again." That was part of his mother's wisdom. Remembering her words, he impulsively drove to see his mother. She now lived in Sunnyside. In Queens. A little queen surrounded by sunflowers and gardens. The aunts who kept his mother company, knitting shawls or playing cards together, had died. His mother remained, a great lady among sunflowers. Driving in his limousine to see her he felt as he got closer to her that he must pay more attention to her. He stopped the car at a candy store and bought her favorite candies. The limousine stopped in front of the small brick house where his mother lived. She was sitting on the porch as if she were waiting for him. His father was in the back of the house with his fingers in the earth. His mother rose to greet him. Her red lips were always carefully made up, her skin had the same brown toughness that he had inherited from her. He gave her the candy.

"So thoughtful. Jerry, you have always been so thoughtful!"

"I have pain in my soul," he said to her in the kitchen. She was making tea.

"I know."

"How do you know?"

"I sense you."

"I'm at a point, Mother, when I have to change everything. I feel anxiety. I feel as if a catastrophe is about to happen."

"Is it a conflict? Or a crisis?"

"Aren't they the same, Mother?"

"No. There's a difference. If your son were sick again, that would be a crisis. But if you are thinking of hurting him by leaving Lillian and you don't know what to do—that is a conflict. Do you see the difference?"

"How do you know me, Mother, so well?"

"I brought you into the world. We are alike. We don't like mediocrity. We don't like sameness. When you are in *pain* it is not physical, or financial. It's because some deeper discontent has eaten into you. I know you, Jerry."

"It's true. My senses are dull. I don't make people laugh anymore."

"You make me laugh, you big overgrown boy. I think we sometimes expect too *little* in life. And when we get too much we feel frightened. You have everything that you wanted. You didn't expect so much."

"But I'm missing so much, too."

"What?"

"I'm not happy with the labels of my life. I live in the Dakota.

29

My wife is a lawyer. My son is at Deerfield. My luggage is Vuiton. My chauffeur drives a Lincoln limousine. Avedon takes my portrait. Cartier sends my Christmas presents or Chanukah presents depending on who I'm trying to impress. I travel around the world buying and selling art, which might as well be shoe polish. And deep down, in the shoe, in my real shoe, there's an annoying pebble. And that's the thing I have no *label* for. You see, Mom, I think that under the sanity your son has cultivated—he's deeply and unforgivably angry."

She laughed. "Who isn't?"

"A thriving person isn't mad. A person who has self-awareness. A person who accepts his life. You see, Mom, besides all the anxiety, I just don't accept being me."

"Who would you like to be?"

"I don't know."

"What would you like to do?"

"I don't know."

"What are your doubts?"

"About Lillian. About my career. About my son. About my body. About age. Most of all about age. It never occurred to me that—don't laugh—I would grow old. That I would meet people whom I knew a long time ago and think that they changed not thinking how I had *changed*. There is, in my sanest hours, a thought that arises that my *identity* is not the one I wanted. That I don't want to be just a husband, father, art dealer—if all these things are me I don't want to be them. I don't want to be a serious writer either, because I know that just means person. I want to hide in some tree somewhere in the country and crawl inside it until, like a bear, I have hibernated long enough to know who I am."

"I know, son. In this country everyone wants to be what they are not. It's the American cancer. Rich want to be poor. Poor want to be rich. Black want to be white. White want to be black. Everyone wants what they are not. It's a sickness. It's an immigrant sickness and everyone is an immigrant somewhere in his soul."

Jerry thought, as he held his mother the way he used to when she was his whole world, "She understands."

8.

Living in New York City by herself at twenty-two, Mary Reagan was trying to be tough. But secretly, she missed her family in California. Her mother had been a tall blonde Irish beauty—a model. Her father was an engineer. They met during the Depression. They had driven across the country together in a blue sedan after they were married. Mary always romanticized that trip—she imagined her father honking the horn across America, her mother taking sandwiches out of a bag and peeling fruit. In California, her father got a job. At night he worked as an inventor. He invented a new kind of folding chair that Roosevelt had bought for the White House. The president sent for her parents to drive across the country and sit on her father's white folding chairs on the White House lawn. Her mother remembered FDR and her father shaking hands. Her mother had photographs of the event, framed all over the apartment, pictures of the president in silver polished frames with white folding chairs blurred in the background.

Mary thought of all these things as she jogged around the park. One thought remained constant: keep going. Her legs were beginning to ache. She had just started jogging about a month ago, and already, her body was promoting the supply and use of oxygen; she felt her body demanding it and circulating it into her system.

Mary enjoyed running.
She was too young to be afraid of growing old. She was young enough to run without a curative purpose. She ran not because she might have a heart attack or because she needed to take the cellulite out of her thighs, but for the sheer joy of being free.

Running. Mary felt her second breath coming. This was the time when the other Mary, the Mary of the clear mind, the Mary of the good impulses came through. Broke through the other Mary. Mary was a journalist, and as such was trained to examine everything. Over her desk was a wary set of instructions scrawled in her large, neat print:

Get the jogging habit.
Practice the hard-easy principle.
Take the time to warm up and warm down.
Make your jogging hour into a sacred period.

Mary Reagan recited these mantras in her mind. A chant to hold on to. That was what she had to do. Put her mind on jogging every day and build up stamina so that she could run in the Marathon. She had already won running medals at the track meets held every Sunday in Central Park.

She had always been contrary. Her radicalization had not started at twenty-two. She had been born questioning, according to her parents. At ten, she was already leaving school early to take part in demonstrations against the upper classes. *Struggle. Change. Protest. Demands.* These had long been key words in Mary's vocabulary. She had left California one summer to work in New York. She had written to her mother that she was involved in the "National Anti-Imperialist Movement in Solidarity with Africa."

"Fancy that," said Mary's mother.

She bought flowers once a week for her room. Flowers. Posters of Che and Castro. Pictures of children in shanties in South Africa. A huge sticker over her bed that read: *South Africa! Hands Off Angola.* (She loved Shirley Chisholm, Florynce Kennedy, Patty Hearst. Pictures of them were glued on the bathroom mirror.) Candles. Books on the Cuban Revolution and Latin America were on the floor. She was doing research for an article she was writing for a media workshop collective. Sunlight on the floor. So many people in New York, she thought, were bummed out. They ran around trying to impress each other with their wealth, their success. Mary felt alienated in New York City and secretly wished she was back in the Bay Area or in Los Angeles. She had come to New York to "make it" in the world of journalism. Well, she hadn't done as well as she'd thought. But she still had her savings account, so she didn't have to worry much. She could still afford jazz records. And movies. And lectures. Sun spots fell on her golden floor like halos. As Mary got dressed, she looked in the long gilt mirror and saw that her body was getting thinner. That must be from jogging. She brushed out her hair. She couldn't wait to jog. To change from a sparkling woman into rhythmic machinery of feet, legs, and arms. She put her socks on carefully and then her white cotton underwear. Then her green jogging pants. Finally, her jogging shoes. She felt good in her jogging shoes. Life was flight and movement. Life was the landscape of running. Mary felt joy. And then the next moment anxiety. She would slip into her running shoes before she had time to think.

9.

Not to think was the main thing.

For Mary, running was therapy.

She had not been having good luck lately in her personal life. The guys her own age whom she met were juvenile and had no political awareness. She found it hard to relate to them. To talk to them. She had gotten used to going out with radical guys, a few of the people who worked up at Columbia in the Network Project, but they all turned out to be married or living with someone. She had tried older men. That had been a disaster. One man she knew, a good-looking white-haired guy called Nat, was the producer of a television humor show. He had once gone with a movie star, which made him seem glamorous by association. The producer had turned out to be impotent. He seemed only to be interested in her when she didn't want him.

"You've come into my life as a gift," Nat said. When he spoke he had a habit of wobbling his head.

"I'm not sure I'm in your life."

"Well, I like knowing you." He was supposed to be a comedy writer, but she never heard him say anything humorous. He had a double chin and false modesty and loved to take her to Elaine's, where he pretended not to be looking at the celebrities. He had black hairs all over his arms and legs and his body was still good.

At first she had thought he was modest and charming. He had invited her to his apartment one afternoon and from his window, she could see a white dove. He had a charming apartment filled with books and pictures and a large hat rack filled with hats he never wore. His voice was soft and he didn't talk much. She noticed that he put everyone down. Once she had had an assignment to write about Ralph Nader for *Crawdaddy* magazine, for the bio section, where they often used free-lance writers as long as you could "deliver" the person you said you wanted to interview. They didn't believe Nader would let a twenty-two-year-old interview him, and they gave her the assignment—and she had called him and he remembered her clearly from her days in San Francisco when she was agitating for consumer controls. She had been given the cover story and when she finished the interview, Nat had said, "Don't you think enough has been written about Nader already?" He always tried to put her down. On the other hand, at times he would twist his lips into a smile, and try to be funny, saying "Did anyone ever tell you you were perfect?" He was an oddball Pinocchio—a Pinocchio with white hair. He seemed to be hiding something. Was it that he was Jewish? That he was secretly frightened of not being the class act he pretended to be? The day she decided to sleep with him in his apartment was the day he began to lose interest in her. It was the Don Juan syndrome. She had encountered it often. She thought Nat would have been happier as a fag.

Nat was a loser. Most of the men she met in New York were losers. They weren't healthy. They drank too much. Were on coke. Speed. They were either fops—like Juan, the Venezuelan she went out with who called everyone "darling" and broke appointments with her by sending her flowers with little cards that read, "Sorry, darling, but I must fly tonight to Venezuela"—or they were, like Nat, forgers of their own identities. Mary chose to find something more in life than the stupidity of relationships that were not love, but something else, where sadness and joy were only played at. She lived with the dilemma of wanting to be close to someone and share her life with someone—and desperately needing to be alone at the same time. The only person she met in New York whom she liked enormously was a script writer called Lem. Lem had gotten fed up with show business and writing scripts, and at the age of forty-five had started studying to be an analyst. He now practiced on the West Side where he treated a lot of hippies and radicals without charge. He was good-looking and she loved looking at his large blue eyes. But he was as fucked-up as anyone. They had long raps at his house where he cooked dinner for her and walked around in his old jeans.

"What do you feel really bothers you as a man?" she asked him.

"Why do you say *man* all the time? All the feminists make such a large thing out of man and woman. Two neurotics have more in common than most men and most women have in common with people of their own sex. It's not what do I want as a man, but what do I want just as a human being?"

She put her arm around him and hugged him till he calmed down. "I'm just trying to ask you what is it that makes you unhappy?"

He started to laugh. "What makes me unhappy?" He was bitter.

"Yes, I'm serious."

"Lack of self-esteem. The same thing that makes everybody unhappy. I think having a good opinion of yourself is the hardest thing in the world for me."

"But why, Lem? You're a neat-looking guy. You're smart. You're good at what you do. You're political. Why shouldn't you think well of yourself?"

His voice got very low. "It goes back to childhood. My parents never thought much of me. I guess I'd need a lot to think well of myself."

"What would you need?"

"Well, I'd like to be at the top of my profession as a writer. That isn't going so well. I'd like to find some kind of financial security. I'd like to have a female companion that I could be with, and share things with, when I wanted to be with her, and not be with her, when I didn't want to be with her."

"Why don't you be with me, Lem?"

"What do you mean?"

"I'm not kidding. I like you. And I'm tired of living in the Gramercy Park Hotel. Besides, I can't afford it. We could share a place and I'd write and you'd write and analyze."

He smiled. It made him happy that she liked him. "It only works because we're not involved. The moment we had sex it would all be over."

Sex, for, Lem, was the great destroyer.

"Why?"

"Are you kidding? It would set up anxieties between you and me that neither of us could cope with."

"Does sex always lead to the nuthouse? Does it have to lead to anxieties?"

"For some people. I'm beginning to think I'm a person who can't ever be with anyone, and it depresses me. Maybe the reason I don't have successful relationships is my own fault."

"What's the main problem?"

"I can't leave. I get involved with a girl and then I feel guilty. I've been in the worst fucking relationships for years. If someone is nice, I don't want to hurt her feelings. Guilt keeps me with her."

"I've heard about Jewish guilt. Since I've been in New York, I'm beginning to understand what it is. It's like a disease. All the Jewish guys have it. It's like spiritual eczema." They laughed.

"I don't know, Mary. It's hard for me to relate. Once I'm in a sexual relationship, I feel trapped."

"But don't you think it can be done?"

"I know it can. I know of some couples who are really happy, who like each other and grow together. I've just never done that."

"What about your friends?"

38

It was a painful question.

"I have no friends."

"Why not?"

"I spend so many hours at classes and analytic meetings, I don't have time for friends. I have one friend only. Ubi Frank. He's also an analyst. But he's just the *opposite* of me. He only likes one woman at a time. When he does, he devotes himself to her *totally*. If she cuts her finger, he'd run twenty miles to get a Band-Aid. All he does is want to please her. I'm not like that."

"How could I help you to feel more self-esteem?" Another hug.

"Keep being my friend. Women are my only friends. I have to say that almost all of my patients are women. I have one woman now, who used to be two hundred and fifty pounds and she's now a hundred and twenty pounds. She screws twelve men a day. She was just divorced. Has seven kids. She fucks constantly."

"Gee, could you ask her where she finds them? I'm getting horny."

They both laughed and smoked a joint. "I love you, Lem."

That night, in her hotel room Mary watched cable television. She had made arrangements with the hotel to pay extra and have it hooked up to her room. On the box were two married women from White Plains, arguing about the meaning of sex. Both of them confessed that they "fooled around." Mary loved cable TV. It was her Old Vic. And talk shows were the modern comedies and tragedies. The modern *Electra* and *The Birds* could be seen every night on cable TV. One of the women from White Plains looked out from her black eyelashes and mask of white shoe polish, or whatever it was, and confessed to her partner: "I want a cock I can count on."

"So do I," the other woman said. "But is a cock really everything?"

"For me it is."

"Well, for me it isn't. I would much prefer my husband or a

39

lover feeling me all over, sucking my boobs, and then giving me a hand job. I find it's much more exciting than someone flopping all over me."

"Not flop. Pound. I don't like a flopper, but I love a pounder."

"Well, what about going down? You like that, don't you?"

"Of course I do. Who doesn't?"

"So you prove my point. A guy without a cock still has fingers and a tongue. So why all this bullshit about getting it up?"

Mary listened and laughed until she wept. The Globe Theatre of the modern world was lodged in her bedroom at the Gramercy Park. Only Shakespeare wasn't needed. These two hags were modern Rosencrantz and Guildenstern. The problem was, they weren't just the "asides" or the "minor" actors. They were the whole show. Suddenly she switched channels. She loved to do that. Just switch to another world. It was too bad people couldn't do that in life. If something got heavy, just switch channels. She switched to a cosmic-con show. A man with a beard was saying, "Self-awareness is the condition for healthy living." How true! She switched back to the fuck-suck show. That didn't interest her. It made her too horny. She switched to a late movie. Gun shots. Her life was a jangle of talk shows, articles, dreams. It was all hilarious.

As she lay in bed on clean, cold, white sheets, her mind drifted to memories. Her parents had worried about her and sent her to a convent school. At sixteen she had organized, with some friends, a strike in support of the Coalition of Black Trade Unionists. When her father had questioned her about this, she had tried to get him to come to a meeting. He was stubborn. Sucked on a pipe. Shook his head.

"I won't go, Mary."

"Why, Pop? You've got to wake up and see that the majority of humanity are living in a way that is indecent. Capitalism contributes to this."

"Where the hell would *you* be without capitalism?"

"What do you mean?"

"If you were growing up in Russia, you'd probably be in one of those Archipelagos. At least here, you have the freedom to talk all the blarney you want."

"It's not blarney. You can't talk about freedom when you have racism and injustice everywhere. Freedom isn't neutral." He called her an "injustice collector." She wept and she left California. That was the traumatic time of her life. It had been hard for her to leave. It wasn't just that she loved her mom and old man— it was hard to leave the beauty of the hills and sea of California. Ripe vegetables. The sea's sound on the beach. The sun. In New York, she often felt cold. She looked in the mirror. She looked like a foal. She had long legs. Long black hair. Eyes that were large and green. Large lips. Mary O'Shea Reagan, a product of Dorothy O'Shea and Bill Reagan.

Mary woke in her room at the Gramercy Park and realized it was a good morning for running. The room was small. There was no air conditioning and it was hot. But at least there were no cockroaches in the room the way there had been in the tiny apartment she had lived in before. In the jungle of New York. What was she, Mary, really like? Fact: She had a big heart. Fact: She was a good researcher and was bright enough to understand history as it was happening every moment. Fact: She had enough money to live on for another month. She could always go back to a job in the Bay Area. Fact: She was beautiful and could go out with anyone she wanted. Fact: Politics was the way to help the poetry emerge for the souls of those who didn't have any hope. Fact: She was lonely. Fact: She was frightened.

Mary rose, and opened the window. Breathed. Fact: There was nothing to be frightened of. If she wanted money, she had to stop writing so many articles for nothing and go out and hustle more. If she was depressed she'd have to jog. Mary took her jogging pants out of a drawer, and smiled.

"I want to be a political journalist," she had told the editor of her hometown newspaper. She remembered how kind he had been. She was only sixteen. It was her last year of high school. She was tall, gawky, shy.

"Tell me exactly why, Mary," he said from behind his desk piled with newsprint.

"Because I want to expose things that stink in this country," she said. She had forced herself to be bold. "I'm already an active part of the local civil rights movement. I've agitated at nuclear plants in the Bay Area, I've been in marches, worked as a gofer in the offices of the women's strike for peace and agitated for abortions."

"But what journalism experience have you had?"

"None, outside of the high-school newspaper where I was an editor."

"So you want to be a top reporter?"

"I really do, sir."

She was a beggar, a supplicant, she had been so serious then. Had her attitude amused him? He allowed her to work as a stringer. And surprisingly (even to herself), she had pulled in some of the best stories. She had interviewed people in emergency rooms, in family court, she had been concerned about education and health and children's schools. She had interviewed Ronald Reagan and gone back to her high school and interviewed her teacher, who had once been his girlfriend. That was a scoop.

"Good work, Mary," he had said.

"Thank you."

"When you finish college there's always a job for you here, Mary."

She had gone back during college summer vacations. She had chosen to major in economics at Berkeley and every summer worked on the paper. She had interviewed freaks, radicals, Hell's Angels, hippies, yippies, Weathermen and ex-Weathermen, Black Muslims, former SDS leaders, poets, Chicanos, grape pickers and members of La Huelga, rock and rollers, drug addicts, whores, Prostitutes for a Democratic Society, CYOTE members, go-go dancers, freedom fighters, nonparents, gays, communists, agrarian revolutionaries, environmentalists, and freaked-out astronauts.

"Aren't you interested in boys?" her father had asked when she graduated from college.

"Aren't you ever gonna get married, Mary? And give us grandchildren?" her mother had pleaded.

"Mother, don't be so corny. I'm not a nun or a spinster at twenty-one."

"Her mind's on other things," her father said, resigned to his tomboy.

"But it might be nice if we saw her just once in a dress."

She was a tomboy. She always wore jeans and a cap on her head. She thought it made her look like an English cab driver. She was radical. A firecracker. She learned karate. Spent nights reading Rimbaud, listening to the Stones, and studying self-protection. She pored over *History Will Absolve Me*, and worshiped Castro and Pablo Neruda. Secretly, her heroine was the Chilean, Violetta Para, who had committed suicide. Violetta Para, musician, feminist, poet, artist, had established folklore centers and made the peasants of Chile aware of their own richness in their poverty. Mary read Violetta's *Thanks to Life* every night to herself in Spanish:

En mi triste diario
Restaurant El Tordo Azul;
allí conocí a un gandul
de profesión ferroviario

"You should go to New York," her editor had told her. "You belong in the big city. You'd be the best there is, Mary."

She had left California. Been in New York a year. She hadn't taken the easy path, wrote a few commercial pieces, and slaved at the media workshop collective. She had written pamphlets for the Network Project. But no one knew where the Network Project was. Professionally she was nowhere. Her name was known only by the police, who had arrested her twice in demonstrations and let her go. She had no love life because of her career. And she had no career.

She had no love life and no profession. The only time she went out and had fun was when she went to political meetings. That's what she thought as she ran. Mary, Mary quite contrary, had grown up to be radical Mary. Mary in New York.

"I'm sorry, Miss Reagan, Mr. Berendt is busy. If you have an idea, send us a letter."

She sent letters every day. But there were only two editors who gave her any work. Both were editors of porno magazines. She would die if her parents found out she was writing for sex magazines. The world of *Beaver* and *Chains* was not where she wanted to succeed. But only the porno editors appreciated her mind. Her name appeared in *High Society*. "The Meat Market of Mary Reagan" was one article she had penned for cash. It was about her sexual fantasies. (She still managed to include her point of view about imperialism. Her point was that people had to have pornographic fantasies because they were politically oppressed. "In a free society," she wrote, "there will be love, not sex." After she'd written those sentiments, *High Society* dropped her.) For cash, she was now so desperate, she was dreaming up cooking articles during the day and writing about imperialism in Angola at night. And she had to study recipes at the New York Public Library to know what she was doing. To support her contributions to the Liberation Movements of Southern Africa she took an advance for an idea which she thought no one would be interested in. But they were. She had been given two grand to write *The Jewish Princess Cookbook*. It was ironic. She had never known any Jews, personally, until she came to New York. She had wound up an ersatz cook. While others pored over the racing forms she pored over Jewish recipes. Hope was the only thing that kept her going. As a goy, she didn't know the difference between a matzo ball and a meatball.

10.

Feet wriggling in shoes. Get there! Where? Anywhere. This morning it would be uptown to the reservoir. Mary on the street. Long strides. Shoulders above her hips. People on the streets watching her run. Long antelope Mary. Shoulders above her hips. Hips over her feet. Head straight up and set on her shoulders. Not satisfied to look ahead, but staring around a lot. An animal hunted. Mary. Running and loping, running one way and then another. Letting her arms dangle, long strides, breathing in rhythm with her steps and then forgetting who she was. Mary changed pace, encountering the pain that every runner feels and the dry rhythms which lift you like sky diving, into a rhythmical universe. Yes, running was better than anyone could imagine. Her own world. Her own streets. The rhythm of the body suddenly given back. The world womb. Lifting and rising above it. Feeling lifted above life.

Running. Air in lungs. Out of lungs. The jogging high.

Mary began feeling that she was running against time. She remembered her mother pulling on her, tugging on her to stay in one place. Her mother was part Irish, part mystic, part miracle woman. She had written two books (bound in blue cloth, which could be purchased or ordered for twenty dollars), called *A Course in Miracles*. "The Course does not aim at teaching the meaning of love, for that is beyond what can be taught. It does aim, however, at removing the blocks to the awareness of love's presence, which is your natural inheritance. The opposite of love is fear, but what is all encompassing can have no opposite. Nothing real can be threatened. Nothing unreal exists. Herein lies the peace of God." It was the God part that bothered Mary. But her mother soft-pedaled the God part. It was as if she were a peaceable seamstress, stitching little maxims into the fabric of Mary's life.

Mary had grown up hearing her mother's thoughts.

"Spirit cannot be taught. But the ego must be. Learning is frightening because it leads to the relinquishing of the spirit. Yet teaching and learning are your greatest strengths, Mary." Mary had taken down the lessons of her mother at night the way one puts stitches in embroidery. But she had also needed to be herself. She had wanted to run away from her mother's apartment in San Diego with its hanging flowers, bookshelves filled with the books bound in blue cloth, the candles, quills, antiques, tiles, flowers, tentacles that held her to each moment of her mother's life.

"I'm leaving for New York," she had told her mother.

Her mother had heard her the way a mute person hears—her face seemed to recognize that something had been communicated—but her ears had not heard anything.

"Leaving? Why leave? There's work to be done here, Mary, in San Diego."

"I'm afraid if I stay here, Mother, I won't find out if I can be the journalist I know I am."

"God is not the author of fear. You are. You have chosen to create, unlike him, and have therefore made fear for yourself.

You are not at peace because you are not fulfilling your function."

"Why do you say that?" (*What does it all mean?*)

"You have a lofty function which you are not meeting, Mary. Release yourself and release others. Do not present a false and unworthy picture of yourself to others. The ego has built a shabby home for you. You cannot run away from God by going to New York."

(Is she sane? wondered Mary.)

But that's just what Mary had done. Run from her mother and her mother's truth and her small bedroom. Run. To another life.

Mary felt her second breath coming as she ran. It was as if she was getting to the real Mary. The Mary who felt pain. She didn't like thinking about her major love affair in New York. It had ended with a phone call that had been a disaster.

"I want to take you out, Mary," Johnny said. He was a trombone player, the only white member of a black jazz band. She was attracted to him and gave him her number, but didn't think he would call her.

"Where are you?" she asked.

"In a phone booth."

"Where?"

"In New Jersey."

"What's happening?"

"I want to see you." She could hear the cars going by on the freeway.

"When?"

"Tonight."

He had arrived in an hour.

They had talked all night about his life, his music. He was from Minnesota and grew up on a farm. His mother was a music teacher and his father was a truck driver. It was a bad marriage but he grew up always hearing music. He had run away from home when he was fourteen. He was now thirty and had been through some heavy scenes. He told her, right away, that he lived with two other women. One in Florida, one in The Bronx.

47

"Then why are you with me?" she asked.

"I'm looking for the perfect woman," he said.

"What would that be like?"

"Like you," he laughed. He sounded spaced out.

"Why like me?"

"I don't know. You feel good to me."

She could tell he was spaced out. And not too bright. But in some odd way she understood his *search*. Everyone in New York was *searching* for something. Adopted children were searching for their real parents. Black people were searching for their roots in Africa. Gays were searching for the right beach on Fire Island. Middle-class women in the suburbs who were nailed to boredom were searching for the exciting life they never knew. The ultimate, outermost fuck. Why shouldn't Johnny be searching for the *right* relationship? Everyone else was searching for something. A good relationship was as good as anything else to be searching for.

The first time she went to bed with him, she learned that he was a master.

There are some guys, she thought, who are not too bright except when they go to bed and there they know everything there is to know. In bed he was a genius. All night long they listened to his music and made love. She felt so high with him. It was the same high she felt in jogging. She let everything go. She loosened up; no bones. At first it was difficult, but she let him turn her around. She was like a white dolphin. She flipped and rolled over in their sea of flesh and sperm.

"You have a tight ass," he said. "It feels good."

She came with her ass.

Afterwards she turned to him.

"Oh, this is good."

His eyes were serious. He was now a child who became serious. "Listen to me, Mary—you have the loveliest ass I've ever seen."

"Thank you."

"People shouldn't thank each other," he began to lecture her. Some people are natural silent lovers. In bed, John loved to talk. To teach. His immediate university was the bed. His only desire in life, she acknowledged, was to be stared at and noticed. He was a fucking-guru. The kind of guru that no woman will listen to unless he's fucking her. The bed was his university podium. He took her in his arms, pressed her close to him, and treated her to a world of sexual experiences that were unusual. He found her naïve, she knew. She had never experienced ice cubes. She had never used vaseline. She had never had need of the *equipment* he brought with him. Yet, in some way, he seemed selfish.

Mary confessed to him once. "All my life I've been called bright."

"You should associate with people on your level," he said mysteriously.

"But it's hard to find people on my level. I've come to grips with the fact that I'm my only friend. Men have been disappointing to me."

"For sure."

"I'm determined to try to find through work the meaning of my life. I'm so used to having my mom and pop doing things for me."

"Once you make friends with yourself, you don't need anyone," he said mystically.

"Well, you need people. What about the woman you live with in Florida?"

"Iza?"

"Is that her name?"

"Yeah. She's attractive. We met three years ago. She has a nine-year-old son. Her husband was a real prick. He left her a restaurant to run and I'm helping her run it. She doesn't understand me. She keeps saying she thinks I'm a moon man."

"I hate that expression."

"Yeah, so do I. She's so organized. Everything has to be figured out in advance. We're business partners. And she's been good to me. But I feel a change coming. One thing's for sure. You feel good to me."

He drove his old white Jaguar convertible to New York once a month and came to visit her. They sat in her hot hotel room, smoking grass, making love. They took showers together and she washed his white skin. She enjoyed being with him because he was beautiful to look at. His body was slim and when he was naked the tiny curls of blond hair were so soft as she took him inside her mouth.

"Suck my cock, lady," he always said. He often showed her some of the songs he wrote. They were simple songs with one-line refrains:

Your good people.
Your good people.
Your good people.

They seemed innocent. One day she realized Johnny was just a boy who had never grown up. He would also treat her to some of his memories.

"Tying my shoe in sixth grade, I tried to look up Leona Purdy's dress." One day she realized he was deeply into coke. He was always so spaced out. That accounted for the fact that he would talk slowly and stare beyond her. One day she put one of his records on the phonograph she kept in her hotel room.

"I can see people doing a ballet to this music. It's so sacred. It's so beautiful." He began crying. Something was working in his head. He often seemed like a beautiful retarded child. Under his milky innocent persona, which included guruesque conversations about the "cosmic eye" and the "meaning of light" and "dreams of a holy family," were a lot of hostilities. He was constantly talking about being ripped off and his greatest fear in life was that his CB radio would be stolen from his car. He wrapped a scarf that Florence had knitted for him around the radio.

"Why do you alternate between these women?"

"Iza isn't enough for me."

"Why not?"

"She's not very bright." (Who was he? Einstein?)

"What about me?" she fished for a little flattery.

"You're bright. Brighter than either of the two women I live with."

She often wondered if he was a liar. If he made up these women. Sometimes when his eyes would seem watery and he didn't know whether to get up and go, or stay with her (he always had spaced-out decisions to cope with), she realized he had no sense of time. "What is time?" he would ask.

"What are you thinking, Johnny?"

"Is it something that ticks? Is it something that tocks?"

"Time is now," she said.

"Now will be past," he said slowly.

It was conversations like this that made her wonder if she were out of her fucking mind to be carrying on such a stupid, pointless affair. But she was lonely. There was the animal heat. She clung to him because the city frightened her. In many ways she knew he was the only warm body she could come near. A few of her friends, who were couples, thought about her only as an afterthought. They were involved in child rearing and social clients. An old friend from school was married to an actor. Whenever Mary tried to make a date to see her for dinner she would say she was sorry, but "Irwin has a producer coming for dinner." She would call up all her friends when she felt she had time on her hands. They were all busy. Johnny was the only person who had time for her.

One day he was sitting with her in the white car. They were parked near the Hudson to look at the boats. "I have something to tell you. I'm the confirmation of your life," he said.

"Why do you say that?" she asked.

"Because I have been given a mission. To be your confirmation," he said in a serious voice.

"Why do you think I have to be *confirmed*?"

"All of us are here for a mission. Mine is to be your confirmation."

"If you're my confirmation, why don't you come and live with me? I'd like that a lot, Johnny. That way, I wouldn't be so lonely."

"I am your confirmation. But not in a personal sense."

"In what sense?"

"In a psychic sense. I don't want to ball anymore."

She began to think he was mad. Every time he made love to her now he touched her forehead to "adjust her psychic eye." She realized, wearily, that he had a Jesus Christ complex. He believed that his music was a "message to the world" and that he was to confirm her being, the way saints were confirmed.

Suddenly Mary realized that she was so desperate to live out her dream of being loved that she had attracted a loony. Loonies and loneliness were all mixed up. Was he really a loony? Or a horny musician? Or a nut who was wearing sandals and wanted to play Jesus Christ in the big city? Why did she attract this kind of person? Was she nuts? Writing alone at night, she wondered if Johnny would call her.

The problem with New York City, Mary thought, is that you get so lonely you'll accept almost anybody as a friend. Even a lunatic. She thought of this as she walked through the streets near Gramercy Park. Looking at the bag women on the streets, the old women with swollen legs, fierce eyes, filthy mop hair, the women who were stranded in life, who carried shopping bags and had shoes with holes in them—looking at them she identified with them. They were beyond pain. Beyond suffering. They didn't have to fuck lunatics who played trumpets and pretended to be messengers of God. They didn't have to write sell-out articles for pornographic magazines. They weren't doing research on Jewish cuisine in the public library. The whole world was a matzo ball. The whole world was a knish. The world was mamaligga. She had been learning about Jewish food. It was the loneliness. She, a goy, was bleeding inside for warmth. Sometimes, as she ate alone in a restaurant, she would long to talk to the other strangers sitting nearby. Once, eating at Ratner's (dairy dishes), where she hoped to steal some of the menu ideas, she saw an old man with a small black hat on his head. He had a long beard. Who was he? She asked the waiter.

"He's a rabbi. He's the holy man in the neighborhood."

She wondered if he was *really* a rabbi or if he worked for the CIA. A master spy in Hong Kong had been a Hasidic rabbi.

Suddenly, she felt like crying. She closed her eyes. She was so paranoid.

"Is something wrong?" the waiter asked. He had a thick accent that seemed Slavic. His face was old and bruised and she wondered what life had done to destroy him.

The sign on the wall said, "Capacity 200." But there were only two people eating in the restaurant. Herself and the rabbi. Hunger brought him there. She was brought by the desire to have an ethnic experience and study the menu for future cookbooks. Life seemed absurd. She was really hungry for love.

"I'm just feeling a little lonely in New York," she said, smiling at the waiter.

"Ach! I know the feeling. A nice girl like you. You should be married."

"Thanks. I just broke up with my boyfriend."

"So—find another boyfriend. Men are like taxis. When one goes by another comes along."

She felt reassured.

As she was jogging, Mary thought of the last phone conversation she had had with her mother.

"Are you safe, in that hotel, Mary? Is it a firetrap?"

"Mother, I'm fine. Don't worry. New York is not what you read about in California. There are no muggers. Don't worry. No one is out to destroy me, Mom, like the big bad wolf."

"Do you have any girl friends, Mary? Girl friends are very important. You get to meet their folks. You get to meet their friends. Have you met any nice young men?"

"I meet a lot of different people here. You can't imagine how many kinds of people you meet in New York."

"Well, watch out, Mary, for men who just want to make out with you and use you. I remember from when I was young. A man thought just because he bought you dinner he could pet with you."

"Mother. Everyone's gay. Not everyone, but everyone I meet who's not married or crazy. I've been going out with a musician called Johnny, but he's involved with two other women and he's only made me unhappy."

"Forget him. There's no happiness in a situation like that. Aren't there any healthy, serious, Christian young men?"

"I haven't met any. But don't worry. I'm so busy finding work I don't have time for men. That's not where my head is at."

"Mary, don't forget that before you know it, life passes you by. Remember to stay wholly free of fears, and miracles will befall you."

No miracle had befallen her.

She was out of breath. Her life was out of breath too. She had been jogging. But what else did she have? Johnny was supposed to call her at six o'clock for the hundredth time but she realized her life couldn't depend on his telephone calls. What would she do if he didn't phone? She was leading life above the surface of writing and looking for work. But underneath it, in that secret place of her soul, she was still waiting for a stranger to contact her. Wasn't it all a false hope? It was possible that Johnny was coked out and just couldn't get himself out of the quicksand of his life and Bucks County. She had, out of deep loneliness, expected him to love her. Then everything would have been good. But she was smarter than that now. He was just another freaked-out musician.

Johnny broke all his dates. He could never *get it together.* One night when she was writing a piece for *Crawdaddy* on the sale of armaments, Johnny telephoned. He was calling from a phone booth near the Lincoln Tunnel. He was high.

"Everyone says I'm a moon man."

"I told you I hate that expression," she said into the phone.

"Tonight I can't see you. I've got a rehearsal, sugar. That's what I called to tell you." He always had another rehearsal.

She knew. "Well, hang loose."

So they went from *hello* to *good-bye* in two months.

11.

Then she had met Liza Smith, a twelve-year-old black girl. She had glasses, tattered clothes, buckteeth, the worst education, and the best sense of humor. She was a tough little warrior in the world where eating doesn't always happen on time.

She met Liza in a storefront in Harlem where she did volunteer work teaching art one night a week. Mary had taught Liza how to use paint, how to paint old houses orange and blue and green. And how to use words, to use *herself* as the subject of a poem. Often she had felt that it was there, in the storefront, that Liza and the other students made life meaningful. Bearable. She had taught them to believe in their feelings, to find them, to hold on to them. Tears, troubles, fears—these were all precious, Mary taught them. They were not to be thrown away in the garbage. So many kids in Harlem were unwilling consumers of television programs that instructed them how to be happy. According to the messages they received, happiness was a new car, a permanent, or a new breakfast cereal. How grotesque these images were for these kids, who were taught that unless they could buy something, they would be nobody. Mary taught them to have nonsense detectors—how to think of the nonsense in their lives.

Mary felt less lonely at the storefront teaching children who had nothing—she would show them it was possible to have a voice in the wilderness.

Mary ran.

"I love Liza," she thought. "She's the only person I really love in New York."

12.

Jerry remembered his past. His father and mother had been immigrants from Germany. They settled in Brooklyn, in a small brick house with a garden. Jacob Hess silently searched out a new life. His trade of gunsmith helped him find a job at the Metropolitan Museum as an armorer. Here in this country, he found a peaceful life. Jerry remembered his large breakfasts, the tunes he sang, and the long good-byes in the morning. Sometimes Jerry's mother took him to New York City to visit the enormous museum, and showed him the different collections. Jerry would look at the Impressionists and memorize their names, and his mother would take books out of the library for him to read. Down in the bowels, Jacob worked at a large worktable, caring for the armory, the axes, shields, bronzes; he polished and checked the pieces of horse bit, the placques engraved with horsemen. At home, his mother lived in the calvary of her kitchen, the spoons and forks and knives, which she polished daily. His father bought an old black sputtering car with a rumble seat. Jerry would sit in the open seat with his dog while his father drove the car to the beach. They would rent a boat and go fishing. Sitting in the fishing boat, his father would be silent. His mother, wearing a large yellow straw hat, would wave from the shore. Driving home, he would hear his father and mother in the front seat singing Viennese lieder. His black-and-white dog would lick him. It was a happy boyhood.

Memory.

Jerry remembered the party, the first time he had seen Ursule. He was nineteen, a schoolboy in a tuxedo who loved classical music, and had won a scholarship to Juilliard. It had been after a concert. He had wandered into the large room of the partygoers. And he had seen Ursule standing alone, a tall woman, perhaps forty—or fifty— it was difficult to tell. She looked like a goddess and seemed to shine in the darkness. Her dress was long and green and around her neck were green stones. She had magnetic black eyes. He seemed to be sucked into them.

"What are you doing here?" she asked him, and he couldn't take his eyes from her face, her polished, shining skin, her beautiful eyes. Although she was the most beautiful woman in the room, she seemed to have no escort.

"What is your name?" she had asked him.

"Jerry Hess," he said shyly.

"And what do you do, Jerry?" she asked, lighting a cigarette. He noticed she lit her own cigarette—defying anyone to help her. Her fingers were slightly veined and freckled and had no nail polish—the aging hands of a child. She was breathtaking. A child-woman. An electric woman. A black-eyed goddess. He recognized her, she was a famous actress, whose family had been pioneers in the Berliner Art Theatre.

"I'm a student," he remembered saying.

She stood close to him. She was as tall as he was.

"Of what?" she asked.

"Of the Renaissance."

"Of the golden age of the Renaissance? Are you a Renaissance man?"

"I'd like to think so," Jerry had said.

The intensity of her expression changed. She began talking about the masters, Brunelleschi, Donatello, Filippo Lippi, the Paduan circle of controversial masters and students. But he didn't hear her harmonious voice that was so deep and flattering. The party circled around her—she was interrupted by men who kissed her hand, or stopped to kiss her cheek. He wondered why she was bothering with him. As the evening wore on she gave him her arm and asked him to take her home. He felt as if he were moving in a strange dream. Her home was filled with family portraits. Her father had been a friend of Reinhardt and Brecht. By her bed was a picture of her beloved father and Bertolt Brecht, arm and arm.

He adored Ursule. It was a passion beyond what he hoped for. Her eyes. He wanted to live inside her huge black eyes. He remembered the first summer when she took him to Italy with her on vacation. She had taught him everything, about Europe, the Renaissance, the great inspirations of the masters. They had summered with Bernhard Berenson. He had followed behind her, her sheepdog, her servant, his large puppy eyes adoring her as she made her entrances into the great hotels—the Ritz in Paris, the Gritti in Venice. At first, she had paid for everything—and then, as he began to buy and sell old masters, he deliberately moved away from the image of a young boy kept by the famous actress and teacher to that of the young impresario. He had learned from her about traveling, the texture of the skin, how to hang draperies, how to love, and how to find fine Italian Renaissance paintings. How to jostle. How to speculate. How to convince families needing money to part with their local art. He became a merchant of pictures, a banker, he moved with Ursule and the international set, he became, in short, a young aristocrat. It was

Jerry who had found, thanks to Ursule, the Bellinis, the Donatellos; how to trace in Padua's ceilings and attics the sources of art.

They loved each other for years.

It was hard to remember exactly why they had parted the first time. She had said she was getting too old and that she needed a change, and she perfected the art of discontent.

"How well you know how to hurt me," he had said.

"I have given you everything you have to have for your life," she had answered him. Her large black eyes turned against him. And suddenly she had resented him. Accused him of trying to turn her into a "normal human being," accused him of wanting to stifle her and ruin her freedom with his domesticity. It was true. He wanted nothing more than to love to touch her forever. To lie in her arms forever.

"Don't leave me," he begged her. His parents had been scandalized by his love affair with a flamboyant older woman. Their son with an "old woman" who taunted them by the very difference of her life. She had alienated their son, had made him into a dazzling stranger, mesmerized him, changed him so that he hardly came home. "Jerry, this woman has *obsessed* you."

"I can't help it, Mother. It's the only time in my life I've loved anyone."

"You love her? She's so much older than you. For shame."

"She knows everything, Mother. About history, the arts, theatre, opera, lieder. She's known Picasso and Stanislavski and Piscator. Her mind is electric. And you have to admit, she's beautiful."

"In a theatrical way."

"Mother, why do I have to love the kind of person you want me to love? Don't you understand that love doesn't have to have practical *reasons*?"

"I loved your father because he was a good man."

"Ursule's good."

"Good for what? That deep phony voice. Her boobies exposed all the time. Those fake jewels. And those sycophants who follow behind her. Son, how can you bear to be humiliated? Following behind her with her two Labradors on a leash."

"Princess and Duke and I are friends."

"You're friends with *her dogs?*"

"To us they're not dogs."

"What's this '*to us*'? What are you using now? The royal '*we*'?"

"Mom, cut it out. You wanted me to be independent. Ursule is different from the kind of woman you might have wanted—"

"Different? She's a tragedy. Do you want your father and me to sit shivah? Listen, son, there's a nice girl, Clarissa Roche, she lives in Bayside. Her father works at the museum. He's a curator. She's going to Vassar. She rides horses. With a helmet and everything. I saw a picture of her, her father showed it to me."

"Please, Mom. I love Ursule. And that's it."

"Don't tell me you're gonna marry her. Because if you marry her I'll die, immediately. If I don't kill myself with a kitchen knife I'll walk in front of a truck. Married to someone twenty years older than you? Thirty, what do I mean twenty."

"Did you ever see her walk into a room, Mother? How everyone turns around?"

"I saw her walk into my house. With her two dogs. That was enough."

"I've been reading the myth of Demeter," she said one night, walking around her living room filled with golden antiques. Her body was white and beautifully formed. She wore only a black lace slip and high heels with straps that were her trademark.

"I've forgotten the myth," he said. He was miserable. He knew she was going to leave him. He wondered how he could stall the pain, put it off.

"Demeter was the goddess of grain. The mother of Persephone.

Remember when she was taken to Hades? Demeter made everything cold. She was miserable without her daughter."

Jerry knew what she was going to say next.

"I miss my daughter, Jerry. She needs me. She's the person I love most in the world. She's living in California, just had her fourth baby, and I have to go to her. You're sweet. But *you're* not my baby. You're a darling person and I've had three wonderful years with you. We've gone everywhere—met everyone—done everything. But I must leave you. Don't you see?"

"Is it really for your daughter?"

"That, and we don't belong together, darling. You're starting your own business now—I think you'll be very good at art dealing. And I have my school. Not one child but hundreds. Now don't be pouty. Everything that happens in this life is to make us richer. Everything changes. You mustn't fight change, Jerry. You must accept it."

He had hated her then. The door slammed. He could hear it slam for the rest of his life. An odd assortment of desperate and remarkable acts followed. He followed her. Shadowed her. Threatened to kill her, to kill himself. Sent flowers. Telegrams. Engraved bracelets. Grew a beard. Adopted a dog. Two dogs. It was all useless and he knew it. And then he did the only humiliating thing that he had ever done in his life. He tried, like an alcoholic, to forget her. He lived one day after another, trying to just get through the day without running to the telephone to phone Ursule. He tried not to phone her daughter, sister, friends. He tried not to take her name to his lips. He tried to get rid of her image. But he never forgot Ursule. Her perfume, her skin, her extravagant love of candles, flowers, gold negligees, her scenes with friends, her treats for her family, her tears for children—her wisdom—he followed in her shadow. Until he became the man she had made him into.

Looking out of the window, Jerry remembered how he had loved Ursule for the best years of his life. Passionately and without doubt. With her help, he had opened his gallery for selling art privately in New York, on Fifty-seventh Street, the "Tangiers" of the city. She had become a legend and they traveled together during the long summers. She had encouraged him to entertain. Give banquets. She had taught him how to cut his hair. How to listen carefully. How to speak. The three years passed. Life easily found its way to confirm his love for Ursule. Until one evening, just as she had appeared in his life, she left him. Just as she had expanded his life, through history and travel—just as she had brought him into the renaissance of his own life—she dropped him. The grand hotels, receptions, summer houses, limousines, all disappeared.

He remembered the nights he made love to her. Her home had been a cathedral for him. The terraces were lit with bright lights and he could see the windows glowing. Her bedroom was always perfumed with Rigaud, and there were satin sheets on which her white body seemed perfect. He felt as if he had met a dark goddess, and he melted inside her—their lovemaking had been passionate. He kissed her until she came to life in his arms. Could he ever forget that? The long nights of romance, the secret meetings, the embraces, the days of studying and running to be with her. She was gone.

She left him many times. Then impulsively she came back to him. He had moved out of her apartment when she called and told him she missed him. Just as she had been determined to end their relationship she now wanted him back. He felt like a prisoner who had been given a reprieve before being shot. He couldn't believe it. Ursule took him back.

"I missed you."

"I missed you, too."

"Let's never fight, Jerry."

"We won't ever again."

They made love. She fixed his favorite drink. Bought him a present—a golden heart from Tiffany's. After a fight their love quietly went back to where it was. He sold paintings. She brought him clients. He hosted her dinner parties like a young prince. She surrounded him with poets, editors, dancers—the jabber of the wealthy and successful. But he was always afraid. Afraid of what? That she would leave. They had their months of good moments. Their months on edge when she would turn on him and call him a fool. He would get angry at her also and hate himself afterwards.

"You give me all the garbage to do. The bookkeeping. Everything you don't want to do you throw onto me," he complained.

"Would you rather that I do the garbage?" Nothing was reciprocal. Nothing worked in the end. Some days it would be like magic. Other days her moods would irritate them both. His parents sat quietly in their house in Queens and called Jerry's life with Ursule a disaster.

He remembered another scene they had.

They had been to a party. Ursule wearing her trademark of black lace gloves, a black chiffon dress and pearls, large floppy velvet black hat, her sables, her high heels. She had made her usual grand entrance into a room. She had surveyed the room with the purpose of locating a target for her charms. Her charms were little darts that always hit the bull's-eye. Jerry had trailed behind her with the dogs. He helped himself to a buffet dinner and stood in the corner talking to one of Ursule's students. He watched Ursule without her knowing it. She was talking to a young man, even younger than he, who had suddenly become a rival. He watched numbly as Ursule bent down and whispered to him. They both laughed. He watched him handing Ursule his card. Watched as she slid it into her bag. He saw enough. He put down his plate, walked over to them, seized her, and began pulling her out of the room—dogs, sables, and all. No one was aware that he was dragging her out of the apartment. He pulled her into the elevator. She began screaming at him as soon as the door closed.

"Who do you think you are?"

"I'm your lover. And even though I was just a cultural wetback when we met, just a boy from Queens in awe of you, I'm now paying most of the bills. I don't like you fucking me over in public."

"This is just a power play, Jerry, and absurd. I'm not interested in that young man. He wants to study with me. You forget who I am."

"I know who you are. You're a whore."

She slapped him. Just before the elevator door opened. Then she ran into the street looking for a cab. He ran after her. When he caught up with her he saw the black mascara running down her cheeks, making long black lines that wavered on her beautiful skin. Her black eyes were filled with water and were red. It was snowing. He remembered the snow coming down and the way they were screaming on the street. No one was on Fifth Avenue and they were in the darkness screaming at each other.

"I'm sorry, Ursule. I didn't know what I was saying. I was jealous."

Tears ran down her face. "I hate you."

"Forgive me. We need each other, Ursule. Sometimes you treat me like an employee. Employer and employee. I do everything you want. We need each other, but be fair with me. Don't go too far."

"If you needed me, you should have thought about it before you said what you said."

"I was jealous."

"You have no right to be."

"Love—does the word mean anything to you? Or is it just an acting exercise? I love you, Ursule. You're my life. When I see you with another man who might fuck you, I can't stand it."

"Why did you think I would *fuck* him?"

"That's how we started, remember. I can see him replacing me."

Then they had found a cab. Gone home embracing each other. That night, they made love as if nothing had happened. They had become closer and still more distant.

His parents no longer invited them to visit. His mother never phoned. It was as if they had given him up forever. He always wrote to them when he went abroad. Sent them presents. Wrote them postcards from all over the world. But they could not disguise their sorrow.

13.

His parents had taken their troubles to the temple, wept to
the rabbi, cursed the harlot, and walked away shaken and
mystified by the loss of their only son to this bold woman. They
had taken their grief to their hearts and wondered why their son
had replaced his visits with envelopes with great colored stamps
that arrived from all corners of the globe. His mother withdrew
from him, punishing him for living with Ursule. His father
never spoke. Jacob took him fishing whenever he returned
home, just as he had when he was a boy, but they were two
silent men, one large, one small, in a boat. He had no family.
He had only a blind puppy faith in his goddess, Ursule. And
she had left him for good. He remembered with pain. With
tears. One night they had arrived at his apartment and she had
refused to hold him, refused to undress. She spoke only in odd
choppy words that were seductive but not quite connected.
"Leave." "Teach." "Go." They were all baby words.

"I'm leaving you for the last time." That much he remembered. "I must teach at the Festival of Spoleto. I must leave you and go. You can find your life when you write. You have things to do." There was an atmosphere of suspicion. He suspected she had found someone else. He would kill himself, he told her.

"Don't be absurd. That's tyranny I won't accept. Your life will take on a whole new shape, my sweet baby. Let's not give the end of this affair a monstrous architecture. We will always be close. Close friends if not lovers."

He went on buying trips. Bought paintings at auctions. Taught. Read. Fished in the elegant seas of the world where they had never been. But it was all too painful, because Ursule seemed to shadow him. Once, in the red poppy fields of France, where he and Ursule had once gone walking, where she had held his arm, he returned like a deranged person looking for her shadow where no shadow was. He thought of taking his life. Finding her. Every telephone which could be a medium of reaching her became the enemy. He tried calling her from health spas where he went to find his own sanity but could not forget her. She was never in—she hid herself behind others, behind men, behind her friends, behind maids. Three years of calling to her didn't help. Until one day, he forced himself to find another woman. This was Lillian. Lillian had been an antidote for the poison. He had found Lillian because she had been the opposite of Ursule.

That had been his lost period. His mind took in the memories. He met Lillian in a café in Copenhagen. And slowly life had taken on its rhythm. He was living through his life. But in some odd way his life was living him and he had never forgotten Ursule.

He had never really loved Lillian. But she made sense to him. She was brilliant. She had studied law at Harvard and she was just entering a large law firm. Her soft voice, her discipline, her coldness appealed to him. He was tired of traveling. He wanted children. A home. A career without wondering what he was going to be or do. They married in a church in Copenhagen. And then a civil ceremony. She told him she wanted to convert to Judaism to please his parents. He told her not to bother. They would love her. And they did. And everything was good for a while.

There were moments when Lillian, alone, faced the person that she had become after she married Jerry Hess. He had transformed her with his magic wand into a different person than she had been before him. Growing up in New York City as part of the International Danish Consulate—she had been shy, studious, feminine. Jerry had made her "go out" to the world—and still she thought she had overdone her role as wife. It was a zeal to please him. To love him. An abundance of love that had led to the disastrous personality that she now owned. It was so easy to become a boss. One uses the "aggressive" personality for deals, for one's work, and soon one becomes the public self. Such was the case for Lillian. Her lawyer's mask became her own face. It was difficult now to tell where the mask stopped and the skin began.

Lillian thought often about separations. What would life be like without Jerry?

She often thought of that. What would it be like to have Jerry move his clothes out of the closet? His medicine out of the medicine cabinet? What would it be like to face a medicine cabinet without valuable cologne (which she bought him) and constipation pills? Why was Jerry so constipated anyway? What would it be like to face the odds-and-ends closet in the bathroom without his hair massager? What would it be like to live without his scotch? Without his shoe bags filled with shoes? She had become as attached to "his" objects as to her own. And what if they were all to disappear? What would she miss most about Jerry? His madness? His affection? What would he miss about her? Deep beneath her lawyer's personality, beneath her "sensible" mask was another Lillian whom Jerry never knew. A frightened person with whom even she had never made friends. A Lillian who always longed to wear high heels that were much too high, a Lillian who ached to be less sensible. Jerry was a magician. He had made her body feel whole for twenty years. Now their lovemaking had slackened and stopped. It was, perhaps, her fault. She wondered what had happened. It was as if one day an enormous cold wind had blown over them, chilling their passion and isolating them. Now when she reached out he was there. But not there. She remembered when she first met Jerry, the long talks that had not stopped with their lovemaking. He had held her in his arms and kissed her so many times, then loved her, then talked. He had told her about his parents and his life in Queens, where he looked for beauty and found only tomatoes falling out of a shoe box. She had whispered to him about the consulate lunches that her mother (now dead in an airplane crash with her father) had taken her to, how she had been dressed in white pinafores and how the whole world seemed to speak Danish and Swedish. She spoke about memories of Denmark during summers, the Tivoli Gardens, and her mother taking her to the public library. The long days when she crawled inside of books at Harvard to forget her life, and how proud her parents had been when she graduated.

Lillian had given her deepest feelings to Jerry. When he first undressed her she had been a virgin. He had stroked her body as if she were a precious flower that he dare not pick, and she had encouraged him to make love to her. Now, she was not his loved one. Their passion had cooled, turned to friendship and later to deep intimacy. They had sat together, shoulder to shoulder, at funerals, weddings, bar mitzvahs, christenings, dinners, they had walked hand in hand through summers and falls and winters. He could not really make up his mind about things. She had become strong for him, and yet, inside, she knew his tenderness and strength. He had always been thoughtful, bringing little pictures to her, photographs of them together, in small silver frames which he had found in Italy. He had been kind and gentle to her. He had been the one strong person in her life whom she had leaned on after the terrible trauma of hearing about her parents' death. She had never forgotten how he had taken hold of her in his arms and said, "Lillian, I will be your parents. I will take care of you forever," and then taken her away to the cool slopes of Canada where she had finally recovered.

"I love you, Lillian," he had said, as he threw a blanket over her knees and stared up at the sun.

She found herself returning frequently to memories of her childhood in Denmark. One memory in particular recurred. She had skated out on the clear, smooth, cold ice. No one was around. She smelled the lumber from the lumber factory. Suddenly the ice cracked. She fell through to the cold water. Were it not for a fat farmer who saw her waving her hands she would have drowned. Now, it was happening again. She seemed to sense again the cold weather. The smell of lumber. And the ice, cracking. She was petrified that she was losing Jerry. She was going to drown. She was listening to the ice of her marriage crack and she was frightened that without Jerry she would never be able to bob through to the water's surface and live.

14.

Twenty years of marriage. Where had the time gone? Jerry wondered. Lillian's Danish sweetness, her soft voice, had turned to toughness over the years. Gone was the laugh. The kindness. In its place, only practicality. Did Lillian have a lover? What difference did it make anyway? She no longer loved him. That was all that mattered. Lillian did everything she could to annoy him. For example, she had been flirting with the maintenance man at their house in East Hampton. They had one of the big, fairy-tale houses on the ocean front on Lily Pond Lane that required someone's looking after the castle constantly as if it were a child. He had hired a full-time gardener and maintenance fellow who was heavyset, had hands gnarled like tree trunks and a good-looking peasant smile. He could tell that Lillian was attracted to him. She was always finding excuses to go "to the Hamptons" and he suspected that it was more than the pipes that the gardener maintained. Was he Lillian's lover? Did anyone know?

"Are you fucking the gardener?" he asked one night as they sat in the living room reading, or pretending to read.

"Are you crazy?"

"It's Lady Chatterley's lover all over again. O God!"

"My dear Jerry. If Lady Chatterley had married a gardener, she would have been fucking around with rich cripples." It was the first amusing thing she had said in twenty years. "You see, everyone wants what they don't have."

He had to agree.

But weren't there people who loved each other? Wasn't there a happy couple to be found? All those men on their third marriages always seemed to be smiling at the Parke-Bernet sales. They walked through the lobby, hand in hand with their beloveds. They bid on paintings, desks, armchairs they didn't want or need. They seemed to have found at least a last reprieve from old age.

Recently, they ("the model couple—Lil and Jer") had had a spat over the Lehman dinner for crippled children. The dinner had been held at the Waldorf. One of those "benefits" where the list of patrons was impressive and included just the right amount of Jewish Millionaires, Minority Millionaires, and artists to make it chic. Famous song writers. A few movie stars, some artists, some athletes, several movie producers, and a well-known political figure. It was the A List. Lillian was one of the chairwomen. Actually, she was only on the Dinner Committee. The honorary chairman was Mrs. Lehman. It was a black-tie affair and included many of the special directors of special education, directors of the National Information Center for the Handicapped, and directors from the National Association of State Boards of Education. It was all to help handicapped children. Tickets were oversubscribed at two hundred dollars apiece. The handicapped ball! Of course, it was really just to rub shoulders, for the New York philanthropic bullshit artists to remind everyone that they weren't just the aging, decadent rich. For one night, everyone drove in from their homes in the country and snubbed the discotheques to show the reporters from *Women's Wear Daily* and *People* magazine that they, the A List, had hearts! Intellectuals, manufacturers, stars, and ex-glamour kings and queens arrived in their limousines.

At the dinner, Jerry, hitched up in his black tie and dinner jacket, sat on the dais with the Lehmans. Lillian was dancing with a famous tennis player. He noticed with small satisfaction the pieces of David Webb jewelry which shone throughout the room like flashlights. All the Fongs were there. It was a name he'd made up (with a buddy of his who lived in the Dakota) for all the women who appeared at all the premieres, disco-parties, charity dinners, fund raisers, the openings— they had all had their faces lifted so that their eyes all slanted. The Fong faces were the faces he saw at every superchic event. Jesus! He had seen the Fongs everywhere that week. They were the women who never had crêpe chins, never had lines on their faces. Every ten years, their eyes became a little more slanted. In some terrible way, they all resembled each other. They were the New York madly sought-after mandarins. Another Fong affair.

At the Fong affair, Jerry realized how much he disliked the Lehmans. "They're not my favorite couple," he told Lillian.

Fongs and Hamptonites. Moving their asses for charity. Rocking and rolling, hustling, bobbing, shaking, bopping—he looked out over the sea of boobies and suntans. He would make a bet that all of the aging, dancing maniacs were not only tennis players, but like himself, were now into jogging. It was depressing.

After dinner, the deaf children were brought in to sing. It made no sense to have them performing at the dinner. But then, as Lillian explained, "Everyone wants to know where the money is going."

Watching them sing, Jerry felt sick. Who were the disadvantaged? The children with their angelic faces? Or the Fongs?

He remembered whispering to Lillian: "I've got to get out of here. You take the Lehmans home in the car."

"You can't leave in the middle of the program," she hissed back.

"Why not?"

75

"There are speeches." She dug her long artificially wrapped nails into his dinner jacket.

"Whoever arranged this program is sick. It's eleven o'clock. These kids should be home in bed. They shouldn't be performing monkeys."

"But the children enjoy it."

"Well, I don't."

Lillian kept smiling. She was so proud to be on the dais, sitting next to the Whitneys and the Lehmans. Her dress cost a thousand dollars at Martha's—without alterations. The children kept singing in sign language. The guests were all paying attention. The music had stopped. An energetic teacher of the handicapped led the children. The waiters were the only people who made noise as they cleared the dishes. Forks and spoons clattered at the tables. The children continued. Jerry thought how handicapped he was.

"I'm leaving, Lillian, let go of my arm."

"The hell you are," she said through her teeth, smiling.

"If you want to enjoy this misery, you stay. I'm not."

She held his jacket, but he got up and pulled away from her.

"I'm leaving, Lillian. Let go of my arm."

Lillian was enraged. She was afraid someone had heard him. She looked around the table. No one was listening. "Thank God no one heard you. Just a few more moments. Then we can leave. Please, Jerry, don't embarrass me."

"I'm not trying to embarrass you. There's just so much I can take. All the misery that is here tonight makes me sick."

He got up to leave. He looked like a head waiter in a hurry. As he ran down the steps from the grand ballroom, down the blue carpeted hotel lobby, past Peacock Alley, the check-in desk, the Hanae Mori boutique, Ciro's, past the hookers and tourists and into a cab hailed by the doorman, he felt manic. Colors seemed brighter. His energy level was high. His anger level speeded up everything he did. As if he was running, he felt his heart pounding inside him. He couldn't wait to be home.

76

15.

He arrived. She arrived. He was taking a shower.
"Everyone saw you leave," she said.

"Nobody saw me and even if they did, so what?"

"You embarrassed me. At least you could have had the decency to support me. To see this evening through."

"Fuck you!" he screamed from the shower.

"Fuck you."

"You just want a body next to you. I've had it. I've given my body to enough charities. Why don't you drag someone else with you? I'm tired, Lillian." (All this from the shower.)

"What are you tired of?"

"You," he said truthfully. It was elating to tell her the truth. He had read somewhere that Guggenheim had become a mystic. That he had started by giving away all his furniture until he had nothing left. Being free of objects had been electrifyingly easy. That's how he felt now, letting the truth out of his mouth to

Lillian. Free. Oh, could he tell her things. He could really get out of his system what it was like to be married to her. Lillian had taken off her clothes. She was rubbing night cream into her face. She was greased for action.

"I drag myself to all these stupid auctions at Sotheby's and Parke-Bernet. I entertain your clients and art suckers until I'm nauseated by one more dinner party. And when I ask you to do something for me, you humiliate me."

"Since when are handicapped children so meaningful to you? Since when does anything mean anything to you?"

They had stopped screaming at each other. Too tired to continue what both of them knew to be a useless fight. They were deaf and dumb and maimed in the battle of wits. They had fought each other so many times. *They* were the handicapped children.

Jerry wished with all his soul that he could dump Lillian. It was one thing to enjoy the fruits of marriage. It was another thing to have a hysterical woman on your hands. Jerry knew that under Lillian's cool exterior lurked a monster of a woman who could make a lot of trouble if things didn't go her way. She was not about to give up all of the pieces of the jigsaw puzzle they had worked so hard to put together. His recent sale of the Cézanne to the Louvre had brought them a great deal of notoriety. Finally, all of the invitations to all the right parties and charities were coming in. Lillian wasn't about to release him. He realized sadly that he was a prisoner in the very maze that he had created. He was a minotaur who had boxed himself into the maze where he lived, and now that he was there (didn't the fourteen-room apartment seem like a maze?) how the hell was he going to get out?

16.

Slowly he would put on those jogging shoes which held up his frame. And, like a possessed person, begin running from the house, running from Lillian, running from the maids and the dinners and the crap. Running from the lack of freedom—the lasso that Lillian had thrown around him, the straitjacket of his marriage. What was the point of making all this money if he was so unhappy? Like so many poor slobs, he had worked his cojones off to have a better life—but now that the life was here, was it better? Or, just annoying? He had nothing really tying him to Lillian anymore. He would sit with her at the dinner table and think how he disliked her.

He was running now.

Running away from Lillian. In his wolfish underwear. In his jogging shoes. In his nylon warm-up pants. In his long-sleeved hooded sweat shirt. Suddenly he saw a vision in front of him that made him wonder if he was hallucinating. It was Ursule! Not as she was now—it was Ursule as he had first seen her. Ursule when he first met her. She was standing and drinking soda pop by a stand with an umbrella. The same crop of black hair around her face. The same long legs and white skin. The same slanted black eyes and smile. He stood there staring at her. It was amazing.

As he got closer, he realized that it wasn't Ursule, but someone he had not seen before. Someone who could have been her double. His opening remark was awkward.

"Soda gives a carbohydrate high." He stood there. She was taller than he was.

"I'm not an orthodox jogger," she shot back. She continued drinking her soda. "Besides, I'm hot. I've run all the way from Gramercy Park." She looked exactly like Ursule.

He was desperate to keep her talking.

"Have you read Jack Batten's book? Anything carbonated is bad for breathing."

"I haven't read any books on jogging. For me, it's not a religion. It's just something I do to keep my head together."

"How long have you been running?"

"I started a couple of years ago. In California."

Yes, she looked exactly like Ursule. Except—in some way she was a slapstick version. There was a comedic element about her. Ursule in an offbeat version.

"You know, jogging is really a science. Like a vegetarian diet. The nutrition one gets out of this exercise is almost like a handful of natural vitamins."

"Oh yeah? Well, I just run because it's fun. It's cheap. It beats snorting coke."

"Since I've started jogging, I just eat yogurt and I've given up smoking, and I can't tell you how much healthier I feel," he said.

"Well"—she was smiling. "Keep jogging."

He was turning into a compulsive jogger jock. The kind who talks compulsive jog-talk.

"I get up earlier. And I do warm-up exercises. And I do a lot of breathing exercises."

"Well, keep jogging." She wanted to jog away. But he was praying inside she wouldn't leave.

"Do you go jogging every day?" he asked.

"Yes. You're supposed to do this regularly. That's what I heard."

"Well, if you're doing your jogging seriously, I'd really like to give you this book I have by Batten that tells you how to be aerobic. It will be helpful. I'll bring it to you tomorrow, let's meet tomorrow at this time and we can run together."

17.

Mary thought about the jogger she had met in the park. She knew nothing about him. Not even his name. There was something about him she liked. He had stood there shivering in his hood.

What was it like to be an art dealer?

He told her that he sold paintings. Had a great private collection of art. He spoke about himself as they walked to the reservoir.

"What is it that makes you a good art dealer?" she asked.

"My understanding of people."

"Is that what has made you so successful?"

"Well," he said modestly, "I have a good eye. I look where other people look. But I look closely. At the Van Richmond sale in London, everyone was bidding so high for the Rembrandt drawings. My eye happened to catch a small painting that no one seemed to notice. I bid a thousand dollars for it. It happens to be a Donatello."

"How did you first become an art dealer?"

"I didn't become one. I was a college student selling prints from door to door. Selling pictures that way you learn a lot about selling pictures the hard way. That—knowing how to sell. And grace."

"Grace?"

"I'm different from most art dealers. They usually spend all their time with clients. I spend most of my time reading or writing. I prefer the company of my old friends and a few writers to the art world. Also, one of the things that I did when I first started out was I made friends with the art scholars. I treated the scholars very well. Most art dealers treat them like servants. They're paid consultants and they are not paid very well. I made the scholars my partners."

"Where do you find paintings?"

"I look the same places as anyone else. But I seem to find more paintings. I suppose what's really unique about me is that I'm not a third-generation art dealer. I've studied about art. I traveled where there were good paintings."

"It must be exciting to go to the auctions."

"I don't think so. I don't really find the art world exciting. It's a nice way to make a living. But I really don't like dealing."

"Why not?"

"I don't like dealing with people as commodities. That's what most art dealers have to do."

"Selling painting doesn't excite you?"

"No. Writing excites me. Loving a woman excites me. But selling a picture has never excited me. It's a way of getting money to have the freedom that I want."

"What do you like to do most?"

"Write."

"What else?"

"There are lots of things. And you?"

"I'm not sure. I'm a writer. A journalist."

"You jog every day."

"I try to."

"I jog every day. But can I tell you a secret? One part of me hates jogging."

"I know. Jogging can be a bore," she said truthfully.

"Then you're not passionate about it?" he asked.

"No. Only a narcissist is really passionate about it. Most people who run admit it's hard to have a love affair with it. I'd prefer to catch butterflies or something."

"Then why are you here?"

"It's good for my body. It relaxes me. Some people see jogging the way other people see sex," she said.

"I know. Some people see a shoe the way other people see the Acropolis. But a shoe is still a shoe."

She laughed.

"One of the reasons I'm really here this morning is to see you," he said.

"I don't know if I should believe you."

"Why don't you try it?"

Mary decided to try trusting him. He was an oddball. The patrician art dealer. The next time they met, he told her about his selling trips in Europe. About his apartment at the Dakota. His wife. About Jerry, Jr. Auctions. Wheeling and dealing. Writing. After he told her he was married, she told him she lived alone. They talked about weather. Good times. Fish stories. Icy weather. Childhood. Early mornings. Why they liked writing.

"Who do you write for?" he asked.

He wanted to know about her life.

She wanted to know about his. He always smelled of nice perfume. Something about him reminded her of her Uncle Henry. Not that he was older. The way he talked. Slowly. She liked hearing about his trips. He liked hearing about her writing. The next time they met, they talked. Ran. Talked.

"I'm a political journalist, basically," she told him. They were now at the part of the reservoir where runners stop, and they both slowed down.

"Let's go have a glass of orange juice," he said. He felt thirsty and wanted to keep her with him as long as possible.

"Sure."

Mary found herself following Jerry. It was all new—the stranger in the park—now suddenly becoming her friend. They went to a health bar on Eighty-sixth Street. She wondered if he would, as her mother said, make a pass at her.

"I'm an out-of-work political writer," she laughed, "because there's no publication for me to put my work into."

"What do you mean?"

"I mean that most things political—deep down political—just don't get out in the press. The press is really self-censored." She paused to check his interest. She added, "The political information one gets from the press is *owned* by sponsorship and advertisers and doesn't allow the real facts of what is happening to be known. Sure, you can turn on television and see programs of the holocaust after the events—but what about the holocausts that are happening now?"

18.

They met often and ran.

When she was with him she felt elated, happy. She looked forward to seeing him. They ran together now every morning. She told him about California and her mother. Wasted years. Being an oddball. Wanting to be political. Dates. And how strange it felt hanging around New York.

"To tell you the truth, I thought I'd be famous right away. Now I really think I'm semi-famous. I'm known in the underground papers. And I thought I'd be rich. Now, I'm semi-rich. I pay for my hotel room but that's all really. I'm Miss Semi. Semi-everything. I get a semi-good table at Elaine's. I go to semi-literary parties where I'm semi-known. I have a semi-definite publisher. Meanwhile, I'm nowhere special."

They both laughed. She could make fun of herself. For the first time since Ursule, he was having a good time. He wondered if he was starting to really love her.

Mary. Who was she? She looked like someone who had accumulated nothing. He asked her out to a bar. His favorite. P. J. Moriarty's. This was their first "date." He was frightened she wouldn't be there. He waited. And suddenly she walked in. She looked as if she were held together by push-pins. It was the first time he had seen her out of her jogging suit. Her hair was long and messy, and she had braided the front parts of her hair so that she looked like one of the Renaissance painters' women. Her sweater was purple and her pants were red canvas. She wore high-heeled red leather boots. A gold chain around her waist.

The drinks arrived, the amenities bridge crossed. "I've just been interviewing a media freak," she said, suddenly. "He wants the latest information immediately before it can cool and be superseded. He was king of the hippies. Now he's looking for a place to perform. He's haunted by his past. Blissed out. He's now putting together nonpolitical seminars which are being held in his living room, and he's writing a television special based on the insights which come out of the seminars. He keeps talking about inner light, the faith, and cosmic consciousness. He keeps telling me he's in touch with his feelings and *creative energy*." She paused and studied Jerry. "You know, those guys who find new ways to breathe and eat and meditate—he's trying to get the answers without even finding a way to the question."

Jerry was ricocheted by the machine-gun bullets of her conversation. She stood there at the bar, six feet of woman, filled with that light energy to which he was attracted.

19.

Jerry felt a little uncomfortable. He wanted to get laid. Instead, he was getting a political oration. He was willing to put up with it for the moment. She kept talking in her double-time voice. He had once heard Billie Holiday speak on a television talk show. She had been brilliant, comic, and spoke so quickly it was hard to understand exactly what she was saying. She sounded like her. Not what she said. But the way she said it.

"You see, a journalist feels about the news the way a whore feels about jewelry. She loves it. And she wants it to be truthful. Look at the *Times* this morning. We're going to war in Africa and nobody cares. Carter is trying to get this country to intervene again in Angola. Carter's trying to support a political faction that was defeated in the War of Independence."

"What War of Independence?" Jerry asked.

"Angola's War of Independence. This could be worse than Vietnam."

"I'm not sure I understand the situation. Who the hell knows where Angola is? Why are you so concerned about Angola?"

"Who knew about Vietnam? Until America mucked around, nobody knew where Vietnam was."

They stood drinking.

"Have you ever been to Sri Lanka?" he asked.

"No. Why?"

"Well, they have a magic ceremony there called Tovil. It's white magic. They believe that when someone falls ill and finds no relief they seek the advice of a priest or yakadura who specializes in the curing of spirit attacks. It involves drumming, dancing, and chanting. It's called charming."

"Why are you telling me this?"

"I thought I'd charm you."

They walked slowly in the streets to her hotel. He was anxious to make love to her and she could tell the signs. He couldn't stop talking about exorcism and ghosts and ceremonial systems.

"As a Tovil ceremony begins, a dancer whirls to drumbeats and chants. Tovil songs and dances honor Buddha, appease demons, and appeal to gods who hold sway over evil spirits."

He took her clothes off slowly.

"You're a master of spells," Mary said.

"You're pretty adept at charming yourself."

"This is better than homeopathic medicine," Mary whispered to him.

"Let's just fuck," he said.

"Don't you know a more poetic way of saying that?" she asked.

"Can I make love to you?"

"For sure."

He was a good lover. She didn't expect this. Her mind wandered back to Johnny. Jerry was so different from him. Johnny kept saying, "Suck my cock, lady," in a way that he thought

90

would turn her on. Jerry talked about charms. Tribes. Dancers. She held her breasts to him.

"I want you, Mary," he said.

She hadn't felt anyone care for her for a long time.

He was funny. "Do you know that fable about the War Between the Rats and the Weasels?"

"I thought you'd never ask."

"Seriously. It's a fable by La Fontaine."

"How does it go?"

"Weasels were ever foes. Like cats. All of ratkind. And their long spines would wind through rat holes, I suppose, to stalk the prey to his bedroom, except that every rat secures his habitat with insufficient headroom."

"What's the moral?"

"I forget."

They laughed. And loved. And laughed. Then she wept. Took out some gin and poured him some. He took her in his arms.

"Under the whale, you're a white dolphin," he said. He didn't know what he was saying. "The frog expressed some doubt that he could swim without a helping hand, but she soon found a remedy by taking a reed for tether to tie their feet together."

She was pink and white. In the dark she looked so much like Ursule. They took a shower. Her arms were round and soft as they embraced him. He picked her up in the shower. She slid soapy and warm out of his arms. When they came out of the shower, he made love to her again.

"A partridge and a hare are wont to share."

It wasn't frantic. It was the way she had hoped making love with a man would be again, in the loneliness of her soul. Why did men think that harshness was sex? He held her in his arms, crooned her name over and over. This was where she felt at home. She forgot everything as he kissed her and moved in and out of her body. She forgot her articles, Angola, the sadness of being alone in New York. For a moment, she belonged to someone. This wasn't a vaudeville of sex in a hotel with a stranger whose name she didn't know. This was Jerry, a man she just met jogging, but whom she knew she was going to have a long and deep relationship with. She felt good as her head filled the pillow. This was deeper than sex. This was like coming home.

After making love they were both hungry. It was only nine o'clock and he took her for dinner at Orsini's. He was known by the captain, who said, "Oh, Mr. Hess. You don't need a reservation. We always have a table for you."

He led them into a dark room where couples sat on couches and candles lit the room. Mary felt uneasy in this restaurant because she was wearing pants and everyone else was in a dress. "I feel uncomfortable," she whispered to Jerry.

"Well, don't." He ordered a bottle of champagne and looked at her. "To our lives," he said.

"Well, this is a far cry from McDonald's," she said. "I'm used to ordering Kentucky fried chicken in a take-out bag. I don't know what to order first."

He ordered for her. "We'll start with some fried mozzarella and then we will both have the veal piccata and a rugola salad." The captain bowed.

"We have to watch our bodies if we're jogging," Jerry said, and held her hand under the table.

"Now," he said, "you listen to me, Mary Reagan."

She looked at him.

"If you really want to write for a magazine, I know the publishers of *Fortune*, *Time-Life*, *Art News*, *New York*, *Esquire*. All of these people are art people, also my clients. I can call anyone. I have the connections that most writers only dream about. You tell me what you want and I'll get it for you."

Mary sipped her champagne. "I feel like Alice in Wonderland," she said. "Only I'm not really suited to those magazines, Jerry."

"What difference does it make? Get in a situation where you make some money and get your name known and then you can write all that shit about Angola for anyone you want. Would you like to write for *The New Yorker*? Brendan Gill comes to dinner at my house once a week. He's helpful to young people. Brendan could introduce you to William Shawn and you could write 'Talk of the Town' pieces for *The New Yorker*. That's just to begin with."

Mary was eating her mozzarella without stopping. "Hey, this food is delicious," she said.

"Or you can write for *Scientific American*."

"Look, Jerry. I have to live on the edge and do something that's truthful and dangerous. I'm a working woman. That's true, but if I wanted to sell out, I could be writing under my own by-line in Los Angeles, the way I did when I was a kid."

He took another glass of champagne. "OK, kid. You tell me what you want to do. I'm ready to help you as long as I don't have to believe in what you're doing."

20.

At the Dakota, Lillian was planning to confront Jerry.
On the evening of confrontation, she dressed the part of a wife who is going to have things clarified. She was tired of white. She had bought, just for this occasion, a dress by Bill Blass that was made of gold mesh. Golden in her bones, blonde hair woven in a long braid, a Gauloise carefully placed in her mouth. She sat in the den waiting for Jerry to arrive back from his meeting. The den annoyed her. It was wicker. She had been talked into wicker by Sandra Payson's decorator whose influence in homes was seen throughout the wickered playpens of the rich. She had allowed Donghia to put that ghastly marble wallpaper in the den. Why did everything have to look like a bookend? She reminded herself to go to a cocktail party for Brenda Feigen Fasteau, who was running for the senate—the state senate. Another woman lawyer was trying to break through the barriers. She made a mental note to send Brenda a check for a thousand dollars. Where the hell was

Jerry? It was better to get this scene over with. Jerry opened the door. She heard him in the corridor of the apartment.

"Are we going to the theatre?" Jerry asked as he made himself a drink and sat down across from Lillian on the wicker sofa. "What play are you dragging me to?"

"No, we are not going to the theatre. We are going to have our own little comedy right here. Unfortunately it won't be a musical comedy—but I do hope you will find it amusing."

Jerry looked at her and said, "I hate your sense of humor, Lillian. You're much easier to take when you talk like a lawyer."

Jerry hated confrontations. He avoided truths as much as possible. This evening was going to be a drag.

"All right. Let's start reviewing the case. Three months ago, you began behaving oddly. You refused to go out to dinner, no longer took an interest in the friends we have generally seen together over a period of eighteen years. You were no longer interested in the son we share in boarding school and forgot to mail him his letter and his check. You canceled all your business luncheons, did not appear at many of the meetings that took place in this house, leaving your clients to be entertained by Rosa, who is a cook, not an art dealer. Your certificates of registration for the paintings arrived from Paris and you never opened them. The book on forgeries arrived after having been sent by messenger through the mails in Holland and you never opened it. Your jogging which began at eight in the morning has extended to eight in the evening. You look all jogged out, darling. And yet, no one has seen you running recently."

Jerry sipped on his drink. "Would you care to summarize your case, Mrs. Hess? Or should I say—Judge Hess? Since you seem to be judging me about things which are really none of your business."

"I happen to think this is my business, darling, since I happen to be your wife."

"Since when?"

"What do you mean, Jerry?"

96

"I mean that you really stopped being my wife several years ago. You're really just another one of my art clients. And I'm your client. I sell you pretty pictures. You sell me your educated guesses concerning how I should proceed. And we have a housekeeper in every house to handle the details of living. We're two professional people. Sharing property. Memories. And destiny. But you can hardly be called a wife, Lillian."

"I think the courts would think differently."

"Since when have you been thinking of legal action?"

"I always think of legal action. Professional courtesy. You remember the joke about the sharks who parted in the water thanks to professional courtesy?"

"You don't really have to put everything into small print, Lillian."

"I wouldn't get insulting, Jerry. I could blow the whistle on you any time I choose."

"Are you blackmailing me?"

"Not emotionally. The way you blackmail me. Let's not call it blackmail. Let us just say that you have left out some very interesting details of your recent jogging life. Does the name Mary Reagan mean anything to you?"

"You know it does."

"Does the fact that your adultery is not only insulting to me, but can cost you all your property, all your paintings, your houses—does this fact annoy you?"

Jerry sipped on his drink. "It would be very annoying," he said in a low voice.

"In other words, how would you feel about my ruining you?" Lillian asked in that matter-of-fact voice of hers.

"Don't tell me you want to save this marriage," Jerry said sarcastically. "What about our East Hampton?"

"What about him?"

"Haven't you been a little more than employer and employee?"

"No. Do you have any proof to the contrary?"

Jerry relaxed. "Look, I hate scenes. What do you want?"

"What does a woman want?" Lillian asked suddenly. "Freud was supposed to have asked that question. Actually he never wrote that. But what do I want? Honesty. A better relationship with options to grow and love. I want you to dump Mary Reagan before it's too late."

"Too late for what? It's already too late. I love her, Lillian."

Her eyes narrowed. "How touching. I can remember when you loved me because Ursule didn't want you. Now I'm quite sure you love Mary because Lillian doesn't understand you. Only I do understand you. And you can jog your life away with your hippie. You can play tycoon, rebel, radical rake. You can choose Mary as your slut. Choice is the mark of a healthy person, Jerry. But I can choose to remain Lillian Hess. I don't happen to feel like throwing away my investment in your life. You may think you can dump me after eighteen years of marriage. But I'm an aristocrat, if you please. I'm the one who will do the dumping when I choose. And I don't choose. I would do anything in the world to keep you with me. Including making sure you had no recourse to money."

"What good would that do you?"

"No good. Except to ruin you. The way you choose to want to ruin me in life."

"What do you want?" Jerry asked. He was beginning to see the dynamics of health; as Lillian became angrier her face grew younger. She had the same rosy skin she had when he met her in Denmark—she seemed to look less used, less tired, as she glowed with anger. She changed back to the sympathetic young Danish girl who had listened to his confidences, aspirations. "You look healthier than I've seen you look in years," he said.

"Healthy people don't get depressed."

"Let's work out our arrangement," Jerry said warily.

"All right."

"What are your conditions?"

"I want you to be with me on weekends and two nights a week. I want you to see Reagan in private—and if you go anywhere, use the limousine. I don't want you to flaunt in public this aberration. Also—zip your fly." She walked out of the room.

98

21.

It was after the scene with Lillian that Jerry began to wonder if he could find the strength to make a new life without Lillian. The more she held on to him the more he wanted to leave. He thought again about Ursule. On a whim, he called her theatre to find out where she was. They said she was now acting in California but that she would be in New York for two days the following week to receive a special award. She would be staying, her secretary said, at the Stanhope Hotel. Jerry rang up the Stanhope and made sure that she was arriving. He sent a dozen white peonies and white roses—her favorite flowers—and a bottle of their favorite champagne. He prepared to call her. Why did he want to see her? Everything had gone wrong. Lillian, whom he had married on the rebound, was now preparing to ruin him and hold him to her by blackmail. Mary Reagan? The truth was, he didn't know who Mary really was—except that he knew that she was a ghost of Ursule. Was it unhealthy to look for carbon copies—to chase shadows? Ursule was the source of anxiety. The source of all his voyaging. Meeting Ursule again was important to him now. He looked in the mirror as he dressed. His hair was greying, but he was aging well. He was considered handsome; now his body was sleek from jogging, his skin was tan. How long had it been since he had seen her? Nine years. At her last husband's funeral. It frightened him to meet her again. But he was eager for her.

"Come in, Jerry," he heard her slow sensual voice call from the suite. He opened the door and was surprised to see how well she still looked. Face lifts and exercise had kept her young, embalmed in her own legend. How old was she now? Seventy? Older? Ursule was still a great beauty.

Jerry, despite all efforts, felt like her slave again.

"Jerry, you've aged well."

"You don't look so bad yourself," he said in a high, boyish voice that he used only with her.

"You mean for an old woman? Let me tell you about my recent life. I fell desperately in love with Michael, my sixth husband, as you know. It was the greatest love affair of my life—after you, darling. Well, you knew Michael. You knew what a great composer he was. Perhaps one of the most interesting men of our generation. His only problem was his modesty. When he died, after the funeral I hid myself in my apartment. I even gave up acting. But slowly the life juices returned. And my thoughts, oddly enough, began turning to you, Jerry."

"In what way?"

"You were like a kite—a beautiful young boy—a kite that I let go. Never be afraid to let anything go, I said to myself. But suddenly I wanted to pull you back to me. But I knew of your commitment to Lillian. She saved your life, poor darling, when I left you. And my conscience wouldn't allow me to interfere in your marriage."

"I always missed you," Jerry said.

"And so you've searched me out?" Ursule was smiling. She was wearing a sheer dress and he could see her skin, beautifully white, unwrinkled and still exciting under her black dress. The white gloves seemed to bring a certain formality to the occasion. Otherwise, he knew, she would have been wearing one of her negligees. On the coffee table was the unopened champagne and two volumes of Brecht. He walked over to the champagne and popped the cork. It flew to the air and sounded like a gun exploding. But she didn't move.

"Champagne?" Jerry asked. He poured a glass for her.

"Thank you," she said with the familiar sensuous look which meant she still found him interesting.

"Are you still interested in me as a lover?" Jerry blurted out abruptly. He realized that he still found her smell, her perfume exciting.

"No. Of course not, darling."

"What do you want?" he asked.

"I just want to be friends with you," Ursule said.

He looked at her. "I have this odd feeling about the past, Ursule. It's as if I want to go back to it. And I can't. I seem to be moving ahead in my life and backwards at the same time. When I knew you first, there was just one woman in my life. Now there are three."

Ursule sat and listened.

Her extraordinary eyes, huge brown-black eyes, took everything in.

Finally she said in her low voice, "I hope *I'm* the most extraordinary one."

Jerry laughed. "Sometimes I wonder why one woman isn't *enough* for me? Am I looking for a mother? Am I a fag?"

"Don't be ridiculous, Jerry."

"It's not ridiculous. Every man wonders about that."

"Oh, God. Everyone's a fag. All my *homosexual* students are getting married."

"Why do they do that? To cover up?" Jerry asked.

"Don't ask me. I could never understand why a homosexual got married. But then I could never understand why a heterosexual got married either. Marriage is ridiculous."

"I wish we had gotten married, Ursule."

"I know. We loved each other."

"Why did you leave me?"

"There must have been a reason. I just can't think of it." She lit a cigarette and placed it in her ivory holder.

"I always think of you," Jerry said, nervously looking away from her eyes.

"Even now that you're so successful? My God, Jerry, I read about you everywhere. That Cézanne that you just sold to the Louvre was written about in the *Times*. *The Wall Street Journal*. Even *Variety*. That was quite a coup. I loved the piece in the *Times* saying you were an exceptional art dealer but that you really preferred to write elegant essays. That was a marvelous picture of you and Lillian. How is Lillian, by the way?"

"It's over."

"What is?"

"Our marriage."

"Don't be dramatic."

"Just stating the facts."

"Why over? She's intelligent. She's been an excellent wife."

"The woman's revolution is really the man's revolution, Ursule."

"What does all this have to do with Lillian?"

"It's not love that keeps us in the dining room, course after course, fierce and silent. It's not love that keeps us in the same bed. It's not even indolence. Or passion. Or indifference. It's not habit, which no one can explain."

"What is it then, darling?"

"Fear of loneliness and money."

"Why should you ever have to be lonely?"

"Because I'm impossible to live with. We all are."

"That's true. But everyone puts up with each other."

"I'm having a hard time putting up with Lillian. I ask myself is that why I'm running around like a rat? Because I no longer want to make love to Lillian?"

"There's a perverse thrill in asking yourself questions like that," Ursule said.

"Nel mezzo del bloody well comin di nostra vita mi retrovai dans una bloody selva oscura qui la derita via era smarita. Remember that? The *Divina*

Commedia? You read it to me in Florence, Ursule, when I was twenty. Dante found himself lost in the middle of his life. Couldn't find the straight path out. And Vergil was his teacher? That was you, Ursule. My Vergil. Except I wasn't lost then. I'm lost now. Help me."

"You're not really lost, Jerry." She blew smoke at him.

"You're the only person in my past who can come to the aid of my future."

"What can I do?"

"Step out of the past and be part of my life now."

"You have me. Here I am. I'm real. I'm here. Talk to me."

"I wish I could talk to Lillian."

"Why can't you?"

"She doesn't understand anything. About the poetry of living. About growing old. Especially about growing old. Whenever I stir up monsters inside myself—she doesn't understand."

"How about the young girl? What's her name?"

"Mary, Mary Reagan. I feel politically speechless with her. To her, I don't exist politically. And she doesn't understand me as a Jew."

"She's not Jewish, darling."

"But all I'm talking about is the gap that exists between us. Though I try to fill the gap and pretend to ignore it, it's there. As a Jew I'm heir to a cultural experience she doesn't even share. Lillian tried to. She studied and immersed herself in the world of paintings and art. Mary doesn't care about tradition and culture. She told me she never wants to live in the world of my misfortunes."

"Well, she's young and easy under the apple boughs. She doesn't really know what she wants, Jerry. How about you? What do you want?"

"I feel that I am face to face with new choices. And new changes. These past few years, I feel myself becoming a new me. I feel different."

"How are you different?" He studied her large eyes, staring at him. Jerry thought of how Ursule had changed. It used to be that she could only look at a man with the desire to *seduce*. Now she was listening. Really listening to him. It was thrilling to have the great Ursule's total attention.

"I care about fucking." He averted his eyes, turned his gaze to the floor.

"That's normal."

"I need *women* more than ever. I'm being honest, I see them not as *them*, but as an obsessive horny need. The spirit's necessary anchor."

"Well, I spoiled you, darling. To make up for me, you now need many women." She crossed her legs, smiled.

"Sometimes I imagine us back in the Greek village where we used to go in the summer. I remember the village without crosses. I remember how I kissed you until you came to life in my arms," he said to her.

"That's all past."

"The past is still a place."

"A place to leave."

"This isn't the past. It's now."

"Well, I wanted to see you too. To find out how you were. And now I see that you're excellent. You're alive. Living. Filled with questions. Doubts. Passions. And your son?"

"In school. I adore him."

"And your work?"

"I told you dealing in art is a profession. No longer a passion. It doesn't mean all that much to me. I walk through the sales and auctions. But thinking about other things."

"What do you think about?"

She was now the old Ursule, the great actress. She put her hand on her breasts. He could see through her blouse. Her lips were moist. He hadn't felt excited and wanted a woman the way he wanted her, *ever* in his life. If she encouraged him to he would stay and make love to her.

"I know what you're thinking, darling. Well, not today. I have to get ready for dinner at '21.'" She stood up.

He got up and sniffed the air for the aphrodisiacal scent of her. It had been paradise to be with her. Even for a little while.

22.

After Jerry left Ursule, he thought with desire about Mary. He ran to her apartment. When he found her she was working against an article deadline. Mary was in a calmer mood than Jerry had seen her before. Since she had begun the article, she had become quiet, centered, a serious and determined person—a new Mary. She wore her glasses on her head and sat in a room filled with papers. She had unplugged the phones.

"My sometime roommate has returned," she said, running to him and kissing him. "Listen to this, what do you think of the title of this article? 'Boom. Should We Arm for Nuclear Defense?' "

"I think it sounds good—it has a hand-grenades sound to it. Now stop working and listen to me. I think you should put some poetry into this article. How's this?

There was a young girl called Sara
Who slept with her own Che Guevara.

When Che was away
Some new guy would stay
And only her lover could bear her.

What do you think?"

"I think I love you, you crazy mammal. Social progress is the only thing I love more than you. Now I'm ready to screw."

23.

As she lay in bed with Jerry, Mary thought of Johnny. Of the past. Of other men she had been with when she had been lonely.

"I'm going to do it," Johnny had said that morning on the phone.
"Do what?"
"Take a break from you."
"A break from me? I haven't seen you in weeks."
"Mary, I just can't handle it. You. Iza. The band. Our relationship. I have a lot of responsibility to people. It's too much. And don't call me in Florida. I thought that we had something together. We don't have."
"Go toot your horn," Mary had said, and hung up.
That was Johnny. Before him there was Hal Becker, porno king. His schtick was to get her to write a movie script.
"You can't afford me, Hal," she said. "Besides, your porno crap doesn't interest me."

"Don't call it porno. Call it exploitation. And when you introduce me to your friends, don't tell them I make porno films. Tell
them I'm a new-wave film maker."

But, like Johnny, he had seemed nice in the beginning. (Everyone seemed nice in the beginning.) His hair always looked as if he
had just blown it dry, and he had a small body—like the body of a
boy, not a man. He was half her size. In bed, she was always afraid
he would be crushed. For a sexologist, he knew *nothing* about
making love. She had gone into her bathroom to get undressed
the first time they made love and when she came out of the
bathroom, he was lying naked on the bed. She imagined he was
posing for one of his "insertion" shots in *Under the Yellow Window,* his
prick pic which had made so much money. She remembered Hal,
the pornographer. No heart. No feeling. Only hustles and hypes.
Hal and Johnny were two losers she had fancied. She imagined
what her mother would say about Johnny, about his coke habit,
his filthy nylon shirt, and there was his cosmic arrogance, his
pretensions toward stardom—"You like me only because I'm in
the public eye," he'd once said to Mary.

"Public eye? Who's ever heard of your band?"

"They haven't." He added, "But they will."

What would her mother have said?

She imagined her mother sitting at home with her book of
miracles. She would say something to Mary about both of these
losers. "Make welcome the state of grace, Mary. Rid yourself of
the swine."

Johnny was now out of her life. The last time she had seen
him, she had thought she was flipping out. They had been driving
around all night in Johnny's white Jaguar and smoking grass.
Suddenly, she had begun to cry. It must have been the grass but
her whole life started pouring out. She told Johnny how difficult
it had been all her life to be smart.

"Retards get all the attention. But the bright people have
problems. There's no one to talk to. In California, I always felt so

isolated all my life. I would hear voices talking to me and telling me to write, to care about others, to look at things and get them down on paper. It wasn't anything I told anyone. I would hear the voices—and I would write furiously. I remember in the convent school, I would sit on the lawn and I would imagine I heard God's voice telling me to do things for others. Help the poor. To write the truth. It frightened me."

"Don't be frightened," Johnny had said. "It's just that you live on a different level from other people. A higher level."

"Do you think so?" Mary had asked.

"Yes, I do."

And then, Mary remembered, Johnny had done something that frightened the shit out of her. He had raised his right hand and he had said, "I am your confirmation on earth of all you believe."

It had scared her. She sat in that white Jaguar wondering if she was flipping out. She wondered, "Is this how the Blessed Virgin felt at the Annunciation? Am I a saint that an angel has come to bless? Am I a holy messenger?" Her senses were agog. This blond man was sitting in front of her, staring with those blank eyes and talking to her as if she were a saint.

"I know I'm a good person. But I am not a fucking saint. Stop it, Johnny. Stop saying things like that."

"I can't help what is your destiny. I am your confirmation about why you have come to earth. You have a mission, Mary. It is a sacred one." His hand was raised. Was it real? Or had it been a con? She had begged him to start the car. She felt nauseated.

"Please, Johnny. Hurry. Start the car. I can't bear being in the middle of an annunciation."

Her experiences, except for Jerry, had all been with retards, coke freaks, or nuts. Once she had been asked to wear a nurse's uniform by a sick journalist from the *Enquirer,* who had given her a pair of black nylons, with a garter belt. She had met sick people. Especially Johnny, with his cosmic con, who was more sick than sick. He was playing Jesus Christ with her head. She had watched him and she knew the signs. His life bulged with an egotist's desire to manipulate women. To play God. To be worshiped. Well, he had picked the wrong number. Mary had gotten rid of all the creeps. Now there was only Jerry.

She thought of these things as she lay in bed with him. He was spoiled and rich. His confusions bored her. He was another guy with problems. Why were they attracted to her?

It had all been part of her first experiences in New York. She hadn't known any better. She didn't know a freak from a fag. A millionaire from a mugger. The people she met were so different from the friendly people in California. And it hadn't been as easy as she'd thought to get work. The publishers weren't dying for political truths from the mouth of Mary Reagan. It had been rough. She had clung to Johnny because she thought he was hip and open and honest. Instead he was just another freaked-out musician. It was hard to tell who was truly talented, who was good, who to hold on to. Here she was now, with Jerry. He seemed to be a regular guy. A little on the overprivileged white male side—he had too much in his life, not too little. But he was at least trying to choose and to change. There was something touching about him. Under the Dunhill tailored clothes, the credit cards and the cash, and the middle-aged sophistication, was an author manqué waiting to break out. She had met lesser men. He was like a magical Harvard professor, or a yippie she had once danced with under the turrets of San Francisco, a yippie who had once been a priest. He had passion. But he had missed something in life. He had come to her, like a fugitive, from a world of art, a world of money and manners and summer plans. A world of weekends and expensive restaurants and domestic problems and wife problems and child problems and servant problems and veterinarian problems. Behind him stood a tailor, an analyst, a broker, a chauffeur, a hairdresser on Madison Avenue, a travel agent, a masseur, a secretary, an accountant, a bookkeeper, a lawyer on retainer, a tennis pro, a world of financial advisors and art advisors, and bankers—and brokers. Then there was his wife. His son. His parents. And his friends. She could lay a magical finger on his life which included so many people she could never meet. Art. Love. Empires. Men were supposed to be what they *do*. Which was a mistake. Because she knew that Jerry wasn't what he did. He was what he wanted to be. He was his own museum of oddments and inklings. She really was beginning to feel good with him sometimes.

24.

Another day.
Lovemaking with Mary.
Jerry felt that she was wet and wanted him. He took her clothes off slowly. He kissed her face and her ears. He carried her gently to the bed and whispered to her how much he loved her.

"I love you too," she said and they giggled to be alive and feel how joyful it was to know what it was like to only want each other. And there she was—his "Renaissance woman" in his arms. He held her and noticed how each curl of hair twisted around her neck, her dark muffin hair, her large breasts and the serene look on her face when he kissed her. For too many years he had forgotten the wonder of making love. He had forgotten what it felt like to discover the texture of flesh, the feel of skin under his rough hands. He had been afraid to show the joy in covering a woman with kisses. He had to get rid of that fear, had to manifest his feelings. It frightened him. He alternated between elation and anxiety.

25.

Then there was the homecoming. He remembered that day after he returned. His son was waiting for him in the den. Jerry, Jr., had come down to look for a summer job and was spending the weekend at home before going back to school.

"Dad, what do you think?" Jerry, Jr., asked.

"About what?"

"About you and Mom."

"I think we are no happier and no unhappier than most people," Jerry said, looking across the room to a Monet water lily painting that hung in the end portion of the den. He was admiring the track lighting that had been created for it. Then there was the *Woman and Anemones* of Matisse that he had just bought at an auction. He loved the blue of Matisse's brush—the blue inspired by aviaries and bird feathers—the slanted eyes—the woman lying in the picture looked so much like Mary, Jerry thought, Mary with her slanted eyes, what was she doing, was she typing?

Where was she? A phone call away, a dial away, a telephone cord stretching from his lifeline to hers.

"It's all bullshit, Dad," his son said. Jerry had forgotten what they were talking about.

"Look, aren't you butting into things that are none of your business?" Jerry asked him.

"It's my business, Dad. When I came home this afternoon, Mom was crying. I saw her standing by the window looking as if she were going to jump. That isn't like her. Something is wrong between you. And I know what it is."

"How do you know?"

"Mom told me."

Jerry made a mental list of things he would never do. He would never take Mary to lunch at the Russian Tea Room. He would never put his money in a joint bank account. He would never go with anyone to the track. He would never tell his son he fucked anyone but his mother. He would never let Lillian blackmail him again. He would never sell his house in the Hamptons or his apartment in Paris. He would never invest in a motion picture or a Broadway show.

"Dad, I think Mom is going to kill herself."

Suddenly Jerry heard his son talking. The impact of what he said almost made his nose bleed.

"Why do you say that, son?"

"She told me about this person you're seeing. Mary Reagan. She said that you've taken her all around town including Orsini's, and that you're going to leave us and live with this person."

"I don't plan to do that."

"Mom thinks you're going to."

"Why does she tell you these things?"

"Because she is desperate. Desperate people do odd things, Dad."

"Why should she be desperate? Because I have another relationship? Is that so odd?"

"Because she loves you. Because she couldn't bear the humiliation. She's Danish and has a different code of honor than you think. And because the habit of our family and home mean so much to her. You know how proud she is. She thrives on the sameness of things. She can't bear everything to change."

"Well, things do change. Once I started jogging, everything started to change. My body changed and my mind changed."

"We're not talking about jogging, Dad. We're talking about Mom."

Jerry was now feeling like shit. He loved his son. But he couldn't stand Lillian. How do you tell a child you hate his mother?

"I think you should take her away for a few weeks. She needs a rest. She's nervous and on edge. I saw her taking tranquilizers and drinking wine to wash them down when I came home from school yesterday. I know there are lots of girls around, Dad. And you're an attractive man. I understand that you don't live by the Ten Commandments. But please, Dad, I love her. One day she's holding my hand and taking me out on Sundays to the fair at Asia House, and the next day she's cutting my hair and getting me ready for boarding school, and now, I'm grown up. But she's given me all the confidence that I need in life. No one wants her. She eats dinner by herself in the dining room, Dad. She waits for you to come home." The words tumbled out.

He loved his son. The earthquake of the whole relationship was about to erupt. He suddenly saw all the rooms of his son's life. There was the first room, the baby room with the wallpaper in it. He had loved his son so much he would come back from selling trips and bring him gifts. A papier-mâché elephant from Switzerland. A football from Paris. That was Riverside Drive. Then there was Jerry, Jr.'s room filled with hockey sticks, posters, and books. Yes, he loved his son too much. He remembered him being in a hospital room. The fever. The cracking ice. He had sat there all afternoon reading to him. "Please, God, let my son live and I'll do anything." Then the world became filled with alcohol and parties and Lillian entertaining too much. Too many people. He pulled the rooms of his son's life out of his mind. And still they were strangers.

"Please, Dad."

His son looked at him. He had Lillian's face. Lillian's curly blonde hair and light skin and large eyes.

"Can't we have a peace talk, son?"

"Don't leave Mom, Dad. She can't take it."

26.

"I am the plaintiff of my own life. You the defendant of yours," Lillian said.

These words went through Jerry's mind at the hospital. The doctor was saying, "She will live." Lillian had made a suicide attempt. It was a dramatic tactic that hadn't worked. The maid had called him in Paris and told him. He had taken the plane home. When he arrived, Jerry, Jr., and the doctor were in the apartment. They were all strangely polite. As if it were a nightmare. Would his son ever forgive him? It was hard to know those things. Would he ever forgive himself?

27.

He had flown to California on business. Staying in Los Angeles was always dreamlike. He'd have a limousine drive him to the Beverly Wilshire. Ursule was working every day, rehearsing. That night Ursule came to his suite. She was wearing long chiffon.

"I'm sorry about Lillian's trying to commit suicide. I hope she's all right," Ursule said.

"I want to talk about us, not about Lillian."

"She loved you."

"And I love you, Ursule."

"I'll always be your friend, Jerry."

"But I don't want you as my friend, Ursule. I want to be with you."

"I'm too old, Jerry, for love. I've told you I have my work. I have my roles. My life is working. Go back—to where you came from. I've done everything in life I can do for you. I wish you only the best, darling. Sort out your life with that young girl." She was kind but distant.

A few nights later, the dreams began. He was back with Lillian. He was jogging with her in the park with their son. Three joggers. It all pained him so much. He could hardly bear it. He left Los Angeles after selling one of the underrated Utrillos to a millionaire's personal museum.

28.

On a summer day, back in New York, Jerry sat in his dentist's office waiting for his dentist to see him. It was a new dentist and he wasn't sure that he liked him. He was Italian and his nurse instructed Jerry to watch a cassette which would "explain" what the dentist would be doing. Jerry wasn't sure he liked all these things. He had a toothache. Wasn't that enough? The nurse entered. "Dr. Veretti will see you in five minutes. Meanwhile, he wishes you to watch this picture which will explain what the doctor will be doing."

He watched her slide on the cassette.

A picture of a huge tooth was shown on a television screen. He saw pictures of the nerves. The pulp. Impacted teeth. It was all too much. A new lover. A new dentist. Too many news in his life. He began sweating. Suddenly he got up and left.

The limousine was downstairs in front of the dentist's office. He said to the chauffeur, "Drive me anywhere," and the chauffeur obeyed. He was no longer able to decide where to go. To Mary's. To Lillian's. Ursule.

29.

He went to Mary's and they made love.

Touching her—stroking her—he felt better. Just knowing she was out there. Being with her made his tooth stop aching. She touched some nerve in him that brought him comfort. When he left, he felt that he must stay with her forever. He loathed going home to the Dakota. He dressed for jogging and circled the park for an hour, thinking of Mary's curative powers. He was on edge. He couldn't take the affair. He was always anxious.

30.

As he alternated between Lillian and Ursule and Mary, Jerry felt that he was skydiving. He knew the clouds of marriage. Dark. Rainy. The sun came out when he dipped into his past. Mary was easy sailing. Skydiving? *Thigh* diving was more like it. He was obsessed with making love. Sex obsessed. Men who weren't lovers were lesser men. He thought of writing his autobiography. Once upon a time there was a boy called Jerry, who rode on the subway and thought about breasts. He grew up in Brooklyn, and imagined what it would be like to live in a castle of women. Once upon a time, there was a dirty old man. Once upon a time there was a great lover. Once upon a thigh there was a dreamer whose life was a miracle. But an intellectual one.

He made a mental list of things he loved. He loved the game of dealing. He loved making money. He loved writing in his journal. He loved jogging. He loved pictures. He loved the country. He loved dancing. He was a lover of life. (That was what Lillian never understood.) He was exuberant. (She always interrupted him. Ruined his jokes. She never really promoted him. She pooh-poohed jogging. She always talked about men being "supportive" of women. Well, why the hell wasn't she *supportive*? What was so fucking *supportive* about her?) That was it! He loved Ursule because she was supportive. That was it. Under all the talk about understanding, and love, and cathexis, and interaction, under all the therapy and conjugal understanding and relating to, was the key—supportiveness. Ursule believed in him. She introduced him to new worlds. She thought he was special. She had created him as a man by thinking everything he did was fabulous. Who cared if she was twenty years older? She *approved* of him. Was that all men and women wanted? Approval? Maybe that was the key. An "older" person could teach you. Could approve of you. Could open up worlds of love. Lillian had always been competitive. Mary was charming— but too innocent. How tired he was getting of her political rhetoric. If only she would fuck and shut up. Jerry realized that all those questions the women were asking themselves, the deep questions of *identity* and self-awareness, were the same questions he was asking himself. What changes a middle-aged art dealer into a philosopher? Into a runner? Into a clown? Self-awareness was the key. Maybe he should just shove the whole art business. With his body, he could be a dancer, or a professional runner. He was limber enough to start living through his body. Why not? All his life he had been zigging when he should have been zagging. Was it too late? Why hadn't he been living above the base line? Why had he been satisfied with the present? Instead of jogging into the future? He had read recently something which had jolted him. He had read (in a book by Richard Grossman called *Choosing and Changing*): "What lies above the base-line zero is the unknown."

What was his purposeful activity? Was he really confronting his life? Which was the woman he wanted to have as a partner? Did he want a partner? What about his secret fear? That he would grow old without having realized himself fully? He was looking for answers in the dark. And they could be found—those answers—in mercury in back of the mirror. He jogged and knew that the man in motion could become the thinking man. Jogging helped produce answers.

31.

That crazy man who stood for husband's lib—the oddball down at Rockefeller Center—he was the modern hero, the modern Lazarus who came back from the dead, to tell the world what everyone should know. It wasn't just the women who were getting fucked over. It was everyone in the pathological society. Didn't the women realize that? He, Jerry Hess, realized it. He was a feminist. He was the embodiment of everything the new woman stood for. He was, after all, just like Dante—trying to find his way—or jog his way—out of the wilderness of the modern nightmare.

32.

He'd taken to visiting Mary at her apartment (she had moved from the Gramercy Park to a tiny studio), and they were always laughing and glad to see each other. Mary was childlike in her appreciation of Jerry. She would hug him and make coffee for him and make him tell her about how he sold art in Europe, about the painters he knew, and how he had found the collection of El Grecos in a basement in Greece which he had sold for twelve million dollars. She imagined him lost among the rich clients. He had to tell her how he bid for pictures at Parke-Bernet. He was endlessly a source of information to her.

They jogged together. They kept pace with each other. She was faster than he was. They did calisthenics together. They jogged every day. Their stamina was keeping up with each other.

He loved embracing her.

He wrote poems about her.
He talked about her in his sleep.
To his doctor.

She introduced him to Liza, her little black girl friend from Harlem. With Liza they bought ice-cream cones and visited the Statue of Liberty and rode on the Staten Island Ferry. He gave books to Liza. She liked him. One entire day the three of them bummed around New York. He bought Liza a jogging suit.

Mary became obsessed with jogging.
She was in better shape than ever.
She was writing a long article on Castro's road to power. She had been studying a document in which Castro proposed that Judge Manuel Urrutia should become president after Batista's fall. She sat in the tiny studio in her jeans and a bra, typing the article. She heard the door open. Jerry was back from Los Angeles.

"What are you writing?"

"I'm writing about how Fidel sent his brother with about fifty men to the Sierra Cristal, a mountain region in the Province of—"

"Come away from your typewriter," Jerry interrupted. He hoped it didn't sound like an order.

She obeyed him.

"I saw Ursule in Los Angeles."

"I know," Mary said.

"I still love her," Jerry said. He began crying. "What the fuck am I supposed to do? What the fuck am I supposed to do?"

Mary ran five miles a day now.

She had found that her jogging speed was picking up. Jogging left her mind with time to think. She thought of Jerry as she ran.

They were half living together. His son had accepted her. She was doing well. She was eating a lot and running a lot. She was working a lot. She suddenly realized that her life was talking to a typewriter. Jerry rarely talked. He was now a consultant to the Whitney, the Guggenheim, the Metropolitan, and the National Gallery. They often ate together at Mary's place. Chinese food. Jerry saw few of his old friends. He had changed. He had declared himself. And committed himself. The act of loving was always an act of will. He had added deep-breathing exercises to his daily ritual. He had more courage than ever.

33.

Jerry was writing poetry. At night, he would sit in the room next to Mary while she studied and wrote. He wrote also. He wrote down the words:

Energy
Sweat
Hunger
Desire

Jerry looked at himself in the mirror. He wondered if he should go back to writing and start publishing small editions of books. He knew that was crazy. The art business had been good to him—he was respected, rich. Under Lillian's legal guidance he had grown from a man with a few paintings to one of the legends in the art world. He had banked millions of dollars. The wheeling and dealing had appealed to him. But the pressures now seemed inhuman. He decided to seek out his old friend, Dr. Friedman. Bart Friedman had been his friend in Bayside High School. They had been the dreamers of Queens. Jerry wanting to be a writer, and Friedman wanting to make films. He wanted to seek Friedman out. Talk to him about life-changes. He told Mary he was leaving.

"I'll be back in a few hours."

Mary never nagged. Never asked, "Where are you going?" Never made him produce Exhibit A, Exhibit B, Exhibit C of his whereabouts. Was that because she was from another generation? Mary accepted. Was it because she didn't care?

"Please don't wake me," Mary said, "in case I'm asleep."

In his life now, he was fêted with pizza. His social life consisted of sitting in on meetings at the apartment where Mary debriefed various visitors about Latin America or Africa. The Steven Biko inquest. The diagnosis of the Brazilian crisis. The crisis of under-development. The economic growth of Cuba. The intellectual development of Latin America. The conundrums of social change. These were the bread and butter of his new life with Mary. He had never realized that he had a social conscience. As he walked in the hot summer streets of Manhattan, he thought about his manhood, the long days lost in an empty city, the early days. He suddenly quickened his walk and began thinking about Friedman, who had lost the sight in his left eye. He lived on West End Avenue. He had stopped writing film scripts. Had he gotten old?

34.

In front of Friedman's apartment house Jerry stopped for a moment and rested. He had walked from the East Side. The jogging had kept him in shape. He wondered what the hell he wanted from Friedman. He had recently become a psychiatrist. Given up scripts. Changed his life completely. Left his wife. Married someone else. He was now treating patients from his apartment. The building was old. Smelled of urine. Unhappiness came creeping out of the hallways. He went in. The watchman told him which apartment was Friedman's.

Friedman looked ten years older than Jerry. He had a paunch.

"You should jog," were Jerry's first words to him. But he had a wisdom in his eyes and his laugh was good to hear.

"Not the same boy from Bayside?" Friedman said.

Jerry entered the apartment. It was dingy. The books in

bookcases were dusty. Artificial flowers. Pictures of Friedman's daughter were everywhere in gold frames. The kind of frames that came from Woolworth's.

"Come into my office," Friedman said. (Friedman had lost his hair.)

He had come for a friendly talk. He knew Friedman would tell him the truth.

"What's up?" Friedman asked. He sat in a large chair and lit a pipe. He wore his thick glasses over his large nose. His skin was yellow. He had all the accoutrements of an analyst. Diplomas on the wall. Learned journals piled upon tables. Beyond all that Friedman looked like a wise man. He had suffering written on his face. He had been tortured by life's relationships. He had failed in his career as a movie writer. He had been left by his wife. He had succeeded as an academic. He had produced a beautiful child who was now in college and whom he obviously loved. He was a wise man who had gone in and out of humiliations the way a needle darts in and out of embroidery. He had sewn up his mistakes. He had lived.

"I want to talk to you about health," Jerry said.

"Go ahead."

"OK. Friedman. You know my life. Small-town boys play stick ball. Dream of money. They dream of getting out of Queens." *I know*, was written on Friedman's face.

Jerry sat on the couch and felt at home. He was talking. He had found an ear. Was that all he wanted? An ear?

"Women, I want to tell you about women. I don't know where to start."

"Start anyplace."

Suddenly without his controlling it, tears welled out of Jerry's eyes. He was embarrassed. It was like wetting his bed. He remembered peeing in his bed as a kid—wet sheets, wet rubber mat, wet pajamas. The towels and embarrassment. Now the wet was going down his cheeks. He couldn't hold it back. Life was a mess. His own life? Tears ran down his cheeks.

"It's good to cry," Friedman said. He sat in his chair impassively

138

smoking his pipe. Jerry felt as if he had taken his clothes off in front of Friedman. He had never cried in front of another man. Only his mother and Ursule—and Mary—had seen him cry. Words broke through.

"I met Ursule when I was still a kid in Queens. She was the only woman I ever loved. She taught me everything I know. Wised me up. I was a kid gawking at the world. She showed me Europe. Introduced me to cities. Museums. Wines. Paintings. Through her I saw the money that could be made in selling paintings. And I began dealing. She left me. I met Lillian in Copenhagen. We married. You know all this. My son's in prep school. Last year I took up jogging. My body needed—to do something. I felt that to run was to live. Everything else was just waiting. Running made me feel alive. I saw my muscles change. My body changed. A new body took its place."

"Go on," Friedman said. He sat very still. Listening.

"While I was running, I met a girl who reminded me of Ursule. Name is Mary. Something happened. I wanted to follow her. Be with her. You understand?"

"I understand."

"I spent a lot of time with her. Lillian began to notice what was happening."

"And?"

"Lillian tried to kill herself."

"I heard."

"You heard. Now what?"

"What do you want?"

"I don't know. I want to give up some of my influence. I want to stop buying and selling paintings. I want to change my life."

"And Mary?"

"Mary loves putting radical words on paper. For her, change is a part of her life, continuously. For me? I don't know. My sense of purpose isn't clear. I have to give up a lot of things. But I feel I have more energy available."

"Go on."

"I've hated myself for so long. I hated liking my life. I hated being married to Lillian. One day I woke up and couldn't take it anymore. I started running. Nobody knows that hatred can kill you. I felt like a dead man trading paintings in Vienna, Zurich, Paris. When I started running I felt increased energy available. I felt new."

Friedman sounded like a rabbi. "Well, I'm sure that you have been living through that deep woods where everything is lost."

"I have," Jerry said.

"You'll find the Paradise," Friedman said.

It was hope from a boy from Brooklyn.

35.

Jerry wound around Central Park. He wondered about Mary. Did he love her? Did he want to live with her? He didn't know. He thought about teaching. Suddenly he felt the energy increase in his body. He felt like a Rouault clown running. That was it. He was a running clown. Dressed in red terry cloth. White shoes. Painted bright red he might be a stained-glass clown. Or a comedian. Was that all that life had to offer? The running from one way station to another? A clown on the run? It didn't matter.

"Our own identity is our personal truth," Friedman had said. Jerry thought about that while he ran. It occurred to him that he was an ancient clown. He was jogging right into old age. That was how he kept his life going. Jogging was moving the wheels. He wasn't moving the wheels of progress. He was moving the soles of his feet. He was moving his toes. He was moving. He began to feel the high.

36.

When Jerry jogged there was release—nothing to fear. Jogging had a great deal of pain connected to it. But it was good pain. It was not punishment. Putting on his shoes, the shoes he loved, was like putting on the real Jerry. Jogging through the park, he felt all of the symptoms that he loved. He felt his runner's humid skin. He felt the wet, the rise in body temperature. He felt himself pushing his body as if it were a machine that only he could regulate. And suddenly he entered a new country. It was a country where there was no depression. The high that he felt was almost as if he had stepped slowly out of his own identity, and into a new Jerry. He didn't have to be Jerry the boy from Queens. He stepped out of that skin, shedding it just as if it were a jogging suit. He no longer was locked into that boyhood of empty days and loneliness when he would sit and read in his bed and dream of being rich and important. He wasn't that fat boy who wanted to be *somebody*. He was no longer the puppy following behind Ursule in all of the best hotels. He wasn't the young stranger who sat in cafés and waited hours for Ursule to return from her shopping trips. He wasn't the Jerry who sat by the canals in Venice staring at garbage in the water, and looking at his watch, wondering when Ursule would arrive. He wasn't the Jerry who married Lillian and spent his life looking for paintings in the nooks and crannies of Europe. Jerry who drove his child around on weekends, or who spent his life commuting between the country and city. He was no longer the Jerry who couldn't find out who he was. As he ran, all of these people were no longer him. He could step out of each moment of his life until he became another person, heart pumping, lungs pumping, he became the new person he was. He was *lifted* out of the old Jerry as he ran. And in that new country that he now inhabited he could build houses, design dreamscapes, he could dream, he could make millions, he could dog step, he could see his lost friends and lost lives and still look at himself and feel himself. That was it. He could feel himself becoming the person he always wanted to be. The swift marathon runner that lay buried in the aging art dealer. And because of this, Jerry ran faster, faster.

Touching Mary made him feel alive. That was the best part of Mary. She made him jog with her. Made him exercise with her. She taught him the Achilles stretch.

"Place your left leg forward and take a comfortable large step in front of you. Make certain both feet are in a straight line. Watch out that the back of the foot isn't turned out like a duck's." He found it easy to have fun with her.

"Here's the leg pull. Do each side three times."

She was his teacher. They did the stretching exercises and stretched for the sky. Then out at the beginning of the morning to run up the path of the river. Jogging by the river he watched the city come alive. In the morning. It was just the two of them, against the steel and grey and concrete. In doing all these things he had begun to feel his life changing. Not that he was a different person. It was only that he felt different. For the first time he saw his rib cage. It was coming out of him like a huge plant. Running on the concrete with Mary, along the East River, he felt the surface under his feet. He was his arms and legs and mind and fists, he was his knees and weight and breath—he was his breath coming in and out of him. He was his heart beating and he was the pain. What was pain? He began to understand it as he ran. The pain in his life was harder to understand than the pain in his legs. The pain in his legs was real. He felt a pain in his side. The side stitch that he felt so often. But it was a good pain. It reminded him that he was running. Suddenly he felt beyond pains. It was the high. He felt it. Mary felt it too.

37.

Mary took Jerry to one of the meetings concerning South Africa. The meeting was to plan a concert at the Felt Forum for the children of Soweto. Jerry dressed in jeans, no longer the tycoon; he felt oddly out of place with these radicals. The world of the Hamptons, Regine's, Parke-Bernet, the worlds of privilege, money and taken-for-granted luxuries were light-years away.

He experienced an ecstatic moment when a black man from Ghana pressed his hand in his and said, "Brother—I'm glad you're here."

The meeting came to order.

He sat on the floor with Mary and crossed his legs. Did anyone know that he was a refugee? A stranger to Africa's demands? A black man called Jonas, the executive secretary of the National Imperialist

Movement in Solidarity with African Liberation, stood up and began speaking. He wore a dark blue sweater, a white shirt, and spoke in a soft voice that had a slight sad accent of the South. Everyone strained to hear his voice.

"The sharpening struggle is brilliant evidence that the desire for freedom and independence is indestructible. Today, the tide of liberation engulfs southern Africa, striking at the heart of the illegal and colonial regimes in South Africa, Namibia, and Zimbabwe. The task of bringing freedom and peace to Africa is not just the task of the peoples of southern Africa. . . ."

Everyone applauded. The young man continued to speak, his voice growing louder. Smoke filled the room. Jerry listened carefully, wondering if anyone was staring at him. Was he the alienated capitalist in this room filled with dedicated activists? In some strange way, he felt good in this room. He remembered how he used to be when he was a boy and filled with the concept of *helping* the world and *social* justice. He had dropped all of this idealism in his quest for fame and status. The world of Ursule was the world of impressing people, the world of pearls, status, theatre and mansions, feasts, and "items" in the columns. The world of white gloves and artistic pretense. Lillian's world of organized wealth. A world of dinner parties. Everyone in Lillian's world lived by the season—the Winter Season, the Summer Season. Lillian kept track of weekends, dinner parties—it was a world that they enjoyed because it was comfortable. He didn't have to think for himself. But Mary was opening up another world to him. In her orderless ways, she had introduced him to Imperialism, Solidarity, and Struggle. Her world was a fight for understanding, freedom, a fight against colonialism, racism, sexism—all of these words were new ones for him. New worlds. Mary's world was outside of the world of wealth. It was contrary to everything he knew. He felt excited. And good. As if he could have a voice for the first time. A woman stood up to speak. She had a black button on that said SOUTH AFRICA HANDS OFF ANGOLA, she wore a long white African robe, golden earrings, her hair was in an Afro. Perspiration was on her nose, and her nostrils flared as she spoke. Unlike Jonas, her voice was not soft. It was a voice that was almost like a song. Jerry felt as if he was sitting in a floating gallery—black canvases of faces angry and compassionate—the woman continued to talk in her *singing* voice.

"Henry Kissinger has now assumed the spotlight in an effort to preserve the structures of colonialism and racism, albeit, in a modified form, in southern Africa. He has aligned himself with the most vicious racist leader of our planet. John Vorster, the admitted Nazi, who heads the regime in South Africa, and Ian Smith, the racist leader of Rhodesia, have both welcomed Kissinger. As Ian Smith puts it, 'Dr. Kissinger assured me that we both share a common aim and a common purpose, namely to keep Rhodesia and the free world—from Communist penetration.' "

When the meeting ended, Jerry was introduced to all of the leaders. He shook hands with them and felt how good it was to finally *belong* to something real. He felt more comfortable than he had felt for a long time.

In bed with Mary, after making love. She turned to him and asked him, "What does it feel like to be you?"

"Why do you ask me that?"

"Because you seem so removed from me. I want to know what you're thinking."

"I'm thinking how far away from my own world the African National Congress is. How far away from the world of The Market, the Rainbow Room, Picassos. The restaurant days at Quo Vadis, the cassettes, the lightweight conversations. I'm so used to hearing discussions about the decline of the dollar. I'm so used to dinner parties in which I hear conversations about capital investments, portability, quality control, structural stability, it's quite a change to hear about 'Power to the People.' "

She held him in her arms and smiled.

"You're not sorry you're with me?"

"No, I'm just living in a jigsaw puzzle. I'm trying to put the pieces together. One day I started jogging around the reservoir and my life changed."

"I know that."

"I love you, Mary. I want you to have a lovely life. I don't know how good I am for you."

"You're good for me," she said.

He took her in his arms. Hugged her. She pushed him away.

"You know what? I've changed my life, too. My old playmates in California—the ones I had in high school—they were so stupid. All they cared about was surfing and skiing and being popular. They all wanted to grow up and be consumers, just the way television taught them to be. They were like dishes I ate from. I never really judged them. I just loved moving with them—after balls, on bikes, into water. Now they exist in cupboards I can't even find. They live in worlds where hunger and loneliness don't exist. They live in places where everyone says 'sure' and 'nifty' and 'super.' They live in a CB radio world, but the same things are always played on the same station. They spend Sundays with their kids and dogs that lick their faces. And here I am—so many worlds and words away from them that I can't find them anymore. Sometimes when I'm alone in this room, putting together articles, I can hear the furniture breathe, I can hear the carpet growing, and I wonder if I'm alone in all this struggle, forever. I think of the whites grabbing land in Rhodesia. I think of the black children of South Africa who live in shacks. I think of all the victims of apartheid. No one seems to care. And I think of my old playmates in the sun in California and I realize how grateful I am not to be saying 'nifty.' You understand?"

38.

The next evening Lillian was giving one of her dinner parties that mixed twenty of his clients with ten or twelve of hers. That was the whole purpose of dinner parties. To bring together unlikely eggs and they would break each other's shell only slightly—not so the yolk would run out dripping and yellow—just enough so the shell broke. Seated at the large dining-room table was Walter Kestler, Jr. Lillian had lit all the candles. Three maids walked around the table serving cold salmon. The Mitoffs were there. The Lehmans. The Stragers. The Manuccis. All the couples that Lillian worked on. Walter Kestler, Jr., was a tall, good-looking man who ran the National Virginia Museum. Jerry turned to him over the cold salmon, and eye to eye, they caught each other in a net of conversation.

"The variety of your show is remarkable, Walter. I've never seen a show with Ashcan School paintings next to Veroneses."

"It's selections from the Kestler Museum, but it's all Denys Sutton's taste. It's completely his choosing."

"But he's chosen from what you have already chosen. You have the reputation for buying things when other people aren't buying them."

"Don't we all do that all our lives? Doesn't your wife shop carefully? Mine does. So we're shopping for paintings. It's still *shopping*, isn't it, Jerry?"

"I'm curious about what you're buying now. Everyone complains that there's nothing left to buy."

"I'm interested in thirteenth-, fourteenth-, and fifteenth-century paintings. Some of these seem very cheap at the present time. That's why I'm here tonight, Jerry. Lillian's told me about fifteenth-century paintings you have in the warehouse. I'd like to see them."

"Nothing's easier, Walter. But don't expect to walk away with them. My suggestion is that you buy only the large paintings. Everyone else is buying the small ones. It's best to go against the trend. By the way, Walter, I have some interesting Italian Primitives. The Metropolitan deaccessioned some of the Italian Primitives when they thought they weren't in fashion— about two years ago—and I got them. Now they're worth twenty times what I paid for them, and shooting skyward. You must do your own deaccessioning."

"We have committees, Jerry. That's a subject I'd rather not discuss. What painters are you buying now?"

"Delacroix. I have tremendous respect for him. Lillian put me on to Delacroix after one of her clients asked her opinion of how to dispose of an estate that included seven of the finest. At that time—a few years ago—no one was particularly interested in the careful line and in the polished and pristine quality of art, he had gotten his line so refined. But Delacroix has a much broader line than people think. When he began to broaden his line it becomes a little nervous, filled with excitement. You can jump from Delacroix almost to Van Gogh and see things begin to go wild and then to Picasso where the line is completely destroyed, and then to Kline."

Kestler, Jr., asked, "Got any Picassos, Jerry?"

"I have a dozen." He watched Kestler, Jr., almost choke.

"I'd like to look at some of them."

"Are you having an interesting time, my darling?" Lillian asked. She wandered around the table chatting with each of the guests. She bent over and kissed Walter.

"Dear Lillian," Jerry thought, "dressed as usual." As if nothing had changed after her suicide attempt. He always admired the way Lillian brought people together. She was a natural hostess. Her "little dinners" always resulted in business for him or clients for her. They weren't dinners, they were tax deductions. Tomorrow, Kestler would call him and ask to look at the Picassos. It was all part of collecting. He would never be able to pull off these dinners without Lillian. She was so organized. Too bad he didn't love her anymore. But did he love Mary? Or Ursule? That was the question.

The three women became a trinity. Past. Present. And future. He listened to Kestler talk to his other dinner partner. He was an amazingly well-informed man. And a genius at collecting. He almost wished that Lillian were less charming. She was extraordinarily pretty! Through the glow of the candles he watched her drape herself discreetly around Michael Van Burton. They talked about the Franz Kline collection from Hamburg. She had it all perfectly arranged. Dinner. Brandy. And the slight insistence that it was all so much *fun*. Dinner. Money. Sales. Fun. Jerry thought constantly about Mary.

How would she feel about this dinner?

She would probably be revolted.

39.

It was Lillian who finally decided to separate from Jerry. She knew she was taking the blow out of the divorce. A separation was a divorce. She wondered why she was leaving Jerry. But in some part of her brain, she wanted to set herself free as well as him. It was the freedom of facing up to the facts. That's what separation was. She wondered how she would be without him. Perhaps she should take up jogging. It was the only way that she could cope with her life. She would jog until she figured it out. One part of her wanted to go back to Jerry and take back her words. Beg him to call this whole thing off. Make love to him. Cradle him. Love him again as she once had. She ached to love him again. But she remembered a story about chickens she had once heard. A chicken behind a pane of glass would peck its head to death to get at food. A dog would walk around the glass. She was not going to keep on banging her head. She wasn't a chicken.

40.

He'd come back from seeing Mary. And lie in bed. Usually it was Lillian who went to bed first, to get up for work the next day. Now he waited for her. She came home at twelve. He heard her in the hallway. Her heels tapping on the floor. She walked into the large bedroom and started to undress. She wore a white satin robe with her initials on it and went into the bathroom to brush her teeth. He had bought the robe for her at Sulka because he thought he loved her then. He had loved her then. Now he bounced between her and Mary, like a postman delivering his package of love. He made love to Mary. He slept with Lillian. He tried not to think of either one of them as he stared at the magnificent Cézanne he had hung in his bedroom. At least he was sleeping with Cézanne, Monet, Van Gogh, even if he wasn't sleeping with Lillian. She walked into the bedroom and began reading in her chaise longue across from the bed. It was almost as if he wasn't there. Was that what the arrangement meant? That he was no longer there?

"Lillian, just because we have an arrangement, you don't have to ignore me."

"What kind of arrangement?"

"The one you structured. That we see each other a few nights a week. Now we never see each other at all. Is that what you want?"

"No. This is not what I want. I thought it could work out. It hasn't."

"Now what?"

"Jerry, I have news for you. It's true when I first found out you were fucking around with Mary Reagan, I was troubled, desperate, and unhappy. My pride hurt. Especially since I checked into her motives. She is ambitious and common. She's out to get every penny from you that she can. And then dump you for someone of her own kind. Dirty. Radical. A nothing. She has more than street smarts. That much I give her. She's calculating. And she's using you."

"It's not your business who I see, Lillian."

"You're right. And you know what? Since our little scene, I feel immensely relieved. At first, it was hard. But I've gotten more in touch with myself and my work. I do think we would both benefit from separating for a while."

"We don't have to separate. I'm happy with things the way they are."

"Well, I'm not. I've been talking to some people, two of my colleagues, about a separation agreement. I'm not stupid enough to be my own lawyer. I'd like to come to something that isn't messy, such as a legal separation for a year."

"All right. I'll move out of the apartment, Lillian."

"Good. I know you expect me to be noble and offer to move out. But I like it here. It's my home and our son's home. So, I'll expect you to be gone tomorrow night."

Her news was a shock. He hadn't expected Lillian to throw him out. But she had made up her mind. He could always tell when she made up her mind.

"Are you angry with me?" he asked.

"No. Disgusted. Not angry. Most of all, I'm not afraid now to be alone. I realized that I've been alone for several years. You haven't been talking to me. You haven't been making love to me. All I've gotten is your legal work. I've smiled. Kept track of our possessions. I feel relieved. I think I'll take a vacation. Now I must really go to sleep, Jerry. I have work in the morning."

He watched her leave the room and heard her making up the bed in the guest room.

He lay in bed. Looking at the Cézanne hills. He was surprised at Lillian; that it was all done so calmly.

41.

Choosing and changing.

Mary was changing Jerry's life. She began sorting things out in her mind. Jerry was beginning to change. He had left Lillian and was now living in Mary's apartment. There wasn't much he could contribute to her way of life and he often felt cut off from his own friends. He missed the dinner parties, the openings, and even the political cocktail parties for fund-raising. Without his weekends in the Hamptons, he often looked like a fish out of water who flapped around but had no place to go.

"Why don't we drive out to the Hamptons?" he would say.

They would be eating breakfast.

"I'm working on a position paper. You go to the Hamptons, Jerry. I hate it out there. They're all a bunch of old farts. With their tennis games and their benefits for this cause or that cause. What I suggest is that you go to the house and if I can, I'll join you."

Instead, they had spent weekends together going to meetings. There were several meetings concerning South Africa. The Black Consciousness Movement in New York was heating up. One evening they were on the Upper West Side in the home of a white lawyer called Rudin, who was raising money for Soweto. Rudin was addressing a group composed mainly of blacks.

"In analyzing the conflict between the Black Consciousness Movement and the leadership, we have to understand the class origins of an elite dictatorship which builds from the privileges parceled out to it by the apartheid system. Some of us have learned the hard way about the viciousness of elite leadership. The elite use anything—lies, bribes, guns. You will see in Zimbabwe, they will use the army much more efficiently than Ian Smith. And we have to understand and be prepared to fight just as hard to undermine this kind of opportunism."

Jerry listened.

"Teach. Teach," said a black man with kinky hair.

"Taking advantage of the fact that virtually all of the well-known nationalists were banned and jailed last October, Buthelezi has moved quickly to build a base outside KwaZulu."

Jerry's world was spinning. He left the meeting alone and made his way to his favorite jogging paths.

42.

That night Jerry and Mary spoke quietly over pizzas and beer.
"It's all new for me, Mary. A few months ago I was a writer of sorts and an art peddler. I was locked into the Renaissance, pop art, buying and selling pictures. Now I'm at war with everything I believed in. I'm part of an escalating war; I'm emancipating myself. Everything that once fascinated me now makes me sick. I see myself as someone who had put all his energy in the wrong directions. In some odd way, blessings and bruises are all mixed up. It's not as if I have changed *who* I am. I've added to it. I've added to Jerry, a new identity."

"I know," Mary said.

"Tell me something."

"Anything."

"All right. How do you see me in your life?"

"I see you as someone changing your life. As a man rehabilitating himself from East Hampton tennis courts. The Parke-Bernet sales. A man rehabilitating himself from Guggenheim functions and Gucci shoes and other meaningless activities. I see you as someone growing. And that takes guts."

"Is it too late for me?" Jerry felt silly asking this. Did he seem to Mary to be an old clown? An old Borscht Belt comedian? The questions that came out of his mouth seemed soft as foam rubber. He didn't have the hardness that Mary had. Here he had spent his whole life developing charm only to find out in his *new* life charm wasn't wanted? All the tricks he had learned from Ursule, how to charm. To flatter. How to smell. What he didn't count on was that this new person in his life, this tough, hard, charmless beauty, this Botticelli woman of the new Renaissance didn't give a fuck about his manners, his habits. Everything that he had used to make himself successful she considered phony. He had jogged into a life he couldn't quite cope with. Did he really care about Latin America and submission to military rule? Was he really involved with revolutions within revolutions in Africa? What were his fears? He made a list of them in his mind as he walked. He feared:

He would lose his money.
He would lose face.
Mary wouldn't love him.
Lillian would try to destroy him. Lillian would try to
    destroy herself.
Ursule would forget him.
His friends would shun him.
His child would not understand him.
He would die before he sorted all of it out.

In his mind were all the fears of his life jumbling and
    chattering:

Fear of death
Fear of loneliness
Fear of love

Fear of ridicule
Fear of poverty
Fear of stammering

Other fears:

Root-canal poisoning
Murdering
Fire
No hair
Insanity
"Too late" fears, fears of closed-door panic.

Life was all fear—fear of depths, fear of heights, of making
mistakes, of not taking risks. "Don't be afraid of your fears," he
said to himself as he walked with Mary. He was changing. He was
also tired. The change was often too much for him.
    "I think I'll jog tomorrow," he said to Mary.
    "Good idea."
    They walked in the night in silence. Sometimes in the midst
of all this confusion, he found himself desperately wanting to
talk over all these things with Lillian. Twenty years of his life
and memory were entwined with hers. Oddly enough he missed
Lillian.

43.

Ursule was in New York and Jerry wanted Mary to meet her.
Mary was curious. She was beginning to feel so close to
Jerry that anyone who was important in his life had meaning. She
wanted to find out more about him.

Ursule dressed carefully to impress Mary. She was wearing
a black chiffon robe. Her shiny black hair was slightly teased.
She wore her emeralds. The usual Rigaud candles scented the
room. The pink carnations, champagne, all of her trademarks
were in evidence. Her dog followed her to the door. Her
beloved Labrador, Duke, had died, but he was followed by
another Duke and another, so that no matter how old Ursule
became, she always had a black Labrador at her feet. It was
the only thing that never aged. Duke and Ursule stood at the
door. Mary walked down the corridor.

"Darling, Jerry's told me everything about you. But I wanted to see you for myself." Ursule embraced her and led her into her suite. "Sit down, darling," she continued. "I want to look at you. Oh, you're lovely. Just as charming as Jerry said."

"What does it matter if I'm charming or not?" Mary said.

"It does matter. At least to Jerry."

"You mean the Jerry you knew. Not the Jerry I know."

"He hasn't changed all that much. I've spent enough time with him to know that."

"I know you've spent many years with Jerry. I know you were a tremendous influence on his life. But I also understand you haven't really seen him for the past two decades."

"Has it been that long? I am so busy I hardly keep track of time. Jerry loves a woman who is creative, sensitive, and beautiful. And I'm sure you're all of those things. Tell me, do you love him or are you just playing with him?"

"Love? We get along. We practically live together."

"But do you love him? Do you understand him? Most of all, what can you offer him?"

Mary lit a cigarette. "Do I offer him anything? I don't think in those terms. I don't think of offering *anyone* anything. We work together. Live together. We eat together. We make love. Is this an offering?"

"Jerry's an unusual man. Eating and making love is one part of his life, but there's another part. And I wonder if you ever understand it. He's a writer, you know. His language is virtually poetry. I opened his eyes to the great writers. With me, he met Wallace Stevens, Robert Lowell, E.B. White. His work has been published. Do you understand that part of him?"

"Yes. I feel the artistic part of Jerry. In fact he's now writing essays on the Renaissance."

"And what do you do, my dear?"

"I write. Mostly underground newspapers."

"What kinds of things do you cover?"

"What's not covered in the major press."

"For example—raise my understanding. What's not covered?"

"The major press has never reported the mass grass-roots organization at the community level. Since after the Vietnam War many people think the country is moving to the right. On the surface it seems to be doing this. Underneath all this—people are organizing. The establishment doesn't even suspect this. It's not reported about. But it's there."

"How interesting. In other words, you're ferreting out information that no one knows about? The question is, my darling, who cares?"

"Not many people care, because they are too ignorant. But history is on our side. People can be blind for so long. Then one day everybody sees where it's all at, at once. We are preparing for that."

"Well, Mary, this has been a lovely chat. I think that in many ways you're doing for Jerry what I did for him many years ago. You're helping him change. You're opening him up."

"I didn't set out to change him. He became interested in my interests. He's beginning to understand what I'm trying to do."

"I must beg you to excuse me. I'm tired. But I'm happy to have met you." Ursule rose and her negligee swirled around her legs like the delicate petals of a peony.

The meeting was over. Mary waited downstairs in the lobby for Jerry to return from his walk.

"How was it?" Jerry asked.

"She feels my influence on you isn't healthy," Mary said. Then she added, "She hates me."

He called Ursule later. Secretly.

"Horseshit. Since when are you, Jerry Hess, a radical? I remember you with the Woodwards in Switzerland, the Aga Khan in the south of France, the Rothschilds and the Bourbons. Now—suddenly you're hanging out with Mary Reagan, and you're a raving revolutionary."

169

"I love her."

"Why?"

"Because I can't have you. You don't want me. I'd rather be with you than anyone on earth, Ursule. You know that. I adore you."

Ursule sipped her iced tea. She now never drank anything alcoholic because she was afraid it would age her skin.

"If you feel that way—if you really feel that way, come and live with me, Jerry. I'll take you back. Of course, we can't share the same bedroom. I'm too old for that nonsense. But you can live with me in California, darling."

Ursule! Ursule would have him back. He did not have to think twice. He adored her. More than ever.

44.

Ursule telephoned Jerry after she flew back to California.
"I want you to come to California," she commanded.
"When?"
"As soon as possible."
He was on the plane in an hour.
When he arrived, Ursule met him at the airport in a rented limousine. She was not as wealthy as she had once been. But she would never part with the arrogance. She once had to be surrounded constantly by luxury. Luxury was a part of her personality. Luxury. And elegance. And beauty.
The car drove up to a house in Bel Air. It was enormous.
"Who pays for all this?" Jerry asked without malice.
"The repertory theatre is doing well. But the house—it was given to me by one of my grateful students. Marlon is now staying with me. I'm helping him with his new film. He finds it easier to live with me than to spend half of his day calling me."

Jerry couldn't take his eyes off her.

She was still incredibly beautiful. He knew that for him, she was the most exciting woman on earth. Once a young "child prodigy" of the theatre, she was now the "great actress, personality, teacher." Her home still was perfect. He expected as much. It had an indoor and an outdoor swimming pool. The furniture was covered in chintz and white canvas. Fresh peonies and geraniums and tiger lilies were everywhere in Picasso vases. On the walls were the Matisse, the collages from Motherwell, the great paintings he had given her.

"I'm helping the Getty Museum with their collection. And Norton Simon has asked my advice on some of the young painters in Soho. While I'm out here, I intend to research some of the California painters. I'll look in on some studios here, and I might add some new artists to my list. Other than that—I'm all yours, my darling."

He was trembling. Would she notice that his hand was shaking?

Ursule admired herself in the gold mirror. She crossed her legs as she lounged in a red canvas chair. Surrounded by golden mirrors and fresh flowers beside the huge pool, she looked immortal. He wanted to remember her that way.

"I haven't quite told you what I think of Mary," she said.

"You don't have to," Jerry said, sipping his drink. "I already know."

"Well, I hate to beat around the bush. I hate her. I think she's a common, vulgar tramp. She's tough. She's hard. And her apartheid and liberation interests are crap. If she's such a liberal, why is she letting you keep her?"

"I'm helping her. She's trying to make some historic point, and I'm helping—that's all."

"History always has a hard cock," Ursule said. He had never heard her speak vindictively before.

"Her personality is good for me," he said in that babyish funny voice he often had with Ursule. She often reduced him to an infant.

"She has the personality of a dial tone. And I think with her your life would be ruined."

A Japanese houseboy entered carrying iced tea and sandwiches. Ursule took one. He withdrew.

"I find her attractive. I have much more fun with her than I did with Lillian."

"How is it possible for you, Jerry, to go into this trance? Who is this person? Who is her family? What does she do?"

"She writes for a newspaper. She hangs out with her friends. She smokes grass. She plays the guitar. She's involved in world revolution. What can I tell you?"

"You can tell me that you're going out of your mind. Aren't you too smart for male menopause?"

"What do you mean?"

"I don't know what else to call it when a man leaves his wife and runs off with some young body who has nothing in common with him."

"We have a lot in common."

"What? Exactly?"

"Sex. Jogging. Politics."

45.

It was simple.

He'd go back to New York. Say good-bye to Lillian and Mary. Pack a few things. And come back to California. Was this what he wanted *really*? How in the hell did anyone know what they wanted *really*? For years he had been making love to Lillian, pretending she was Ursule. Now he would have his chance to make love to the real Ursule. Would he then pretend she was Mary? "Lovers are lesser men," Friedman had once said. Did Friedman know so fucking much?

"You are like water, and water slips through my hands," Lillian had said. Ursule was the dream woman becoming real. Could one really live out one's fantasies? Was it dangerous to try to go back to the past? Who could advise him? Jerry thought with resentment about his analyst. Why was it that he was always out of town when all the real decisions had to be made? Wasn't the whole point to learn how to make one's own decisions? He felt as if he were wading in a quagmire of impatience and indecision. He had to take risks. He would go. To Ursule. He would risk a new life. He never was sure of the right decision, so why not take a chance?

46.

He called on Lillian.

He no longer lived with his wife, he *called* on her. It was easier that way. Whenever he walked into the Dakota, the doormen were extra polite. He was a known breed—the ex-husband. The ex-husband is treated with great respect. He is almost a hero. A modern hero who pays bills, visits, and silently disappears. As Jerry went to call on Lillian, he wondered how he would feel in his old apartment. When the maid let him in, he felt more comfortable than he'd expected. It was a new maid.

"Mrs. Hess will see you in the den," the maid told him.

So! The den of iniquity. He detested the word "den."

Lillian was sitting with her inevitable yellow pad. He imagined she would die with a legal pad over her breasts.

"Do you have some reason for insisting on seeing me in the middle of the afternoon?" She was wearing her tortoiseshell glasses and now affected a voice of haughty indifference. It was almost as if she had tired of playing Snow White, and now she was playing the Wicked Queen.

"Lillian, I must speak to you. I'm moving back to California."

"With Mary Reagan?"

"No. I'm going back to Ursule."

The news didn't come as a shock to Lillian. "This is what you want, isn't it?"

"Yes."

47.

"You see, Lillian, I've decided to leave Mary." He heard himself say it, but he couldn't believe it was true.

"Have you told her yet?" Lillian asked.

"No, I haven't had the courage."

"I suggest you tell her."

"In a way I don't think she will care."

"I think you're right," Lillian said.

"Is everything in order?"

"Yes, Jerry. I think our separation has been quite successful. Our son has adjusted. Our parents have adjusted. We have adjusted. What else is there to say? Sometimes when I see you I feel sorry that all of this has happened. I want to go back to being with you the way a twin panda aches for its other twin. But then I get over it. I quite enjoy my life without responsibilities. I've become more active in criminal law. I play tennis more. I see more old chums from school. It's not quite as bad as I thought it would be."

"Do you have a lover?"

"I don't quite think that's the business of an ex-husband. Do you?"

"Just curious."

"As a matter of fact I have found someone to while away the time with."

"And who might that be?"

"Your old friend—Friedman. I went to him for help. I found all of this hard to digest. And I found in his openness and sympathy what I always wanted in you but never found."

"I'm glad," Jerry said. (He was shocked—Friedman—the bastard!)

When he left, he wondered why he had left her. She seemed more sympathetic to him than ever. She had organized his life and kept it together. He wondered what his life in California would be like with Ursule. He wanted to make it known to Lillian that life was changing. That the world was turning around. That he was trying to find himself. But perhaps she knew.

48.

Walking to Mary's house, he wondered what Lillian could possibly have in common with Friedman. Friedman was a slob, a good-natured Jewish intellectual slob. He played tennis on the *public* tennis courts. He spent his life having anxiety attacks, or seeing patients, all of whom were not as neurotic as he was. When he reached Mary's apartment, he suddenly felt a panic. How was he going to announce the news to her?

49.

Mary was writing when he arrived.

"What are you working on?" he asked.

"The march for the Rosenbergs. There's a memorial service at Union Square and I'm covering it. Helen Sobell is going to be one of the speakers. I'm having an interview with Michael and Robert Meeropol. It's the twenty-fifth anniversary in tribute to the Rosenbergs."

She paused, staring at him. Then added, "They were killed because they wouldn't lie. I'm inviting the Mobilization for Peace Action's chairman to write a special editorial. So is the head of the National Committee to Reopen the Rosenberg Case."

"I'm going to California," Jerry said.

"When?" Mary asked.

"Tonight."

"When will you be back?"

"I'm not sure."

"Do you want me to join you?"

"Not now."

"Well—you call me whenever you want me. I'll be right here in the city writing."

During this interchange, Jerry had decided not to tell Mary that he was going to see Ursule.

50.

The haute couture.
 The jewels, the graciousness—was he ready for all that? Was it all real? The breasts, the plunging décolletage, the pearls, the hypnotic eyes, the elegant hair, the dogs. Her deep voice—her eyes—theatrical gestures—her limousine and glamour . . .
 Relating to a grande dame isn't simple!

 When Jerry arrived in Los Angeles, life was almost the way it used to be. Ursule had thought of everything. Her limousine picked him up at the airport and brought him "home" to San Isidro Drive, where her house was part of the Beverly Hills tour. It was strictly California architecture—part Spanish, part ranch house, part park, part swimming club, part museum, and part suburban exaggeration. The house had been worth a few hundred thousand when it was built in the 1930s, but now, due to Arab money and the inflation in Beverly Hills real estate, it was worth millions. When Jerry arrived Ursule was swimming in the outdoor heated pool, which had a canvas awning over it on pulls so that "When the leaves fall they won't fall into the pool." What leaves? It also shielded her *skin* from the sun. Ursule thought only about her skin, Jerry thought. Ursule thought about wrinkles. Lillian thought about money, and Mary thought about political struggle. They were his trilogy, and at this *moment* in his life, Ursule appealed to him the most. He couldn't help noting how beautiful she was, swimming in the pool. She swam nude and her body was white—almost perfection. The maid had been trained to stay away from the pool area when she was there nude. He stood at the doorway for several moments, watching her swim.

With a shock, as he stood there, the past came back. Even as he stood there, she called to him in her unmistakable theatrical voice. "Jerry, darling, bring me a towel."

He obediently picked up an oversized brown terry-cloth towel and took it to her. She climbed into the towel and into his arms. The sun was beating down on them. He loved the sun. Suddenly he remembered what it was like to smell Ursule again. The smell of Ursule was there despite the water—nothing could wash it away. He felt himself excited by holding her in his arms. Her face, he noticed, had more pull lines from face-lifting than he remembered, and the skin was taut, but she had the face of a young girl. In many ways, she looked as young as Mary. Silicone had done its trick. He stopped himself from thinking of Mary.

Ursule sat down in a white lounge chair. Beverly Hills was all reclining chairs and chaise longues. It was almost as if nobody sat upright in Beverly Hills. It was a primitive community based on lounging. Ursule sat under a large blue umbrella.

"Come and sit down, Jerry." She beckoned to him in the sun.

He didn't want to sit in the shade. The sun felt good on his back. He felt new, as if the world were shining down inside him and upon him. Sun going into his bones. He stared at the well-cared-for geraniums, bursting in the sun. Their sexual red petals had not been bruised. He looked at the huge lilies and pansies, all shining in the sun. To be with Ursule meant to be out of the sun, so he moved his chair under the shade of her blue umbrella.

"They've made me chairman of the board of the Mark Tapar Forum," Ursule said in her singsong voice. "I don't deserve the honor really, but it means that I'm practically in charge of finding all the talented young people who will be performing next year. I'm happier now than I've ever been," she said. "At first when Mike died, I thought I'd never recover. I didn't know how to be a widow. And I missed his calm voice. He was the one man in a million who knew how to love a woman. I had everything with him. Brilliance. Sex. Friendship." He could see that she was beginning to cry. He hoped she wouldn't cry.

This reunion was more difficult than he had imagined it would be. She was the great Ursule Hirsch of the Berliner Art Theatre. Her brother had started the New School Piscator Theatre—her father was the most famous actor on the Berliner stage. As the daughter of the King of Actors, she had been all over the world, inside the doors of royalty. She was used to the greatest hotels, the great intellectuals; she moved with Lee Strasberg, Elia Kazan, the Cronyns, Laurence Olivier; her students included the millionaire young actors. Many great actors had been her protégés. But the life she led was no longer the life that interested Jerry. What he had found so glamorous as a boy—discussions over glasses of tea—the Café Berliner on York Avenue—the world of theatre, lights, velvet—Ursule herself in the center—the greatest actress of her time—the great beauty—he now saw every crack in the perfection of that life. Her world no longer held the old fascination for him. It was a world that had once had a "social purpose" but now had degenerated into a false lyricism and liberalism.

He didn't like Ursule's theatrical glamour. Not really.

Ursule was holding court in her living room. Her entourage of "pets" came to call for her. One aspiring actress, a girl who was extremely fat, who had acted in repertory with Ursule for twelve years, was at her feet like a lapdog. A homosexual who had just appeared in Marcel Marceau's mimodrama in Paris was lighting her cigarette.

As Jerry entered the room Ursule dramatically held out her hand to him. He had forgotten what it was like to trail after Ursule. Seeing the sycophants around her, so similar to the ones that he had seen come and go, reminded him that one paid *homage* to Ursule, one didn't spend time with her. Her legendary charm had bewitched this new group of people so that no one noticed when he entered the room. He had forgotten how a great actress makes pronouncements constantly. He watched horrified, while Ursule threw her theatrical pearls of wisdom to the group:

"We give our lives to learning how to live. It is the imagination that counts. Making things up. Not our real selves. But our imaginary selves. We turn our knowledge of life into our knowledge of art."

Jerry stood there remembering how he had heard these words over and over again, twenty years ago. It was part of Ursule's shtick, this wisdom which connected life, theatre, proverbs, and nonsense into her own language. She continued offering her wisdom to the supplicants.

"As an actor you must deal with facts of all kinds which come within your experience. That is the secret of acting. Using the interruptions. Isn't it, darling?" She turned to Jerry. It was now his role to agree with her.

"Yes, Ursule, darling."

That was his role. Living with a legend. To agree—to advise. To follow behind. Ursule simply needed him to echo her, to remind her, to bring her things. Everyone got up to leave.

"Jerry, darling, don't forget the dogs."

They were off to the studio. Ursule's theatre was located in a building that she had taken over in Los Angeles.

51.

Driving back to Ursule's house, they sat in the limousine holding hands.

"I have a surprise for you, darling."

"I'm always ready for your surprises," Jerry said.

"This is something I've been planning in my mind all day."

"Ursule? Planning? I thought everything you did was spontaneous."

"This is special, darling." She turned her hypnotic eyes on him, and began whispering like a little girl. "Don't get sulky—but tonight I have a special event."

"Tell me."

"I've decided it was time the writer inside of the tycoon had a chance to speak. Everyone in Beverly Hills knows you sold the Cézanne to the Louvre. It was in all the papers. But not everyone knows how good a writer you are. Nobody knows that *The Great Cup* was nominated for a National Book award or that Bloomsbury Press is publishing your book of essays in England. And so I thought it would be appropriate for you to read one of your essays this evening. And I've invited a few of my friends."

He was stunned.

"Please, Ursule, I came to California to be with you. Not to be paraded in front of people as a writer. You know I only read my work from time to time at conferences, and I would rather just fit into your world silently."

"That's just it, darling. You're fitting into my world. My world is the world of great art. And you're a great essayist. It's all arranged."

"How many people have you invited?"

"Just a few. A director—my favorite. And, of course, some of my children from the studio."

Jerry watched as the servants set up the chairs and turned the house into a small theatre. He was the theatrical event. He sat in his room sipping scotch and thinking about his son. He had just spoken to him on the phone and he was sounding good. As he was sitting in his room looking over manuscripts, Ursule burst in. She was wearing a sheer black robe with nothing underneath. He could see her youthful body under the robe. He wondered if it had all been tampered with the way her face had been. Her makeup was on perfectly. Her long eyelashes emphasized her eyes and she was wearing the diamond pendulum that he had given her in Venice when he sold his first painting.

He could smell and feel her fragrance entering the room, filling it. As he sat in the deep chair looking at her, she came over to him silently and gave him a long, deep kiss. She put her hands on his thighs, and began unzipping his fly, until she held his soft cock in her hands. She moved swiftly.

"I'm going to make it larger," she said in her throaty voice. And then she knelt in front of him and began sucking his cock. He lay back in the chair. This was where Ursule was still a genius. He had never felt anyone suck his cock the way she did. She slipped her tongue over his erection and began teasing him with her tongue. She bit him slightly and began sucking and sucking until he started to sigh. She kept him in her mouth, going up and down gently, then suddenly changed her rhythms until he grabbed her hand. He was about to come and she knew it. Just then she stopped sucking him. She took his cock out of her mouth and held it in her hands and said to him in her deep throaty voice: "Don't come yet, Jerry. I want to excite you even more, darling."

And she went back to sucking him. He finally came and she swallowed, swallowed every morsel of his semen, sucking on it. His eyes were closed.

"That was good," he said softly.

When he opened his eyes, she was lying on the bed. He touched her thighs and felt how wet she was. He began licking her softly and then hurriedly.

"More, more," she called. She was in another kingdom, a kingdom of cum and pleasure. He ate her as if he had never eaten a woman before. She came in his mouth. Then he crawled over the bed to kiss her lips. Gently he took off her robe and began kissing her breasts.

"Don't mess up my hair, Jerry," she said.

Even in bed, she was an actress. He let his hands cover her body and he began touching between her legs. She was wet again. He manipulated her soft clitoris until she was about to have another climax. Then he entered her with his hard cock pressing into her.

"Oh, God, I forgot how good you are." He rode on top of her until they came together. They had both forgotten how much they pleased each other.

"Hurry, Jerry, the guests have arrived." She slowly got up from the bed to exit from Jerry's bedroom. He lay on the bed amazed by her sudden change from lover to hostess. He could still taste her in his mouth. She was the greatest courtesan of all. Now he knew why he had thrown his life aside to come out to California. Everything he remembered about making love with her had only gotten better. The older she was the more she excited him. For some reason that he didn't understand, even the wrinkles, the odd bit of flab accentuated her sensuality. She knew everything about making love. She had forgotten nothing.

She introduced him to her friends.

"Tonight a marvelous artist has come to read to us. He's a man I have known for many years."

Everyone applauded. He stood behind her.

"This is a man whom Edmund Wilson admired. Whom T.S. Eliot sent letters to regularly. Who has known Norman Mailer, Anne Sexton, all the great men and women of letters. Tonight he is going to read from his unpublished works. Jerry Hess runs a private gallery. None of his friends in the art world, his patrons and clients, know that he is a great literary stylist. Jerry Hess, known to all as a tycoon, is truly another person. A writer whose work I will share with you this evening. Jerry Hess." She gestured to him to step forward.

At twelve there were only the flickering candles and Ursule and Jerry left in the large empty house.

"Jerry, darling, bring me a drink."

He obeyed.

"Oh, darling, bring me a cigarette too."

He brought her one and lit it for her.

She sat down in one of the luxurious chairs and put her feet up on a velvet stool.

"Can you take my shoes off, darling? And massage my feet?"

He began to massage her toes. As he massaged her feet, she asked him, "Did you like my friends, darling?"

"Yes. I think they were very polite. Minnelli was the only one who seemed to know anything about art. I quite enjoyed them."

She pulled her feet away. "Darling, this is only the beginning. I want you to meet many people. I group them separately. Tonight was only for the rich and famous. I have a poor group of friends who are just as interesting. In a way, more interesting. You'll meet them tomorrow night. I'm very sensitive to who sees who. Come," she said in her throaty voice. "I want to hold you in my arms all night."

He followed her. The dogs followed him. It was Ursule's procession which led to the bedroom; even when she went to bed, there was a dramatic procession.

52.

Only with difficulty was he able to sort out his feelings after a day of following Ursule and her two black Labradors around town, going shopping with her in the limousine, waiting for her after her classes, driving with her to the ophthalmologist or dentist, chiropractor—so many people made a living from tending to Ursule's body. What Jerry began to see clearly for the first time was how the whole world of sycophants was deftly manipulated by this beautiful woman. It followed that she always got what she wanted, saw whom she wanted to see, her friends, her plans, her games. She needed polymorphous freaks constantly. For breakfast, for lunches. For dinners. He sat through lunch on the terrace where seven freaks admired Ursule, basked in her greatness and talked about food. It seemed that in Beverly Hills food was a constant if neuter topic of conversation. The Killingtons—a couple from Scotland (he was a multimillionaire and she was devoted to needlepoint)—came for Sunday brunch. So did

Armando, a three-hundred-pound out-of-work character actor. So did the Minnenbergs, a nervous couple living on a vacuum cleaner fortune. There was also Lord, a young man with a southern accent. They sat in the sunlight eating ripe melons. And what did they talk about? Guacamole.

"It's our favorite dip," said the Minnenbergs in unison.

Ursule controlled the conversation. She didn't appreciate all this talk about guacamole. They had to talk about her guacamole. Her astronaut salad. Her food. She forbade smoking at the table. She forbade certain topics. She led the conversation round to her, her life, her roles, her dogs, her children, grandchildren, her hot-dog stew. She amused, she shocked, she cajoled. She flirted. She teased. After guacamole came discussions of mime. In Beverly Hills, theatre and food were all mixed up.

"It's a wonderful facial exercise," one of the Minnenbergs said.

Then with a flutter of napkins, cutlery, sunlight, the brunch was over. Everyone went for a swim; water splashed in the sun. Then everyone was gone.

Everyone who worked for Ursule was afraid of her. She would scream. She could cajole. But she could also be hard and cutting.

"Juliet, you burned my blouse. You'll have to pay for a new one," she screamed at a tiny dark student who was also acting as the laundress. Jerry felt sorry for her.

Juliet attracted Jerry.

One afternoon he found her in the laundry room ironing his shirts. "You don't have to iron my shirts, Juliet. I'll send them out."

"Oh, no. Ursule wouldn't like that."

Suddenly he noticed that Juliet wasn't wearing a bra, and that you could see the large nipples of her large breasts through her white uniform. He couldn't believe how big and beautiful her breasts were. He suddenly got hot, erect. He imagined what her breasts would taste like. He moved toward her. Suddenly she stopped ironing and began breathing heavily. She wanted him, too. He aimlessly closed the door. She could see that he was excited. Slowly she began unbuttoning her dress, and as her uniform slipped off, she stood half naked, her brown skin seeming browner against the wall. She was wearing only white bikini panties and her legs were beautifully shaped. She wore high-heeled sandals and stood against the wall, about to let him caress her. As he walked toward her he said her name, "Juliet," and she pushed him gently away.

"Wait," she said. She walked to the door and locked it. As he watched her he took his clothes off. She turned toward him. "Watch me," she said.

She stepped slowly out of her bikini pants. With her forefinger she began rubbing her pink flesh under the mass of curly black hair. She began exciting herself so that she spread her legs, and he could watch her make herself feel pleasure. He had never seen a woman standing in her high heels, making love to herself. He stood there with his cock growing hard, so hard he thought he would explode. Just as she was about to come, she walked over to him and put her hand on his cock. She began to rub him slowly up and down and then got slowly down on her knees so that he moved slowly back and forth in her mouth. He couldn't understand how she could excite him like this. Finally he found himself on top of her, the two of them on the floor. She smelled of laundry, and looked like a little dark fox, a gay-looking fox because her mouth and eyes looked as if they were smiling. A captive fox that scratched and bit and finally lay helpless on the floor after she climaxed. A few moments later he made love to her again, biting her large breasts and kissing her large glossy lips.

"I didn't expect you to be so passionate," she said. As she dressed, he wondered if Ursule had passed by the laundry room while they made love.

"It's funny, one never knows if Ursule is there. Sometimes you don't hear her," he mused. He kissed Juliet passionately. He wondered what he was doing making love to a young girl in a laundry room in California.

"I'll see you tomorrow or later tonight," whispered Juliet.

"Tonight," he whispered.

"When?"

"At about eleven. Come to my room."

Ursule always went to bed at eleven. She retired to her bedroom to get her "beauty rest." Jerry kissed her, and went to his own room. Juliet was a few moments late. He became excited thinking of her fingering herself. When she arrived she wasn't wearing her uniform. She was wearing a tight white turtleneck and a rayon skirt, also white, slit up the side, and the same high-heeled sandals. She looked luscious and he wanted to take her in his arms. He felt in advance how excited she made him and he tried to pace himself. It was almost like jogging. When he felt the blood in his cock, it was painful. He had to remind himself not to come too quickly, to go slowly. He went immediately to the bed. She followed him. He loved to watch her slowly take her clothes off. By the bed was some Coppertone suntan lotion. He began rubbing it on his body. "Your muscles turn me on," she said.

"And you turn me on," he said as he began to rub the oil on his legs.

"Let me do your back."

He turned over. She rubbed the oil on his back and massaged him. Then he poured the oil in his hands and rubbed it over her body. She looked so brown and glowing in the light.

"We have a good thing," she said.

He made love to her until dawn.

There were nights in Beverly Hills when Jerry Hess reviewed his life. Ursule held her court. *Brecht* and *Stanislavski* rang through the rooms like bells, sacred names ringing again and again. Still, as she talked, while Ursule moved through her rooms among her books, her photographs in silver frames, while she planned dinner, cleaned her nails, had her hairdresser, Monsieur Monk, comb out her curls, while she fumed and groomed, Highness Hess was bored. The neglected prince sat with the Labradors in the goddamn den.

"I've gone from Lillian's study to Ursule's," he thought moodily one night.

Ursule entered the room in her red chiffon robe.

"Do you single-handedly support the chiffon industry?" he asked.

"Stop drinking, Jerry. What's bothering you, darling?"

She curled up next to him. The Labradors looked on. Everything they did was recorded by Ursule's Labradors. The dogs were the voyeurs of their lives.

"Everything."

"Begin with one thing."

"You. I know that you're a genuine artist. I know that you're a great actress and teacher, and a legend. I know that you've spent years of your life working upon yourself, training yourself. But you're always acting, Ursule. I feel as if the full mastery that you have of your body, the training you have of your emotions—all of this is no longer exciting to me. The fact is, Ursule, you're always *on*."

"An actress is not an ordinary creature. You, as a writer, know that," she said.

"God, Ursule, why are you always talking about artists? Who the hell cares? Isn't everyone in life an artist?"

"The artist is the person who trains himself or herself to analyze motives and to direct the motives of other people."

"But, Ursule, I've been here with you for two months. I've followed you around Los Angeles, I've watched you give your dinners and draw people into the web of admiring you. Even I used to admire you. But I've stopped wanting an audience for everything I do. You couldn't care less about anyone but yourself. If you gave a fuck about the poor, or the spiritual lives of people who don't have hairdressers, you couldn't possibly live here."

"Jerry—my concern is for the inner image."

"What does that mean, goddamn it?"

"Your problem is that you don't know how to play a scene

197

for your partner. You play every scene for yourself. You plunge into the contemplation of your own feelings and actions. You're more interested in your own contortions than in the entire scene itself. The only satisfaction in performance comes with the right relationship with one's fellow actors. If the actor, like the human being, makes himself clear and understood by his stage partner, the performance will become real."

"Bravo."

"I'm not just teaching my students about acting. Everything I know about life, I've learned from Brecht and Stanislavski. Brecht understood the human condition and the suffering of mankind. Stanislavski understood the psychological makeup of human beings and incorporated it into a philosophy of art. All of life is acting."

"That's just it—it isn't. All of life *isn't* acting. All of life isn't art."

"If you choose to have a negative philosophy, that's your business. If you choose to incorporate the *negative* aspect of life into your consciousness, then you have only to suffer the consequences. Everyone whom you respect conveys who they are through their *bodies* and their language. Right now your voice tells me you want to leave my house. And your body tells me that you are in pain."

"That's perfectly true."

"The philosophy of the Stanislavski system may seem like a cliché to you, Jerry darling, but to me it is, mystically, a philosophy. The creative state of acting is close to the creative state of living. I am *trained* to understand what goes on in the minds of actors. And I think I know exactly what is going on in your mind."

Jerry lit a cigar. "What is going on in my mind?"

"You no longer love me."

"What else?"

"You find Beverly Hills trashy. You see through all of the ugliness of the trappings of wealth. The banality of the conversations has nothing to do with what you consider to be important. I know what you're thinking. Acting is absurd. Astrology ridiculous. There are no poets in Hollywood. Only fools. And you miss New York and little Miss Revolution. Am I right?"

"How perceptive."

"So get the fuck out of my life. Stop eating my food. Stop drinking my liquor. Stop sleeping on beds where I pay for the laundry. And stop fucking my laundress." She rose to leave.

"Wait a minute."

When she turned her eyes were filled with tears. "I was an idiot to take you back."

"Why did you?"

"I don't know. You were my ace in the hole."

"You mean your ass in the hole. Your asshole."

She stepped closer to him. It was all something out of a scene-study class. Why did he feel he was performing?

"I loved you once. You were a bright good-looking kid from Queens without any sophistication or street smarts. Your idea of art was a print of the Mona Lisa you could buy for a quarter. Your idea of life was childlike. You lived by your reflexes, as a child does. By sounds, colors, objects: you were open. I took you into my life and taught you a great deal, Jerry. Above all, I taught you about how exciting the world of the imagination and art can be. I gave you a direction. I showed you how to make a living doing something you didn't hate. And you've done very well thanks to me. I thought you were a poet. That you could look at the world freshly and differently. And that's what I loved about you. Then I left you. Our lives took different paths. You married. Had a child. Finally I married again. I found Michael. We went in separate directions. Then, one moment when I felt vulnerable, you appeared in my life again. Everyone says we can't go back to the past. But I thought we could. I gave us a chance."

"You were just jealous of the fact that I had met a young girl."

She was furious. "I wanted what I can never have. A relationship of one artist to another. I thought that your creative fantasy would spur mine. I was just fooling myself to think that we could create something beautiful."

She was so angry she began crying. The black lines of kohl which she used for mascara ran down her face. She suddenly looked like a statue of Venus that was melting, as if the marble turned into lard. He hated it when Ursule cried. She was a tough, strong person. Why couldn't she stay like that? But that's what's wrong with this whole fucking society, he thought. I can cry. She can cry. We're not gods. He saw her beautiful dark eyes amidst the black.

"It's all right to cry," he said. He put his arms around her.

"I don't feel beautiful. I feel deformed," she said through her tears.

"It will be all right," he said softly.

"It will be?" She looked up, surprised. Light fell on her hair. She looked just like an eight-year-old child.

"Yes. All of life is beautiful. You, Ursule, try to discover beauty everywhere. In young people, through acting, through teaching. You see and abstract beauty from things which a noncreative person overlooks entirely. You are valuable. And I do love you very much."

"Then you will stay with me?"

"I'll try to be good to you. I'll stay."

53.

M ary jogging . . .
She could feel her legs moving. It was a sexual feeling—
to go faster and faster. The running was almost like making love—a
sort of autoeroticism that brought her closely in touch with her own
self. First she felt her legs aching, then the pain of being winded—
and then, there it was—the high—the climax—the sense of not
knowing who she was, the feeling of riding rainbows—of being
lifted above air and mist—the feeling of fighting off reality with the
climax of the run. It was where she wanted to live; she wanted it
never to stop, that feeling of being at the height of herself. Best of
all, she needed no one to "give" her this ecstasy. She could give it to
herself—by pushing her body. It *was* a climax.

Running, Mary wondered about Jerry. He had been gone
a month and had only called her three times. He had sounded

busy—she wondered if he was happy with Ursule. Jerry was tied to the past and Ursule. She realized how hard it was for him, like many men his age, to give birth to himself and live in the present. Some days she felt that Jerry was going to come back to her. Their sexual connection was strong and heated. She remembered the last time she had made love with Jerry before he left for California. His eyes had been closed—he was sleeping. Slowly she had awakened him by putting his cock in her mouth and sucking him until he wanted, so badly, to be inside her. They had fucked for hours, his cock getting hard, then coming, then getting hard again. She knew that her large breasts turned Jerry on. The first time he had begun sucking her nipples she had seen how excited he became, and she had pulled away from him in that instinctual way that she knew could arouse him. She would pull free from him and then hold her breasts in her hands so that he pulled her down and began sliding his tongue over her breasts and then biting her. Jerry might behave like a jerk. He might be uninitiated and unpolitical, but he had the hardest cock she had ever felt inside of her. She thought about *that* as she ran.

54.

Jerry woke up every morning and couldn't wait to be out of Ursule's house and running. The air was cleaner in Beverly Hills. As he jogged past the houses, which looked like well-cared-for mausoleums, he began thinking about *why* he was running. Now he was running away from Ursule's house. But why? It felt good. He was running his own Olympic Marathon against his own life. Jogging in California was different from jogging in New York. It was a whole new high. He could breathe. Running faster and faster, he began reaching that moment when thoughts and muscles combined. It was then that he could run into the wild colors of the gardens and grassiness of roads, run into the dawn, run into the sun. Again, he thought of Mary. When he was with her he had missed Ursule. Now he missed her. He drifted closer and closer to Mary in his thoughts. He suddenly wished he was jogging in the lousy air of New York, past the lousy concrete buildings. He was not a California person. Ursule and the whole Beverly Hills scene was beginning to get on his nerves. Jogging alone was not as much fun as running with a partner. In the California dawn he thought of Mary jogging beside him. He began wondering if he really loved her. For so long he hadn't been able to "feel" anything for anyone except Ursule. Now he missed Mary's face. He saw her face on a canvas in his mind.

55.

That was the end.

That should have been the end.

But Jerry Hess, like most lovers who are really inferior vaudevillians, had his timing off. He was like the tap dancer who sometimes had the feeling he wanted to stay then he had the feeling that he wanted to go—wanta stay—wanta go—wanta stay—wanta go. He couldn't quite shuffle off to Buffalo. Flap. Shuffle tap. He tapped on. The Jewish Fred Astaire. Dressed in a tuxedo for charming dinners. Appearing at screenings with Ursule and the Labradors. Sitting in the back of the classroom while Ursule gave Stanislavski philosophical bonbons to the hungry crew of students and actors who collected at her school from all over the world.

"The actor should not be concerned about his feeling during a play. It will come of itself. Stanislavski maintained that it is important for the actor not to experience, not to make feelings to order, to forget about trying to feel altogether. In life, our feelings come to us by themselves. Against our will. Our willing gives birth to action directed toward the gratification of desire. Thus every feeling is a gratified or nongratified will. At first, a desire arises that becomes the will, then becomes the act consciously aiming toward its gratifications. Therefore the actor, Stanislavski taught, must think first of all about what he wants to obtain at a particular moment and what he is to do, but not about what he is going to feel."

Jerry listened to this at the back of the class. He suddenly felt that the world of Stanislavski, of feeling, of Ursule playing out her legend, all of this was no longer his world. He thought of Mary. Of Liza. Why had he left Mary?

"True creativeness can be realized only when an inner impulse to work is present."

Oh, why doesn't she shut up? Jerry Hess no longer found the creation of a part meaningful. The case history of a role was no longer important to him. Ursule and her adoring actors were characters for whom he felt compassion, not people he admired. He got up and left the classroom. He suddenly began running down the steps. The Labradors ran with him. Ursule's car was poised discreetly by the steps. He gave the chauffeur the dogs. Hailed a cab. Kept the cab waiting. Ran upstairs. Packed. Ran down the steps. Took the cab to the airport. At the airport, he walked into a florist and sent Ursule flowers. He wasn't quite sure what he could write to her.

"I am quite familiar with the play. But I am still completely in the dark. I love you very much. Jerry."

He wasn't sure what the card meant. The phrase, with its ambiguity, would please Ursule. Was he Iago, possessing Satanic energy? How could he leave Ursule so cruelly? God damn it, all of life was not a play. All us people not merely players. He was tired of intellectual Los Angeles and all those chauffeured cars which looked like gondolas—luxurious limousines decorated with fine fabrics—benefiting wealthy teachers of actors. Was he Iago? Or was he Roderigo, who was stupid, stubborn, childish, foolish? It was embarrassing not to know who he was. He knew one thing—he was tired of being a character in the middle of an act. He wasn't Jerry Hess. He was Uriel Acosta. Uncle Vanya. He was Ratkitin in Turgenev's *Month in the Country*. He was Prince Abrezkov in Tolstoy's *Living Corpse*. He no longer felt the tremendous inspiration he had felt when he met Ursule. He felt only that he had to leave her life and find his own.

56.

An aside to the players: Jerry Hess felt good.

On the plane he felt almost like a mystic he had read about in *Town and Country*—William Guggenheim the Third—who had given away a lot of boxes filled with his worldly possessions. And he felt light. To end the relationship with Ursule was to experience freedom. The mixture of conflicting emotions was so interesting that he jotted down in a notebook a poem and a recipe for feeling good. Oh, God! He was experiencing the disease of Los Angeles where everything was a recipe. No. He would tabulate his feelings.

1. Relief at the end of search for a good relationship.
2. Despair at the end of search; no further motive force in life.
3. Horror at cutting himself off from Ursule.
4. Relief at saying good-bye to her forever. What possible

good would come out of making himself into her fool?
5. Relief at cutting himself off from an obsession.
6. Fear that the obsession would come back.
7. Terror at going back to New York.
8. Anticipation of making love to Mary.
9. Intense shame (this was difficult to understand) about Lillian.
10. Willingness to take risk with Mary rather than admit complete defeat with all women.
11. Preference not to face fact that he was growing older.
12. Immense relief at not having to walk Labradors.

It was an odd collection of fragments to put down on paper in an airplane. Unlike Ursule, he was not sure what everything meant. He was a moribund writer escaping with his life from Los Angeles. But what was the point? Should he now join Mary in her desire to reform the capitalist society? Was what she said really true? That a system that is run by a corporate society can have, at bottom, no *love*, only *fear*? Was it true, as Mary the radical brat said, that a society of "haves" and "have nots" will never entertain love, but only breed dissatisfaction? That in order to have love, the way that Mary the brat saw it, you needed to have a sense of satisfaction, contentment with one's work? (But in a capitalist society there was never satisfaction or "brotherhood and sisterhood," only competition.)

He had been with the most beautiful woman who had ever lived. Ursule. He had made love to her, lived with her again as he always dreamed of doing, and now, he had left her. Suddenly he felt deprived of all purpose. He felt that he was swinging from intense joy to a zany intense sadness. He was not sure if this was what was meant by choosing and changing. But he had chosen. Thinking of it all, he felt uplifted. As if there was some funny festival going on inside his brain. He was nervous about seeing Mary. He lay back in his seat on the airplane and tried to relax.

Arriving at the airport, he called Mary. She wasn't in. He wondered about her. If she was at a meeting. Or out on the town? Or with someone else? She was so broad-minded. He wondered if she was angry at him. He checked into the Waldorf Towers. Took a shower. And called her again. This time she was in. He told her he would be right over.

57.

When he arrived, Mary was wearing jeans. She had a drink ready for him. "I'm glad you're back," she said.

"What's been happening?" (He tried to play it cool. Maybe she wouldn't even ask him about Ursule.)

"Nothing much. I just got married a couple of days ago."

"*What?*"

She broke into laughter. "I'm only joking." He didn't think it was funny.

"So what is new?"

"I'm still writing an article about the Cuban Revolution in Latin America for *Crawdaddy*. It's a dynamite article. I can't wait to show it to you."

It was as if he had never left. He got close to her and began kissing her.

"I'm glad you're here," she said before they made love.

58.

Jerry decided to work things out with Mary. At the age of forty-two, in the middle of a hot summer in New York, he realized with some surprise that he *needed* her. Who was he really? Forty-two years of wandering over the earth, he was lover, ex-husband, father, art dealer, and poet, son, friend, and alien to most circles of respectable friends. What motivated him? Once it had been making money, putting together the jigsaw of a life that had all the pieces but didn't fit. He had adventures. Now there was Mary. What kind of couple could they be? To begin with, he'd have to be on her side no matter what she had said. They had talked together the night after he returned and she had looked at him and told him what she thought about a relationship that would work. They sat on the bed talking.

"I want a relationship that's serious. Where no chore is randomly assigned, no power automatically assumed, no slice of toast casually buttered."

"Faithfulness?"

"That's only part of it. I want you to encourage me to make my own decisions and I want to help you, too, Jerry."

"The consequences of two people's genitals happening to get engaged are overemphasized in this society."

"What do you mean?"

"Who knows? I know that men want meaningful relationships as much as women. I know that there are many things that are important to you that could be important to me. And that because of you, I'm *changing*."

"How?"

"When I was in California I began seeing a whole new California. I saw the necessity for *consumption* on a level that made me ill. There is all that talent—the center of the media—and *nothing* to be done with it. A glorification of neurosis. There was no art. No human commitment. No understanding of the human dilemma. I remember the afternoon I met Josh Hiller, who specializes in finding homes for the stars. The houses are showplaces. They must have swimming pools, decks, tennis courts. All of them look like monuments in a cemetery. And while I was surrounded by 'students' and 'artists' and 'quality' Hollywood people, I wondered if in Beverly Hills I wasn't in the center of everything in life I despise. One night just before I left, I talked to a black director, someone who was now doing his own *thing*. I asked him about the film he was directing, and he told me it was a comedy based on a movie that had been made before. It was a blacked-up version of some rock musical. I was surprised. The director had a reputation for being 'serious' and 'political' and yet he was just making another Hollywood product that he didn't believe in. 'Why are you doing this?' I asked him. And the answer was 'Hey, man, I have to make a living so I can do what I really want.' 'But will the time come for you to do what you really want?' I asked him. 'That's heavy,' he said. Then we got into a discussion about freedom and South Africa. I came on with how did he, a black, feel about it? I remember the way that man looked at me. I had ruined his party. He had come to Ursule's for a buffet dinner, he wanted to be seen in his new clothes with a white chick on his arm and have it known how

216

hip and intellectual he was. And there I was confronting him with his own shit. The same questions I ask myself. He was no different from anyone else at the party. A swim, a joint. Close your eyes. Send your kids to an analyst. Maybe the whole anxiety and nightmare of life will go away. Well, that's part of the reason I left Beverly Hills."

Mary looked at him. "You're changing, Jerry."

"I know. But it's hard. I'm so conditioned to live another kind of life. The life with blinders. Pasternak said, 'To live a life is not to cross a green field.' "

"And what about us?"

"I think we should explore whatever we can."

"I've got so much work to do. Articles to write. Sometimes, I yell at myself and ask myself why I'm not thinking of a good relationship and having kids."

"There's plenty of time for that—my God, you're so young, Mary."

"I know. But I think about it. It wouldn't be natural if I didn't. My parents are very religious people. They want me to have a decent life, and I call them every week and assure them I'm not mugged in New York. They wonder what I'm doing here. And I wonder myself. The competition is bad as a free-lance writer. The landlady of this apartment is a kind of a big fat Greek woman. No. Not fat. But very stout. Very stout. Everyday she asks me what I'm doing. I tell her I'm writing an article.

" 'I'm thinking you're crazy,' she says to me. She thinks I should be out swimming or making love or doing something else."

"I need you, Mary. I think we need each other."

"We do, in a way. But you scare me."

"Why?"

"You're a grown-up in many ways. And I'm a child. And, then, in other ways, you're a child and I'm a grown-up. I don't know. You're older than I. And different. You have a kid almost my age. You've been through a lot. And what you've always wanted is different from me."

"I think we want the same things in a way."

"What's that?"

"Caring for each other."

"I cared for you. And one day you left. I came home and realized

217

you were gone. That I had begun to depend on you and that you would just pick up and go whenever you wanted to."

"It's easy to leave. Harder to stay."

"I understand. You had ghosts to work out. Demons that came from the past."

"It was only that I felt so sentimental about my life with Ursule. We had so many good times together. Once upon a time, she opened up my eyes to the world of art and theatre and interesting people. When I was younger it was very exciting. What I learned out in Beverly Hills was that the past is not an elastic band. You can't stretch the past into the present."

"Then why did you try?"

"I used to have unbelievable fantasies about Ursule. You could say I was obsessed with her. I just never gave up. Even when Jerry, Jr., was a little boy and I was becoming a successful art dealer, I never gave up. She was someone that I kept in my mind as my secret. I'd go back to her in my imagination. And yet she wasn't dead. She was alive. I'd read about her in the papers. I'd call her once in a while. When she got married to someone else, I went out on a drunk and ached as if she had just left me."

"Go on."

"Perhaps it sounds odd, but she was what kept me going in life. Every time I sold a painting, I wondered what Ursule would have thought. Perhaps she was like a mother—as I made more and more money, I thought of how she would have been proud of me. I saw things as I thought she might see them. The love that I had for her could never be pulled out of my guts. Not guilt or terror, or all the years of another life could get rid of her. What I felt for her was beyond what we call love. It was something else. Necessity. Illness. Then, when she said she would take me back, I had to live it out. I couldn't resist being back in her arena of excitement and energy. But it was different. It wasn't right. And here I am."

"And now?"

"I'm still going to keep on dealing in art. At least for the moment. I'm also going to find out some things about myself. Who Jerry Hess is. I know it's painful. But I have no choice."

"For sure."

59.

What was his business?
      To charm. To sell. To wheel and deal in art history.

Jerry moved part of his private art collection to the Waldorf Towers. On the walls were the great paintings he had at the Dakota. Many of the pictures were in the warehouse but he had bought many new pictures which he hung one above the other. As usual, he did well without trying. In and out of his suite came patrons and directors, art dealers and fastidious connoisseurs of American and French art. One of his best customers was the director of the Albany Institute of History and Art, and his colleagues—all fat fellows with fat wallets. Jerry knew how to say exactly the right thing and went out of his way to praise Albany. Flattery was his business.

"A delightful city, Albany," Jerry said. He was showing the director and his entourage some newly acquired Fragonards. He was sincere.

"Note the colors in this *Education of the Virgin*," Jerry said, pointing to his new acquisition, which he hoped to unload as quickly as possible. "It's oil on canvas, of course, thirty-three by forty-five. It was first sold to the painter, Folliot, in April, 1843. Since then it's changed hands several times, often anonymously, popping up in the famous Walferdin sale in 1850 and later sold to Wildenstein and Company, and through them to Fleishacker in California. This little picture has been on exhibit in the Fogg, in the Los Angeles Art Association, in the French Painters of the Eighteenth Century exhibit, gentlemen, and it's yours for practically nothing because I think it would complement your collection in Albany. After all, your museum is weak on eighteenth-century French artists. The IBM Corporation and the Baltimore Museum of Art have both put in high bids for this particular Fragonard. But to be blunt—your collection interests me and I prefer to see this hanging in Albany among your Duchamps and new Japanese paintings than lost in Baltimore among the Rodins, Millets, and Picassos."

"That's very generous of you, Mr. Hess," the director said, lighting a cigar. "What do you call practically nothing?"

"A quarter of a million. And it's a steal."

"That's beyond our budget."

"When you consider that Mary Cassatts and Watteaus are selling for a half million, you'll understand what a bargain this is; it's dirt cheap, gentlemen. Especially since I can turn around and sell this to Mr. and Mrs. Raymond Leibowits of Chicago for double the price. Yale is also interested. So is the Sterling and Francine Clark Art Institute."

"We just bought a Redon, shaded blue, scarlet, and gold molluscoid forms floating on a shimmering surface with serpentine animals, from the Goldman Foundation." These men were such idiots, Jerry thought.

"I know the painting well. It was painted in 1905 and comes from Sam Salz. It's not worth anything. This Fragonard is a *treasure*."

"All right, Mr. Hess. We'll take it up with our board of directors."

"I'm sorry, but it will be gone by this afternoon if you don't take it now and write me a check for it."

He knew they were panting for the Fragonard. He could smell profit a mile away.

"That's impossible."

"Good afternoon, gentlemen."

They left. Returned. Wrote a check. Paid, and on went the afternoon. Buyers from the Palisades Museum were followed by gentlemen from the Indianapolis Museum. Jerry was a master at dumping his paintings with discourses on his "fervent belief in the intellectual cooperation between dealer and purchaser." It was all a game. Pin the tail on the Fragonard.

To the Albany buyer, he offered a tip. "I'm enthusiastic about this painting for one reason. Can I speak openly? Several buyers have bid twice as much, and Leslie Hyam, president of Parke-Bernet, has asked me to include this in the next sale. I wouldn't dream of putting this in the catalogue."

And so the days passed. Jerry sold Bonnards, Buffets, Cézannes, Dalis, Daumiers, Degas, Derains, Dufys, Epsteins, Grises and Groszes, Hartungs, Laurencins, Légers—Rouaults and Matisses, Mondrians and Renoirs—to collectors who came in and out of the doors of his suite. To them all, he offered his charm and engaging salesmanship, pitting one museum against the other, making the Philadelphia Museum jealous of what the Fine Arts Museum of San Francisco was buying, arousing the greed of the Horowitzes against the Astors and the Caldwaters against the Childs.

"George Wildenstein would faint if he knew what I was giving this away for," was his operative expression which he used judiciously to the museums and their purchasers. To the French buyers, he offered contemporary Americans. To the Americans he offered magnificent French Impressionists. "I assure you this will give you a place in history," he said to Mrs. Havemeyer. Which was, of course, the same thing he had said a few hours earlier to Mrs. Potter Palmer. "The relationship between New York and French art is extraordinary," he told one of the directors of the Frick as he disposed of two pictures which had belonged to Joseph Bonaparte. Jerry Hess was always "privileged" to sell his paintings as an attractive representative of enlightenment. To Mrs. Nathan Dumpfaster, buying her first Rodin, Jerry threw in a charming Boucher drawing as a gift for her daughter. To the collection of Maurice Morris he gave a tiny Millet charcoal, *Girl with Sheep*. Just as anthropologists studied the habits and beliefs of natives, Jerry Hess studied the habits and beliefs of collectors. Wearing his Dunhill smoking coat, he was at home among the masters. After each patron departed he put down his scotch glass with a click, looked in the mirror and sighed. He ran his fingers through his hair. He understood "people" and their "need to acquire."

Every day another deal.
Every day, another possibility to sell art.
Jerry was getting tired of the art racket. That's what it was in the end—a racket. Every modern painter, he knew, was ripped off by the galleries. They bought his paintings for a small price. Sold the painting to an off-shore company. The company sold it to other buyers. And the price was jacked up. Creating a false value was the job of the galleries. They were being indicted. Jerry knew the racket well. He had begun, recently, separately buying young artists. At least he would be giving them a chance. But even that was a certain connery. He would buy a Kawabata, sell it to a museum, buy it back, sell it to a collector, and build up credentials, buy it back, and then sell it to a larger museum. He would buy Tsutakas, Akanas, Shinodas, Yamamotos, Isumis, and turn them over quickly for cash. He was the only one collecting these Japanese artists and he sold them along with Picassos, El Grecos, and Monets. Every day another deal. Every day more sales.

To the Japanese elitist, he sold American. To the American elitist, Japanese. To the Europeans he sold Asiatic. Everyone wanted what they were not. The suite at the Waldorf bustled with painters, collectors. No sooner did the elevator deposit a collector than it took down an artist. Jasper Johns disposed of his early prints. Jerry Hess knew all the artists. Regularly he gave cocktail parties where Castelli, Henry Geldzahler, Kakuzo, Yoshimura, Noguchi, Jenkins, mixed with the buyers. One evening in the summer, he spent his time selling to a particularly difficult customer—the head of the Mikiyami conglomerate who flew from Tokyo to buy Western paintings to hang in the Kikiguchi Museum and in all of the Mikiyami banks and offices. The selling ceremony began. It was just as ordered as a tea ceremony.

Mr. Yagi, chairman of Mikiyami, arrived at the suite. He was wearing a dress kimono. He was alone. He bowed. Jerry Hess bowed. They bowed again and again.

"So, Mr. Hess, I have the honor to meet most famous private American art dealer." Yagi bowed again.

"And I have the honor to meet one of the most famous executives in Japan." Jerry bowed.

Room service was summoned. A waiter popped up from nowhere like a jack-in-the-box.

"I'm having a scotch on the rocks. What can I offer you, Mr. Yagi?"

"Normally I don't drink when I work. Here in your country I break my rule. I take double whiskey and single soda, thank you very much."

The drinks arrived. Jack-in-the-box served.

"What are you interested in buying, Mr. Yagi?"

"American paintings. Very valuable and important American paintings."

"Which period? The Ashcan school? The Earthworks school? Action painters? Pop Art?"

"Too many names, Mr. Hess. I want to cut a path as foremost buyer in Japan of Jasper Johns. I am indebted to critical writings of Leo Steinberg, Barbara Rose, Tatyana Grossman, Ken Tyler, Robert Motherwell for instructing me in interpretation of pictures. I have many errors and misconceptions which you can help me with."

"You have very good taste. Jasper Johns is the most valuable American painter."

"Yes, he is very well known in my country. He visited my country many times. His work very valuable."

"His *sensitivity* is very amazing. And you are very fortunate. I happen to have many of Jasper Johns' works."

"I am very interested."

"You know he has just had a big exhibit at the Whitney. His work is selling like hotcakes. You understand this expression, Mr. Yagi?"

"We have hotcakes in Japan, Mr. Hess."

"Are you interested in circles?" Jerry asked.

"No, I am more interested in flag period. It's more valuable."

"I see you are informed."

"It is logical. Johns is colorist. Colors best in flags. Japan patriotic country. Japanese like flags."

"What about the alphabet period?"

"No. I am interested in numbers. Figure zero to figure nine."

"I do not have any numbers. But let me show you some amazing targets."

Jerry disappeared into a closet. Out came a target painting which he put on a large wooden easel.

"Interesting."

"Would you like to see others?"

"At Minami Gallery we see a lot of Pop Art. Pop Art is biggest influence in Japan. Before that, Marcel Duchamp. Or French. Now Pop Art is very big. Jasper Johns very important. I hear you have recent paintings of Mr. Johns. Recent paintings most valuable. I want barber-tree paintings."

"This is a very important day. I just received a shipment of seven untitled tree pictures. I want to show them to you."

Out of the closet came seven paintings. Jerry Hess lined them up against the wall. Yagi was silent. Jerry began selling.

"This artist is a magician. *Newsweek* calls him the greatest artist in the world. His work is magical—as old as Daedalus and Merlin. His work is humorous and playful, and at the same time provokes anxiety."

Mr. Yagi suddenly took out his magnifying glass from his sleeve pocket. He began looking carefully at the pictures.

"The artist for the moment has settled into a series of paintings which elaborate on patterns of cross-hatching. He has already begun to complicate these patterns in different ways. He is exhausting the potential for mathematical manipulation of the image. These pictures are his most intellectual. They are metaphysical."Yagi was silent. Then he spoke.

"They move upward and onward for benefit and pleasure. I like them better than targets and flags. Better than drawers. How much?"

"Surely you don't have to worry about price."

"I no worry about price. I worry about resale value."

"Mr. Yagi, you are a very good businessman. You understand that at a gallery, at Mr. Johns' gallery, these paintings cost twice as much? You understand *what it is* to deal with a private dealer, not a private gallery?"

"I understand. I save fifty percent. How much?"

"How many of these do you wish to purchase?"

"Oh, Mr. Hess. I must express myself differently. All of them. One two three four five six seven. All of them. All seven."

"I like your attitude. They are a half-million dollars each. For seven they are three and a half million U.S. dollars—you will be the third buyer. Which means the resale price will only go up. I'm giving you a third offering."

"I pay you two million."

"For seven?"

"For all. Yes. Two million."

"Mr.Yagi, you drive a hard bargain. I'll sell them to you for three million. These are not targets. These are the artist's best period. The profound implications of these trees cannot be measured by money. The meanings are elusive. But the work is brilliant."

"Two million."

"An artist cannot fix his meanings. It is an experience that must be explored. I am very sorry. I know how much the Japanese appreciate the work and irony of Jasper Johns. The simple childish play in his work carries philosophical implications that are appreciated in your country where art is sophisticated and the work of art is perceived directly. I love these paintings. As a matter of fact, I bought them for my own collection."

"Two million, Mr. Hess."

"I could not part with all seven for two million."

"Two and one half million."

"Three million."

"Two and one half million."

"Not for seven. Five for two and one half million. Three million for seven."

"Two and one half million. Coat hangers worth more than new work. Two and one half million. Last offer."

"Let's not quibble, Mr. Yagi. Three is my lowest price."

Mr. Yagi bowed.

Jerry Hess bowed.

Mr. Yagi took a check from his pocket. He sighed loudly as he signed away three million dollars for the paintings.

"Thank you, Mr. Hess. You drive a hard bargain. I send my men to pick up pictures in morning."

Jerry Hess bowed as he closed the door. The bastard had gotten a bargain. He had paid two million cash for the pictures that morning. All he had made in a day's work was a million.

60.

Jerry?

Mary knew she could *relate* to Jerry. They would work things out. Then Johnny called. He was coming into town from Pennsylvania and he wanted to talk to her. Couldn't they have breakfast?

"Where?"

"At your pad, where else?"

"Johnny, there's a new guy in my life. He often sleeps here."

"Meet you at the zoo then, sugar. At the cafeteria. You'll recognize me. I'll be wearing a black hat, a red carnation, and a lute around my neck."

"Very funny. Tell you what—I'm trying not to eat. I'll meet you in back of the cafeteria. Next to the polar bear."

They met in front of the polar bear. It was Mary's idea of irony. Johnny with his coked-out personality, his cookie-cutter blue eyes, his platinum mane, his smile, and his soft voice reminded her of the polar bear. He was from a different place. A cold place. An icy place where she could never survive.

"Hi," he said. He had been waiting for her.

There was something so empty about him. He walked quietly, as if he had learned to walk from the Indians. He was an "outdoors" person, and always seemed to be balanced on moccasins. His hair was long, down to his neck, and it was hard to tell where the blond hair stopped and the blond beard began. There was a softness about him that she had forgotten. Softness? Or weakness? He had his face in the sunlight, and his face was turned up to the sun. As if he were trying to get a tan and talk to her at the same time.

"I've given up coke," he said.

"Since when?"

"I decided to stop just as if it were an emergency. Stop dealing in coke. I just couldn't deal anymore. I'm going to concentrate only on my music and helping Iza with her kid and the restaurant."

"What's her kid like?"

"He gets in trouble in school. He has a special tutor. He's not nice. I don't like him. What's the guy like you're making it with? Or isn't it any of my business?"

"It isn't. But I'll tell you anyway. He's great."

"What does he do?"

"He's a dealer."

"Coke?"

"No. Art."

"Sounds good. What kind of paintings?"

"All kinds."

"How's your ass?"

"Great. How's yours?"

"I feel good."

Mary stared at him. It was hard to believe how crazy about him she had been just a few months ago. "I have to go, Johnny. But I'd like to see you again. I was pretty pissed off that you didn't call me the last time we were supposed to meet."

"Well, sometimes a bird just has to fly." He smiled.

"You're not a bird."

"I didn't want to push too hard."

"Well, that was considerate of you. I hope we'll be friends. But I can't say when I can see you again."

She walked away, leaving him staring in front of the polar bear. He was like so many musicians she had known, empty. Deep down there wasn't a heart. There was a saxophone. And a dream of standing in front of a thousand middle-class groupies applauding and bringing their pubescent hysteria to the stage. Johnny seemed only interested in his own fame. Not in anyone else's. Certainly not in *hers*. As she left him standing in front of the polar bear he stared after her with his cold blue eyes of ice. Radar eyes. She felt them on her back. Let him go be famous! Thank God she was over him. He had been nothing but a mistake. He was a cop-out cosmic con loser. He was a creep. A fuck-up!

Jogging, Mary thought about Jerry.

It made her nervous to think that he was pushing for her to meet Jerry, Jr. Why was it so important for all of them to be *together*?

"He's my son."

"I know that, Jerry. But I'm only a couple of years older than he. And he's not going to like me. Why should he? He thinks I took you away from his mother."

"He's going to love you. He loves me. He'll love you. He's a great boy, Mary. If we are talking about spending time together, I'm not going to be happy unless we have him *with* us." That was that.

Mary thought about all of this as she jogged. Running in the park things got all mixed up. Johnny! Forget him. Jerry? A beautiful guy. He really was turning out to be so much better than she thought. Everything was turning around. He was sensitive. The night before they had lain on the bed reading the poetry of Violetta Para. Jogging, hair flying, she realized that had been the best part of the relationship so far. Telling him about her heroine.

"Why is she your heroine?" he had asked.

"Because Violetta Para was the total artist. Innovative and original, and political. She wasn't just a *writer*—she did everything in every medium. She created poems. She wrote songs. Collected folklore. She was an interpreter of Chilean folklore. She was a woman of courage, capable of understanding any effort, going anywhere, of loving and hating with equal intensity. She was always poor, giving away everything. She was a troubadour traveling all over her country, looking for popular singers, speaking directly to young poor people, learning about their lives, their legends, their traditions."

"What happened to her?"

"At the low point of her life, after she came back from Paris, where her tapestries had been exhibited at the Louvre, she created a folklore center in Chile. But nobody—outside of her circle of friends—appreciated her. She was depressed. She had taken up with an adolescent musician, a flutist, who left her. In 1966, she was tired and attempted suicide by slashing her wrists. And in the summer of 1967 she asked to be left alone and wanted to sing her 'Ultimas Composiciones' in Chile which had just been recorded for RCA. Only afterward was the meaning of the title understood. On a Sunday, February fifth, she committed suicide by shooting herself."

They had lain on the bed while Mary read "Las Décimas," which she had translated into English. Violetta Para. White Paper. Tempera. Gold leaf on parchment. Lying with Jerry on the bed. Writing articles. It was all those things that made Mary happy. Why did he have to insist on her meeting his son? It could only mean trouble. She didn't really like other people's children.

Jerry, Jr., was working in New York City for the summer at a bank. He was living with Lillian at the Dakota. Jerry called his son and arranged to have dinner with him at Elaine's.

"I'm inviting Mary, son. I want you to meet her."

"Whatever you want, Dad."

"Good. I knew you'd make it easy for me."

"Dad, I love you. Whatever you do with your *life* is your own business. I feel uncomfortable about meeting Mary because of all the things that Mom says. About her being a couple of years older than I. Shit. Lots of guys at school have young stepmothers, and I'm perfectly willing to show you all the respect I can, Dad."

"Thanks, son."

Jerry resisted the urge to weep. It was going to be a painful meeting but he prepared himself for it. The main thing was to keep cool. Not to show his feelings that were like exposed nerves. He had one more barrier to get over and that was convincing Mary what *fun* it would be for all of them to have dinner.

He spent the morning with Mary. They made love. Then he brought up the idea.

"It doesn't appeal to me. You go have dinner with Jerry, Jr., yourself. I'll stay home and watch television. They're doing a documentary tonight on the life of Noguchi and I'd like to watch it. Thanks anyway."

"Since when are you interested in art?"

"I'm not. I just don't want to play three little bears. I'm sure your son is a lovely boy. I'm just not up to meeting him."

"Look, Mary, this is important to me."

"Why?"

"I want to share a part of my life with you. I love you."

"We share a lot already that's important. It's not that I don't want to meet your son. I do want to meet him. I want to like him because he's part of your past and part of you. But I'm scared shitless that he's going to hate me. And just treat me as if I were some shiksa that picked you up jogging. And I can't hack it. So why *bother?*"

"That sounds like weakness."

"It's not that I'm frightened of meeting your son. It's just that it would be awkward for *him.*"

"He's already said he wants to meet you."

"He has?"

"Yes. And he's looking forward to it. Tonight at Elaine's. Be there at eight o'clock prompt. I have to go now, sweetheart. But I'll see you later." He kissed her good-bye.

Jerry and Jerry, Jr., arrived at Elaine's. It was hard to get into the restaurant and to get a good table unless you knew Elaine. Jerry had known her since the old days. Elaine came from behind the bar and kissed Jerry on the cheek. Holding his hand, she led Jerry and Jerry, Jr., to a table in the back. Jerry couldn't help but notice the women ogling him with interest as he walked down the aisle. He had to say hello to a lot of buddies he knew from his life with Lillian. There was Herb Scharp, his tennis partner from summers in the Hamptons. He looked tan and ten years younger than he was. He was taking out a young girl Jerry hadn't seen before. There was Dee Dee Ryan sitting at another table, surrounded by young men. He stopped to talk with Norman Mailer and his friend Norris, and introduced Jerry, Jr., to Warren Beatty and Diane Keaton, who were sitting together near the back. A group of Germans were clustered around a familiar moustached writer who had just published a new book. The writer got up and held out his arms. It was Günter Grass. Jerry took Jerry, Jr., over to the table. They exchanged bear hugs. When they were seated, Jerry ordered a double Dewars on the rocks.

"Make it two," Jerry, Jr., said.

It was late. Almost nine. Jerry was annoyed that Mary hadn't shown up yet.

"She's nervous, son."

"Why?"

"Because of Mom."

Jerry, Jr., sat looking at his father. Why the hell was he doing this? Was he going to tell him they were getting married? A knot in his stomach developed. He had another drink. He felt sick.

"How's Mom?" Jerry asked.

"She's all right. All I see her do is stay home and read. She's working very hard at the office. She looks all right."

"And the house in the Hamptons?"

"She doesn't go there too much anymore."

Suddenly Mary burst into the restaurant. Jerry watched as everyone looked at her as she came down the aisle. She had her hair curled around her head and was wearing some funky hat she had bought in an antique store. She was tall and filled with energy and almost manic enthusiasm. In a kooky kind of way she was very beautiful. Jerry noticed the deep red gloss of her lips. She sat down.

Mary smiled openly at Jerry, Jr.

"Hi. Your dad talks about you all the time. I'm happy to meet you after talking to you so often on the phone."

"Me too."

"Are you working in New York for the summer?"

"Yes. Then I'm going to Yale in the fall."

"Why did you pick Yale?" She tilted her head.

"I guess where I go to school, everyone goes to Harvard or Yale. Dad thought it was a good school. He doesn't like the idea of my just being a ski bum."

"You are a bum, kid. But I'd like you to be an educated one," Jerry said affectionately.

"What are you going to study?" Mary asked.

"Political science."

"Are you political?"

"Me? Nope. I'm just interested in having a good time and making money."

"Sick." Mary started to laugh almost hysterically.

Jerry ordered a bottle of white wine. The cork popped and a chubby short Italian waiter smilingly poured the wine. As he gave Mary her wine, he took her hand and kissed it. "You could be a movie star," he said.

"So could you," she shot back. She kept laughing. "Why are you just interested in money?" she asked Jerry, Jr., needling him gently.

"Because money gives me the freedom to do what I want."

"What do you want to do?"

"Ski. Go to parties. Take out pretty girls to dinner. Sail. Go to Paris. Buy a house in Vail. Go to discotheques. That all costs a lot."

"I really think you're sick," Mary said. Jerry was trying to pretend she was joking, but it was no joke.

"Look, Mary, I'm sorry to disappoint you. I don't know what my dad told you about me. If he said I'm working for gay rights or that I'm interested in solar energy, I'm afraid he was misleading you. I happen to be a good-time guy. So is Dad, by the way."

The squid arrived. It was fried. Everyone took some in their fingers and began eating.

"Your father is changing."

"Wait a minute—" Jerry said.

"Changing? What are you changing to, Dad? What kind of bullshit are you giving her?"

The squid was followed by pasta and salad. More wine. Everything seemed hazy to Jerry; he was getting drunk.

"You tell me what *you* do," Jerry, Jr., said to Mary.

"I work in a storefront school in Harlem, teaching kids how to read and write. I also write articles for alternate media and some straight magazines. I've written a lot of articles about Africa. Southern Africa mainly. And Latin America."

As dinner continued Jerry, Jr., and Mary battled with each other like rams, locking horns, locking huge round horns, then coming up for air.

"Look, kid," Mary said, smiling. "I didn't think you'd be such a spoiled brat."

"Yep. And I didn't think you'd be a fanatic."

"I'm not a fanatic. In California, we speak our minds. We're not a bunch of hypocrites."

Jerry smiled. He put his arm around Mary. "Christ! You're like a volcano tonight, Mary."

He continued to his son. "And you're probably scared too, Jerry. Somewhere underneath that repressed preppie personality is the son I love."

The dinner was finished, the dessert served, the small brown cookies unwrapped from their colorful pastel tissue. Jerry wanted to go home. He was drunk and tired.

"How are you going to get along with Dad if you're a radical?" Jerry, Jr., asked Mary.

"I'm not a radical. I'm concerned."

"Well, Dad's a dreamer. He's a businessman and a dreamer."

"He always seems to care about people. He cares about you, Jerry."

"I hope you can make Dad happy."

There was an awkward pause. Was the volcano about to erupt?

Jerry wondered in the sadness of his soul why everything had to be so difficult. He hadn't expected the three bears, he had hoped somewhere in his soul that the three bears wouldn't paw at each other.

Mary sensed this. She tried to make chitchat. "Where do you ski?"

"All over."

"East or West?"

"Both. Last year I skied at Heavenly Valley. They hadn't had snow for three years."

Now this was the family scene Jerry wanted. Three little dancing bears. Eating their porridge and squid. Surrounded by celebrities. Eating their curds and fame. On the tuffet of Miss Muffet. If only Mary, Mary quite contrary didn't overdo the political bit. If only she could just *relax*. Why couldn't she take it easy? Why did everything have to be so intense? When she was making love she was so feminine. Otherwise she was more like a sparring partner. Jab. Jab. Punch. Jab.

"Truce?" Jerry said, drinking his coffee.

He looked at Mary over his coffee cup and saw how young and pretty she was. She looked like a Western cowgirl. There was nothing phony or pretentious about her. She looked younger than a lot of the women in the restaurant. The women next to them at another table all wore too much eye makeup, and their clothes might have looked right in São Paulo but looked ridiculous in New York. They were all overdressed bitches drinking and laughing. Mary looked more like a girl who grew up in the sun or by the sea.

"I'm sorry," Mary said to Jerry, Jr. "I wanted things to be better."

"I know," he said. "I'm getting my head together about a lot of the things you talk about. I'm just not very political yet. I like people."

"That's political," she said.

"It is?"

"That's what politics is about. It's personal."

"I don't know. When Dad was married to Mom, they would get all these blue-and-white invitations in the mail. They'd be invited to a summer night's party in support of this or that candidate at some discotheque. On the committee would be Dad's friends or Mom's friends—the Honorable Mr. and Mrs. Angier Biddle Duke, or Mr. and Mrs. David Drexel, the Fourth. Now what the hell did David

Drexel, the Fourth, give a damn about politics? All he cared about was their motorboats, their fox hunts, and their stupid yacht clubs."

"That's not what I mean. That's not what I call politics. I'm talking about blood."

"You mean abortion rights?"

Mary laughed. "I don't mean blood literally." She lit a cigarette. "I'm always difficult when I meet people for the first time, why is it?" she said.

"So am I."

"Are you afraid of me?"

"No. Nor of myself."

"Did you ever imagine your dad with a person like me?"

"I didn't imagine it. But it happened."

Rain was now falling in sheets. Elaine's was very crowded. Lines of people, soaking wet, were waiting for tables.

After dinner Jerry's limousine, which had been waiting outside the restaurant like a huge maroon yacht, carried all of them as it sailed Jerry, Jr., home. As he was leaving the car there was a moment when Jerry looked at his son and wanted to cry.

"I know, Pop," Jerry, Jr., said.

"See you tomorrow?"

"Call me at the bank, Dad."

"I love you, boy," Jerry said as he hugged his son.

"Good night, Miss Reagan," Jerry, Jr., said politely.

It wasn't as bad as they all thought it would be. Jerry listened while the rain fell on top of the car. He took Mary in his arms.

"It was hard, Jerry," she said.

"I know."

He held her tight in his arms.

61.

Later, at Mary's apartment, she lit some candles and put on a record of the Stones. Jerry and she lay in each other's arms.

"I want to be a good writer again," Jerry said. "I want my life to count for something other than dealing and selling."

"That's odd. I just saw an old friend of mine who gave up dealing in coke."

"I want to give up art dealing. It was something I did and did well. But it's not me anymore. I've changed and I want to change what I do."

"I'll help you with that," Mary said.

"When the time comes—"

"When you have your head together, I'll help you."

They stopped speaking. He put out the candles. In the dark they held each other closely, listening to the music.

"Sometimes I feel that you're a life raft," Jerry said.

"Why?"

"Because I want to hold on to you. I want you to float me into another life. Where I don't drown in things I care nothing about. With you I feel as if I've been given a new life. A new chance."

"Even though I was bad with your son?"

"You weren't bad. You were just you. You have to be what you are."

"But I sat there feeling how very frivolous this world was. It made me sad and angry at the same time. To be part of a limousine life with your son, whose mind is only into skiing, making money, having fun, and doesn't give a damn about anyone except you and perhaps his mother. What a waste, damn it! I felt it. And I feel alien to it."

"I agree. But he was brought up in the pastures of our life. Lillian and I are so much more responsible than he is for the way he thinks."

"Let's not talk anymore."

He held her in the dark. She could feel how strong his body was. She held on to his arms, feeling the strong muscles of his arms. He made love to her and thought, afterwards, how much he liked fucking Mary.

62.

At breakfast, Jerry, Jr., confronted his mother.

"What's she like?"

"What's who like?"

"The whore, Mary."

"She was all right."

"All right? What is she like?"

"I hated her, Mom."

"Why?"

"Because she was so smug. She has Dad wrapped around her finger. God, why does he go for her in the first place?"

"Sex."

"But does a man let himself be led around like that so easily? Dad is like a fool when she's around."

"What does she look like?"

"She's young and has black hair. God, Mom, she's not even that pretty!"

"Well, I hate growing old. I don't blame him for liking a young girl."

His mother sat there drinking coffee.

"I think that yoga is going to help me," she said, and got off the chair and began to clear the dishes.

"Why don't you find someone, Mom?"

"How can I find someone?"

"Look. Go out."

"At my age there aren't exactly a group of Rubirosas running around New York."

"Who's Rubirosa?"

"He was a South American playboy. Who played polo. You know—with a mallet. He liked to dance. I keep reading all the articles about where the men are. They're written by fat little girls who work for a hundred dollars a week at the magazines."

"You can find someone."

"Sure, if I were a man with a fourteen-room apartment in the Dakota, I'd be the most popular bachelor in town. But a woman of forty-two? Forget it in the romance department."

"What are you going to do?"

"I don't know. Join the Salvation Army. I just don't want you bumming around with your dad and that girl. Please. It makes me sick."

"Just because I had one dinner with them doesn't mean we're pals."

"Well, don't get chummy with her. That's just what your father wants. She manipulated your father. She'll manipulate you."

"Are you kidding? I wouldn't go with her for anything."

"Thanks."

"What did I say?"

"You said enough. I feel old. Tired. Warned and forearmed and worn out. I keep reading about male menopause. Your father's been having it since he was sixteen."

"Forget him. I love you. You're beautiful. Dad's going to be sorry."

"Why?"

"Because you were good for him. Mary suggested that she and Dad and I go swimming at the United Nations pool. Maybe we could all go swimming and I'll give her a pair of cement shoes to wear in the water."

"That isn't a nice thought. You surprise me, Junior. I must go to review a new estate case now. I'll see you tonight."

Lillian met Sergio at Melon's.

He was sitting at the bar looking moody and handsome. He looked like a thin Valentino, a thin Che Guevara. He was so well dressed. He looked as if he had sambaed his life away. They went to a table.

"I like you so much, Lillian," he said, kissing her hand. They ordered bullshots.

"I'll take a bull without the shot," Lillian said. "I try not to drink during the week. What have you been up to, Sergio?"

"I've been traveling for my country. I just came back for the Miss Black America contest in Namibia. And I'm trying very hard to fall in love. I have so many women in love with me, the question is which one to choose?"

"Who have you met that's interesting?"

"In fact, I just was with a group of women on the island of Deya—all starlets. They kept running after me. I was with a group of six women and one man from Germany. You know what? You mustn't tell anyone—but I went to bed with the man. You know why? He wasn't the least bit interested in me. I can't stand it when people pursue me."

63.

Jerry went jogging. He began thinking of the three women in his life. Lillian was hardly qualified as being "in his life"; he congratulated himself on getting her out of it. But he had once loved her, fiercely. When she was young she had been a person whose voice was music, and her body was impeccable. She had been hopeful for his future, and they had been happy for many years. Trivia had pushed them apart. Did he still love her? Her disposition had changed. Ursule? He had loved her body. It was the body of a tall goddess. A woman who was tall turned him on. He suddenly thought of Mary. As he ran, he was able to remember the first time she had made love with him. She had put his cock in her mouth and gone up and down slowly until he came. He had watched her lips as she slid over him. The way she had made love to him made him breathless. As Jerry ran over a long slow distance he allowed himself to think of Mary. She had hooked him sexually. It was hard to compare her young perfect body, her lovely skin with anyone else's. It was the skin that made her so beautiful. He would run his hands over her breasts. "You smell American," was the first thing he had said to her when they made love. As he ran he thought of his heart rate, of foot landing positions, of the optimum health benefits of running. Suddenly he thought of it all together—healthy running, healthy sex, but was the feeling he had about Mary healthy? Or obsessive? He would desire her when she wasn't around. He would fantasize about fucking her. He would imagine her walking in front of him with nothing on but the high-heeled Brazilian shoes that she often wore, dark blue shoes with high heels and straps around the ankles. As he ran, Jerry thought of carbohydrate overload, of his diet, of how he had to eat to run better and better. He could feel his flat stomach and the sweat coming down it. There was no doubt about it, since he had been running, he felt hornier, as if now that he had perfected his body for sex, he wanted to use it more. Jogging and making love with Mary were all mixed up. He had to confess to himself that he thought about her more and more. She was loose, lusty, and lonely. Was it because of the loneliness that she had accepted him in her life? As she raced from one free-lance job to another, what was she chasing? He had bought her a motorcycle for her birthday and she drove it in the streets, wearing her helmet, and he, hugging her, sat behind her while they bounced through the streets. Lillian had been withdrawn. Ursule, an overly protective star. But Mary? She was a tough customer. It was not that easy to keep up with her.

64.

He was going to ask her to marry him.
He was really getting too old to keep making plans every night, keeping "loose" was a young man's game.

That was it. He'd ask Mary to be his wife. He needed someone to share his life. He wasn't a loner. He had finally worked out the obsession with Ursule. He still loved her, but deep down in that place of the imagination, he loved Mary. He realized it while jogging. Who was he kidding? He loved Mary.

Jerry thought, with whimsy, how nice it would be to fly away with Mary—jog into the sky—the two of them running. Who was Mary? Was she his youth? Didn't all Jewish intellectuals at a certain point look at themselves in the mirror and question about life? Was he a Jewish Ham? A meshugge Hamlet? A sensitive boisterous soul trying to find joie de vivre again? He had

spent so many of kisses and hugs, spent so many of his affec-
tions—and where had it led? He had alternated between three
women—the passionate Ursule, the organized Lillian, and now
the radical Mary. Wasn't it *time* to settle down to one woman? But
was *she* the woman? He had to admit that he felt a *little wrong* with
all of them. With Mary, he often felt out of sync. He was a record
in the wrong groove. Her generation, spawned in the sixties, now
waking up to life was not one that he felt comfortable in. He often
thought of seeking out more contemporary male friends—but he
was out of sync with men too. It was only with women that he
felt most comfortable. In some ways, his love story was with all
women, at least with three of them. He had taken from all of them.
Sensuality from Mary. Glamour from Ursule. A son from Lillian.
Energy from Mary. Understanding from Ursule. Now Mary was
the common denominator that he counted on. He had to reduce
the three to one. He had a selling trip to go on. Perhaps he could
sort everything out while he was in France. Ah! Paris.

65.

Being an art dealer had its compensations.
Every time he went to Paris on a selling trip, or to buy paintings, he felt as he had felt when he was a boy. Adventurous. Paris was still a city of marvels and architectural excitements. He loved the streets. The cafés. The gargoyles and the smell of urine in the city. Paris was his youth, and the times he had spent there with Ursule had been good ones. Paris, city of Mallarmé, Baudelaire, Anaïs Nin, songs, feeling crazy. Surrealist, mad, inventive, outrageous, Paris—he liked feeling boisterous and good. When he arrived at De Gaulle he always felt that he wanted to shout *yippeeee*. Paris, a city of the loved and the loveless, clochards and poets; Paris, city of Proust, of Beckett, Joyce, city of Mary Cassatt and bookstalls and cheese shops and antiques and wine, also, Paris of beautiful whores. He checked into the Ritz, where he always stayed. The dark-haired gentleman, the manager and his friend, who always wore a very dark suit and a smile, greeted him at the desk.

"Bonjour, Mr. Hess. Welcome back to Paris. Did you have a good trip?" He had sent a Telex to the hotel saying he would arrive. His secretary had also sent instructions to have a bottle of his favorite champagne (Dom Perignon) and Iranian caviar waiting for him in his room along with white roses and the day's papers—*Le Figaro* and *Paris Match*. Now as the blue-suited bellboy led Jerry down the old corridors to his suite, he felt that excitement that only the Ritz could give him. He sometimes stayed with his friend, Sam Pisar, the lawyer, but Sam was out of town since it was summer. Jerry enjoyed entering the room, seeing the flowers. He relaxed, opened the papers, sipped some champagne, had some caviar, and enjoyed the room.

The furniture was a chaise longue (the kind Colette liked), and two armchairs. They were pink and shiny and old. There was a desk with an old-fashioned lamp and blue-and-white Ritz stationery. Outside the windows was the Place Vendôme. He remembered Chanel had lived in the hotel. He would see her walking down the aisles and always bowed to her. When he was young, he had seen Irwin Shaw in the Ritz Bar. Now most of the people he knew were dead, or out of town. He had to get up the next morning very early to go to an auction house on the Quai d'Orsay. Once a station for French trains, now it was converted into a great selling place where the greed of art dealers matched the greed of collectors, and masterpieces exchanged hands. Jerry found most of his paintings at auctions.

Oddly enough, Jerry knew that the best paintings and the best buys were right under everyone's nose. That was his secret—he found his *bargains* at the most outrageously expensive auctions. Let the other dealers (the schmucks) go seeking paintings in bars and villas and little towns. He knew what a great dealer must know, how to find the great buys that are overlooked by the untrained eye. He had his spies in Paris—painters who had known him from the old days—who scouted the auctions and phoned him tips about what was selling before he arrived.

He always went right to the Hotel Drouet, brought cash, bid, took his pictures home, and then arranged for the certificates of authenticity to be "certified." It was these certificates, sadly enough, which made the pictures valuable. Those little pieces of paper which determined if the pictures were "real" or "fake." Anyone could forge a passport. But it was almost impossible to forge a certificate of authenticity. And Jerry Hess was known throughout the world of art, in London, at Sotheby's and Christie's, in Paris and at Versailles (where he drove every weekend for the salesrooms where only the art dealers and great collectors did well—the Salle Blache or the Salle Martin or at the L'event des Flora Lilies); he was known as the dealer with the most cash, and the only dealer who submitted his certificates of authenticity to an acid test. Jerry thought that dealing with these certificates was not far removed from trading cards. As a kid in Queens, he had had the best trading-card collection. He had known how to trade his "Blue Boy" for a "Pink Lady" and had built up the greatest collection of trading classic Kem cards in all of Queens. Now it wasn't the classic cards, it was the real thing, the real paintings, but it was no different from cards really. He went to the auctions, sought out the collectors he knew were ready to *sell*, and came home with his catch!

At the Hotel Drouet Jerry was admired. He was modest, charming, well dressed. He looked like an amiable conveyor of art. He wore a carnation in his lapel and shook hands with many of his old colleagues. His French was perfect. When the bidding started, he never hurried. He waited until most of the bidding had gone on and then put in his bid. His knowledge of French art was informed. He knew the eighteenth century well and was able to pick up many of the Louis Quinze painters—Watteau, Fragonard, Pater, Boucher—for much less than he would sell them for back home. He had never studied at the Ecole des Beaux-Arts, but his innocence, knowledge, his *trader's* ability was a legend in Paris.

"He has remarkable taste," Madame Jacques Balsan, née Consuelo Van Bloch, had said about Jerry Hess after he found an Ingres at the Hotel Drouet that everyone had overlooked. Although eighteenth-century French art had lost something of its appeal during the Jazz Age, when in the eyes of the world young Paris was a city of Kiki of Montparnasse, Hemingway, Scott Fitzgerald, and Picasso, Jerry had shown a special interest in this period. (Jerry Hess had felt like a culture carrier.) He had reminded many Americans of the value of eighteenth-century art. He had bought many Ingres for the Royal Dutch Petroleum collection and then arranged to buy them back for Americans, thus raising their value. *Ah, Jerry Hess*, sighed the collectors who envied his ability to walk away with the good deals, the young man from America who also had a wonderful eye for Chinese art, and a love of medieval objects.

66.

And so that summer afternoon Jerry Hess walked out of the auction of the Hotel Drouet, he had the satisfaction of knowing that he had bought what he came for. He had the Picasso for his buddy, Lehman, and the Gris bought for his own special amusement, having paid exactly one-twentieth of what he would sell it for to the McFarlan Museum, which specialized in Miró and Gris. He had also picked up *for a song* a Perronneau portrait of Francis Hastings (the Museum of Fine Arts in Boston would go ape over it) and a tiny Pissarro to give Mary for her beginning collection. Out in the sun walking to the rue Cambon, Jerry Hess felt damned good. It was power. And what was it really? It was all wheeling and dealing. Plus knowledge and the old sixth sense. If he married Mary, would she join him on his great fishing trips into the uncharted waters of the art racket? He wondered about that as he walked down the Paris streets that afternoon.

67.

Jerry couldn't forget his early years in Paris. When he walked in the streets he remembered the days he spent there with Ursule. Heavenly days of making love and meeting new people—the geniuses he had only read about in books. He remembered meeting Picasso with Ursule at the Closerie des Lillas and looking into the pupils of his dark black yes-yes eyes. Picasso had the Spanish fever that said "yes" to everything. He took the world into his gaze. He remembered Ursule introducing him to his God, the painter Giacometti, at a small restaurant in Montparnasse twenty years ago. As he walked down the streets, the pandemonium of his life came back to him. Who had changed his life? He recalled meeting Anaïs Nin. He had been taken to a book-signing party at the English Book Store by a young poet called Harold Norse. Harold had introduced him to a thin, white, paper-faced woman who looked almost Oriental. She was similar to the porcelains that the Chinese created and polished so perfectly—she was a white luminous woman in a velvet dress.

"You are a writer."

"I am what?" he asked.

"How do you do. My name is Anaïs Nin. This is a book-signing party for the magazine, *Two Cities*. And I said you are a writer."

"How did you guess?"

"I didn't have to guess. I know a writer when I see one."

"I do write," Jerry had said, amazed at her perception.

"Would you like me to publish your first book? I think it's important to publish."

He had stood there frightened by the strange beautiful writer who had appeared in the bookstore followed by an entourage of admirers who seemed to worship her.

"Jean, come here," she had said to a young brown man who it turned out was Jean Fonchette, an exile from Mauretia who was both a doctor and the publisher of *Two Cities*, the magazine that Anaïs Nin and Lawrence Durrell co-published. Jerry was not aware of who Anaïs Nin was. She was a cult figure who had helped the literary careers of Henry Miller and Lawrence Durrell and she was destined to become one of the great diarists of her time. Her voice was not symphonic. It was a low whisper. Jean Fonchette walked over to them, he remembered. Anaïs turned to Jerry and asked his name.

"Jean, this is Jerry Hess. I want you to publish his first book. I will pay for it along with Larry Durrell."

Jerry remembered being dumbfounded. This woman did not know his name, had never read his work. But she had "sensed" that he was a writer. And the book had been published. It had come out in 1957, when according to Ursule he was still "a baby." Anaïs had never met Ursule. Years later, when he was traveling on a selling trip in Cambodia, he had met Anaïs Nin again. He had just been thinking of her when his bus pulled up in front of a hotel and she had been standing there. Anaïs. The muse magically disguised as a woman. Why him? Why had she helped him?

68.

Back in the Ritz, safely ensconced and protected by the richness of the furniture in his suite, he climbed into bed. He let himself be covered by the satin bedspread, the clean white linen sheets so perfectly bleached and laundered. There was a little group of buzzers by his bed. He could ring for room service. He could ring for a maid. He could ring for drinks. He could ring for a porter. All he had to do was buzz and someone would arrive. If only he could ring for whatever it was that he truly wanted. If only he had some divine touch in his fingertips that would allow him to ring for *what*? For love? For Mary? If only he could invoke a vision of what he was looking for. He had wealth, prestige. A son. Houses. Clients. Even some friends. Yet he did not have himself at the touch of his fingertips. He had only his broken imagination. His heart, which was oddly discontent. Lonely. He was horrified. He could not speak. Finally he picked up the phone. He called Mary. He wanted to propose to her—to ask her to open her life to him and allow him to marry her. But there was no one at her house. He let the phone ring awhile. Then hung it up in despair. In a way the despair was a relief. He still had the illusion, if it was illusion, of abstract love. He could still live in his imagination where the water clocks of rain or dandelion clocks of the sun had no real time. His love was his alone. His life was his own prose which was never done. He could still unfold the rest of his life, move it from chaos into shape, from fear of death and age into something else, some other rare pattern, some other breath. He slept. And in his intricate dreams, he dreamed of Mary. He saw her in her tall strength, in her light and mystery, in her energy and impatience. Who was she? Was she his deliverer?

He woke.
Tried calling Mary again.
It was dawn in Paris. Which meant it was past midnight in New York. Where was she? At a party? Floating through an evening with a lover? Where the hell was she? He was being irrational. It was silly to expect her to be sitting at home night and day. And yet he could not sleep. He thought of making love. It would be the release. Jerry had always considered the "narcotic" of sex as a healthy release and better than the narcotics of alcohol and drugs. With enthusiasm, he got out of bed. Admired himself in the mirror.

69.

The moment he was on the rue Cambon, it occurred to Jerry that he knew exactly where he was going. He was going to get laid. It felt good. He told the cab driver outside the hotel to take him to Pigalle. When he stepped out of the cab he was in another world. He saw the ladies of love walking the streets, against the neon. He loved whores. As an art dealer, was he not a whore, also? What was the difference between those who sold love and those who sold art? The whore was more honest, he thought. When she offered an arm it was her own arm. Not the extension of some poor painter's arm who had taken brush to canvas in order to survive and which he now sold for a fortune. The whore was the joy of the world. "We are all whores," he thought. And why not?

"Parlez-moi d'amour," sang a whore on the street in front of a nightclub. He was now in the world of Toulouse-Lautrec, the world of red hair that was piled high, cancan dancers, lazy sailors,

257

and lonely art peddlers like himself. It was exciting—the adventure of the unknown. Lust and luck. He heard the whore singing. Was she singing to him?

Vous savez bien
Que dans le fond je n'en crois rien;
Mais, cependant, je veux encore
Ecouter ce mot que j'adore.

And then the refrain, loud, nasal and clear:

Parlez-moi d'amour
Redites-moi des choses tendres
Votre beau discours
Mon coeur n'est pas las de l'entendre . . .

Should he go with her? No. He decided to walk through Pigalle and let his fantasies lightly gloss over the women he saw. Pigalle! Popular. Bawdy. A *quartier*. A place where he could walk alone, Jerry Hess, Jewish intellectual so far from the street of Central Park West, the dull turrets of the Dakota with its doormen and its domestic gloom. Pigalle. He was a stranger oceans away from Mary and her activities of journalism and revolution. Fuck the revolution. He, Jerry Hess, for God's sake was the revolution. He represented the end of the seventies, when America was all fucked up. Mary was right to want to expose everything. But he, Jerry Hess, was the end of the revolution. A man hungry to find out who the hell he was. And what he could do. A lonely narcissist (Wasn't jogging the ultimate lonely sport? Wasn't running the ultimate refuge of the narcissist?) on the lam in Pigalle. His cock led him down the streets. He saw legs in black mesh stockings. He'd like to run his tongue up those unknown legs. High heels which led to heavenly cunts where he could drown himself in the ultimate orgasm. Pigalle! *Pigsville*, Mary would say. But it was a world he felt at home in. A world of vulgarity. It was a million times more pleasant than the Hotel Drouet where the peddlers of art played with the dollars and francs outbidding each other.

It was better to fuck than to think.

Another whore came up to him.

"*Qui est-tu, mon amour?*" she asked him.

Oh yes, the call of the quartier. The call of the vendor of sex. It felt familiar and good. He linked his arm in the arm of the whore. She had shiny lips. Blonde hair. An oval face. Unlike Mary, she wasn't thin. Her face was round. She looked earthy. Mother Earth had come to pick him up. He could see her enormous breasts under her pink sweater. Her hips were round. They weren't the hips of the French models who hung around the Ritz looking for rich men. Models with bones you could stab yourself on. She was round and smelled of heavy perfume. She was propositioning him.

"*Un p'tit jeu?*" she asked.

He liked her. He put his arm around her waist. She walked with him to her hotel. It was a tiny old building like all the other cheap hotels in Pigalle. She climbed the steps in front of him. Led him to a room. He loved Pigalle. Where a hooker was still a hooker. He felt himself grow hard. She was so lovely. In the room he watched her undress. He sat on the bed, which was all that there was in the room. She smiled at him and asked him again, slowly, "*Qui est-tu, mon amour?*"

She didn't seem to want an answer. Her question was sexual. He wasn't going to a personnel department. He was going to bed with one of the greatest-looking whores in Pigalle. He took a hundred-dollar bill out of his wallet. It was all he had—that and some French francs, which would get him home on the Métro. He gave the bill to her. She smiled. It made her happy. Then he watched her take off her sweater. Her breasts were full and lovely. Slowly she stepped out of her miniskirt. She was wearing only her stockings and high heels. It was now her turn to watch him. He unbuttoned his shirt. Took off his pants, his shoes and socks. He was naked. He climbed on the bed. He heard music playing in the street. He felt good. The narcotic was beginning to work.

259

The urge to fuck shot through him like a drug. He felt his cock grow hard. Slowly she climbed on top of him and put him inside her. He watched her enjoy herself. She smiled at him. Slowly he turned her over. He let himself feel the sensitive parts of her back, her thighs. He watched her gently rocking from the back. Somewhere in the room he experienced the loss of loneliness. The loss of pain. The loss of all questions. Inside her he felt as if he were no longer made of flesh. It was only inside of a woman that he felt himself totally at peace. She spoke to him softly in French. *"Parlez-moi d'amour,"* she said.

The words tumbled out of his mouth. Then he dressed. And sadly left. He walked home to his hotel thinking of the whore, and her question. *"Qui est-tu, mon amour?"*

70.

Good protect me from radical women," Jerry said.

Mary was concocting a "welcome home" dinner in her apartment. She was wearing an apron over her jeans and shirt. She was cooking spaghetti with meatballs, his least favorite dish. Oh, well, he'd try not to gag. He had always hated meatballs. They were the only thing Lillian had cooked for him when they had been poor and living on Riverside Drive. Tomato sauce was not his idea of gourmet living. And there was no use telling Mary about the wonders of spaghetti al dente.

"Why protect you?" she asked, shaking the white strands of overcooked spaghetti in the colander.

"Because they're too smart. They can do everything well." He was lying. Mary didn't really do anything well. Except write and fuck. But that was enough. If he wanted gourmet cooking he could always hire a chef. "They can cook. They can think. They can play tennis. They can fuck. They can—"

"Jog," she put in.

"Most of all they can jog. And they can change your life. Marry me, Mary," he heard himself saying.

"Don't be crazy," she said, keeping so cool it offended him. She went right on making the spaghetti.

"Are you kidding?" he asked. "Are you going to turn down a man who is rich, handsome, a great runner? And single? And besides that, a Jewish intellectual."

"That's just what I want. A jogging Jew." She laughed at him.

"But don't you want to get married? And have children?"

"What for?"

"It's an experience everyone should have." He didn't know what to add. Somewhere he thought that any woman would say yes. Especially Mary, who seemed to need a man in her life.

"Don't you want me?" he asked.

"Of course I do, you crazy bastard. But not legally. What's a piece of paper. I don't believe in signing a contract."

"All right. Let's get married in a religious ceremony."

"Buddhist or Hasidic? I know a lot about Hebrew ceremonies. Remember, I'm the girl who used to write Jewish cookbooks."

"Mary, I just got a divorce. I won't tell you what it cost me. Or what my lawyer's bill at Legits and Legits is. I won't bore you with the petty details of my freedom. But I want to make a commitment to you. I want to live with you. And I'd like to have another kid. Maybe two more."

"So have them."

"With you."

"Without me. To begin with, Mr. Hess, I don't believe in marriages. Legal or any other kind. They don't particularly benefit women or men. Secondly, it's much healthier to live in separate spaces. Like Jean-Paul Sartre and Simone de Beauvoir."

"Only I'm not Jean-Paul and you're not Simone."

"I don't think you're really interested in an interrelationship. Because if we were really tight, we wouldn't need marriage."

"You're saying no?"

"Absolutely. And I don't think I could handle my own kids. Not for the moment."

"Up yours."

"Listen. I know it's fashionable to forget about the population explosion. I know it's fashionable to forget about the fact that one out of every two marriages, I believe, ends in divorce. Jerry, you don't want to marry me."

"I don't?"

"Of course not. Haven't you read about battered husbands? The crime no one wants to admit? You don't want to be battered. I don't want to be a battered wife. No one wants to be battered."

"How can we get family counseling if we're not married!" His irony was always lost on her.

"True, that's a point. But seriously, Jer, I love you." He was glad she called him "Jer." It was a turnoff. Now he didn't have to go through life hearing, Jer, do this, Jer, do that. It was bad enough hearing Jerry do this, Jerry do that.

"We don't have to rush, Jer."

"I want to marry you. It should be the other way around. I feel like a jerk saying if you don't want to marry me, maybe we should stop seeing each other."

"Jer—can I tell you something? You're the sweetest man I've ever met. You're just the opposite of every man who's been stereotyped as macho or a pig. You're decent. You're my favorite friend."

"Thank you."

"Why do we have to terminate our love affair with a marriage?"

"The way you use the word 'terminate,' it sounds like 'terminal.' Terminal cancer. Terminal marriage. Sorry, doc. There's no hope. This couple has terminal marriage. The only way to cure them is through sunlamp treatments. Possibly scalp treatments. If you massage the scalp regularly the marriage will go away. Be sure to use cream rinse. Wash three times a day. And watch out for dandruff."

"I thought you were the smartest man in my life."

"That's like saying the tallest midget at the circus."

"Why?"

"Because, smartass—Mary Reagan—all the men in your life have been dumb creeps. When someone who is basically sexy and human comes along—all you can do is turn him down."

"I'm not turning you down. *I'm turning you up*. I'm tuning you in, as Timothy Leary was known to say before he faded away."

"Whatever happened to Spinoza?"

"Can we pretend this little proposal never happened? Are you hungry?"

"For all your radical blarney, you sound like an ad on the boob tube. 'I don't want marriage, but try my spaghetti.' Do you always have to be a cultural wrinkle, Mary? Can't you just be normal?"

"What's normal? To live in the Waldorf Towers and sell oil paintings? For millions of dollars? That's normal? To have a castle on the ocean in East Hampton, where people sit around and complain about their maids, and their hairdressers, and their neurotic kids—that's normal? Or maybe it's normal to drive around in Hollywood with an aging grande dame and take care of her dogs all day? To be a fancy dogcatcher—that's normal?"

"You know what you sound like? You sound like a combination between a new-wave writer and a would-be Jewish Princess. All the things that you put down, you love."

"What do you mean?"

"You wouldn't mind writing for establishment papers if you could. And you'd get used to hairdressers—in fact you go to them yourself all the time. And the upwardly mobile existence you loathe seems to attract you at the same time."

"It does. As long as I don't have to pay the price of selling out."

"And what do you consider selling out?"

"Being Mrs. Hess. What for? I'm Mary Reagan and that's all I ever want to be."

"A lot of people would be happy to be my wife." He had lost the battle. But it didn't feel so bad.

"Lillian? Can you possibly believe that there are women for

whom marriage isn't the pie in the sky it's supposed to be?"

"Then another kind of marriage might work out. One of the understanding and spoken commitment. Look, Mary—I'm tired of living alone. I'm exhausted with the single life."

"So you want to rent a loft and live with me?"

"Roommates?"

"Sort of."

"Let me think it over."

He was secretly glad she said no.

71.

When did you start jogging?"
      "A few years ago."
   "Why?"
   "Because I like it."
   "Any other reason?"
   "I had a girl friend in California who was a really good runner and she showed me how, and I ran with her. And then I got some running shoes. At first it hurt. My body wasn't used to it. I couldn't keep my breath. I ran a little more each day. Then I came to New York. I thought jogging would be a cheap way of getting exercise. And I thought jogging would be fun. Then I saw the New York Marathon. I watched it as a distraction from a friend's loft in Long Island. And I thought, 'I could run in that,' and I began training. It's twenty-six miles and I began running more each day. At first I ran six miles. Then eight miles. And I kept getting better. Then I met Jerry. We ran together."

"Where did you run?"

"All over. We ran to Brooklyn Heights. We ran to the Washington Bridge."

"And do you love him?"

"What do you mean by that, doctor?"

"Why are you with him?"

"Well, at first it was my way of ripping off the system. I saw this really attractive rich guy was interested in me and wanted to help me out. All the guys I went out with were creeps so I thought, Why not?"

"Why not what?"

"Why not *see* him. You know. By any means necessary."

"He was a means to an end?"

"Not to an end. He was just powerful. I wish I could say I fell in love with his eyes. But actually it was because the only way in New York to get ahead is by sometimes connecting with the right Jew. I can't connect with his Jewish guilt. For God's sake, doctor, I had my own Catholic guilt to get rid of."

"Were your parents religious?"

"Very. My mother read to me out of the book of miracles and the Douay Bible. I grew up in a convent." Mary paused a moment, then continued, "About marriage. I just don't see the point. I'm a growing person. And I think Jerry is growing too."

"I understand."

"Now, I've grown to respect him. And I don't like being with him. I just don't see myself as a domesticated person. I don't want to go back to a class reunion and brag that I'm some rich guy's wife. I want something else. It doesn't exclude being with Jerry. He treats me like a human being. I don't see him as the enemy, the way I did when we met. But I can't allow myself to be a mix-and-match team. Like his or hers towels."

"I'm afraid we have to stop now. My next patient is waiting."

"Well, thank you, doctor."

She had done what he wanted. She had seen his doctor. It really didn't hurt. What a sweet guy. He had a lot of degrees on the wall. Trophies of understanding. But she couldn't deliver what he wanted.

What did he want?

What made a person become a shrink, anyway? Inner sadness? If he had any compassion he'd realize that everyone was sick in New York City. There were a lot of people who needed to be cured more than she did. That was for sure.

72.

I've decided to stop dealing in art," Jerry told her when she came to have a drink with him.

"By the way, I've seen your doctor."

"I know. And I think the only thing for me to do is stop all of this peddling and start doing something else."

"You don't have to give it up. You can still keep your rich old biddies and buddies and sell them paintings—but you could do something else with your life that you like a hell of a lot more."

"Like what?"

"Give this up."

"You mean move out of the Waldorf Towers and move into a shack? Towers seem to be my schtick. First the towers of Dakota. Now the Waldorf Towers."

"Untower yourself."

"Can I sing you a song?"

"Go ahead."

"I love you for sentimental reasons. For sent. Tim. Ent. Al. Reasons."

"Did you ever take singing lessons?"

"Nope."

"You could be a singer. Give all this up and be a singer."

"A boulevardier. Singing my song all over the world. A troubadour."

"You crazy son of a bitch. I'm really beginning to love you."

On a hot afternoon, end of summer, Mary rang up Madame Solovieff and asked to see her for tea. There was an urgency in her voice and Madame Solovieff said, "Come at once, darling. Come this afternoon, say around five."

Madame Solovieff lived in an inconspicuous town house crowded between restaurants and office buildings. One would never suspect until one climbed three flights of stairs and entered the apartment that the building's architect was Stanford White. Inside the apartment one was transported back to Russia in the old days—Russia when the French influence dominated the lives of the very rich. The apartment had high ceilings covered with boiserie, a Stanford White fireplace. Antique tables, of gleaming wood that was inlaid, were scattered around Louis Quinze sofas of grey and golden satin. A glass chandelier hung in the middle of the room. Tiny boxes, antiques, statues, ornate candy dishes, malachite cigarette boxes were all illuminated by the tiny Napoleon period French lamps which were now electrified and gave a dim light from under their pink-and-white satin lamp shades. Great satin drapes made the rooms dim and cool. There, surrounded by mementos from past loves, photographs of violinists, great divas, generals, princes, and well-known movie stars from the thirties, Madame Solovieff hid from the world and created her own ambience of polished silver and genteel living. She kissed Mary and brought out tea in silver glasses poured directly from the samovar she had kept polished and in use throughout her adult life. Black Sofranie cigarettes were in tiny vermeil cups and Mary lit one as she began speaking.

"Before you say one word, Mary dear, let me tell you how happy I am to see you. You remind me of your beautiful Irish mother when she was your age—capturing the heart of all the eligible men. It seems like yesterday. Now—how is love?"

"How did you know I had a love problem?"

"Love is always a problem. That is one of its definitions."

"Well, I think I am in love."

"Either you're in love or you're not in love."

"Do you always know?"

"I've been in love many times. And I knew every time. If you don't think you're in love you're not in love."

"I am. But I'm confused."

"That's better. Everyone today is confused. It's an illness. It used to be that people had the gout. Now they are confused. What are your hesitations?"

"His life. The way he leads it. The way he's led it. I met Jerry jogging."

"What exactly is jogging?"

"It's just another word for running. When you run the blood circulates in a different way. It's like sex, which is when the blood goes to the genitals and a rush of excitement comes. In jogging the blood goes to the limbs. It's a rush of blood that makes you stop thinking. If you run long enough you become like an animal, a hunter, you stop being a human and you become in touch with your body in another way. It's almost the feeling you get when you are happy to throw up—it's a visceral feeling—your blood changes. You get worn out. You go on. You push yourself. It's terrific!

"Well, my problem began when I was running and met Jerry. At the time he was married. He felt guilty and left his wife. Then a grande dame who runs a repertory theatre, one of those great glamorous Hollywood prima donnas, came back into his life. She's much older than he is and was once the love of his life. I remember seeing the change in him. She was jealous of me, and beckoned him back into her world. He jumped just like a pony. He went back to this woman and then saw that it was me he loved. But this part freaks me out. He loves me. I love him. But I'm afraid I won't have a good life with him."

"Why not?"

"In some ways he's mature. In other ways he's not together."

"I'm sure he's attracted to your energy."

"Why?"

"As men grow older they want more challenge. Not less. They love female rogues and girls who are difficult to get. They want the chase. The challenge. The more you behave like a brazen brat the more he wants you. For a man to be alive he wants his balls to sing. He wants to feel crazy, excited, and what man in his right mind wouldn't want a long-limbed girl with energy and wit? Chinese, Hottentots, gypsies, simpletons, hyenas, molochs, old lunatics, princes, and shipowners—I've had them all. And what does a man want? To have his nice little nest undone by a free bird that flies out of his reach so he can fly after her."

"There are so many free women in New York, my God!"

"Don't believe it. I have eyes. New York City is filled with these little South American girls with jewelry in bad taste and overly high heels who wear too much makeup on their eyes and spend their days having lunches or going to beauty parlors and looking for rich men to replace their fathers. They all have whining voices. They all cling like weeds around a man's neck. They all have to be called constantly. They are all brainless. These men with brains, like Jerry, get tired of the South American whiners. They want girls with guts and energies—they can only get it up for the others for a little while. Then they get bored. He likes you because you're fun. You're alive. You're energetic. You're probably like a shot of adrenalin for him. What else do you like about him?"

"He's a writer. He has a new collection of essays that he's working on. They're beautiful. They're about *weathering* life. And he makes love to me every morning; he's a fabulous lover. I've never had better."

"A good lover? I've never had a *bad* lover. It depends on how much you want each other."

"Who doesn't make a good lover, Madame Solovieff?"

"Men talking about their mothers. Men who lecture women

and lecture *to* women. Men who sheepishly tell you about their past affairs—men who write about women as creatures who never existed—all of these make lousy lovers."

"You must have been with some great men, Madame Solovieff."

"Great men only exist in fiction."

"Jerry is, in many ways, a great man."

"Then hold on to him, my dear. Or he will fall into the clutch of some little clinging Argentinian whose father is in the fur business and who hopes to be an artiste or better yet a *hostess* in New York. Hold on to him, or he will be caught by the richest and furriest lady available, he will be captured by the great glutinous arms of a divorced hostess with career problems who will see him as her passport to a world of art and money. Beware of everyone—especially enveloping hostesses—every dinner party is a manhunt. You may take it from an expert."

"Should I marry him?"

"Is he a drunk? Does he swig and guzzle? Is he on drugs? Is he cruel? Is he selfish? Does he address all of his remarks to a waiting audience? Is he someone who looks for one-night-stands?"

"No."

"Does he have a double chin?"

"Oh no."

"Does he say boring things like 'I always carry Mallarmé in my pocket'?"

"No. He never says anything like that."

"Is he a catch? You bet he is. With all the androgynous literary ladies and divorced women looking for someone to pay private-school bills and helpless Brazilians and God knows how many other of the man hunters with fangs for fellows who are powerful—equip yourself with a revolver if necessary and keep him close to gunpoint if he leaves you. You, Mary Reagan, are a lucky person. You just don't appreciate it."

And Madame Solovieff chuckled as she drained her tea, washing down her tea with sherry and her sherry with vodka and her vodka with another vodka. It was a merry afternoon.

275

And still Mary thought about the bothersome qualities in Jerry: his guilt, his hurts. Mostly his guilt.

One night they were having dinner at her apartment. Lillian called. He stayed on the phone for an hour. She could almost surmise what was going on.

Jerry's voice was pleading. She walked into the kitchen but she could hear him arguing.

"Lillian, you cannot call me here every time you have a problem with Jerry, Jr."

A long pause.

"I know, but I asked you not to call about every problem. You're a lawyer, for God's sake. Can't you work it out? I've made it clear to you I don't want to be part of your life anymore."

Another pause.

"Of course you can manage. Yes. I'll make it my business to come and talk to you about it. So we had a bad marriage. Let's make it at least a good divorce. No. I can't."

A pause.

"Because I can't. Don't make me feel more guilty. I don't want to hurt you."

A pause.

"I did not abandon you!" (This at the top of his lungs.)

A pause.

"Don't please don't talk about killing yourself. It upsets me. It's emotional blackmail. All right. I'll come over to see you. But this is the last time. Jesus, Lillian, it's eleven o'clock at night. Can't you handle these problems yourself? All right. Hang up. Don't be upset. I'll be right there."

This happened often. Jerry dressed. Left. Came back later.

Lillian was having a bad affair with Sergio.

Lillian couldn't cope with Jerry, Jr.

Lillian didn't know how to invest her money without his advice.

Lillian was lonely.

Lillian who was an expert on corporate estates and could handle a tribunal of judges, Lillian who was one of the world's most capable women, suddenly changed into Lillian the helpless. She couldn't *manage* without Jerry. She wasn't having an anxiety attack. Her whole life was one long anxiety after another. She didn't stop having anxiety long enough to have an attack.

"Lillian," Mary said, "is a fucking pain in the ass."

"But she's the mother of my son, Mary. I'm tied to her forever."

"Forever these phone calls? Forever the phone ringing in the middle of the night? Forever crisis? Jesus. Why doesn't she call a hot line? One of those suicide numbers—the phone clinics which work so well in San Francisco?"

"Mary, be compassionate."

"I am compassionate. Oh, God. There's nothing left of our privacy. We have a ménage à trois. You, me, and Lillian. We all live together, connected by the fucking phone. I think I know more about Lillian than she knows about herself. I could describe where she keeps her douche bag, how many shoes are in her closet, where she shops, where she eats, where she goes to the hairdresser, what her childhood was like, how she loved her family, how difficult it was for her to go through law school. Shit. I know Lillian better than I know you.

"Why don't you go back to her?"

"I'm surprised you ask that. You know our marriage is over."

"Well, if it's over how come she calls you every night?"

"Our lives are still intertwined. I can't hurt her after so many years. I feel I should help her."

"I know. But you're so *guilty*. It's more than that. You enjoy being needed. You get off on it. Why didn't you stay with Lillian, for God's sake? Then you could be calling me in the morning instead of her calling me."

"I can't help it."

"What was wrong with you two?"

"I've told you. Firstly, we didn't fuck. Secondly, we didn't talk. Thirdly, we were all socialed up. With her dinner parties.

And plans. And weekends in the Hamptons. Her boring friends. Her demands what I should do. And—"

"I'm sorry I asked. I'm only wondering what you're going to say was wrong with me after we break up."

"Don't even think that way. It's negative."

"The world does not revolve on its axis of positive thinking. Not everything is *positive*. Sartre said—"

"I'm not talking about existentialism," he cut in. "I'm talking about us."

"Up ours."

"Well, Mary—I do feel this reluctance on your part to really commit yourself to our relationship. You have to make more of an effort."

"I do make an effort. And I love you. And I want us to be happy, but you're caught between two women."

"I'm sorry, Mary. I'll try to fix everything."

73.

Mary decided the three worst words in the English language were "She needs me."

74.

Mary sang a small sad song to herself when she was home. It was hard to make Jerry understand her. Or even to understand him. She took out her diary and wrote, "Love is a way of finding out what we like most about ourselves." All day long she had been writing Jerry a letter in her mind. Some pages were all remembering. She remembered how her body ached for him after they made love. And how she had tried to explain to him the things that mattered. She had tried to teach him about where she *lived* in her mind. She thought about the quarrels that blew up in her body. She had to see Jerry. Talk to him.

"Dear angry one. Don't be mad at me," she said over the phone.
"I'm not, you crazy kid. What are you up to?"
"I'm going to another demonstration. Come with me."
"What kind of demonstration?"

"Demonstration against arms sales to South Africa."

"Oh, shit. All right. I'll disentangle myself and pick you up."

By the time they arrived at the Dag Hammarskjöld Plaza the demonstration had started. It was a protest to draw attention to the debate in the Security Council about the selling of arms to South Africa. About two hundred people had shown up in the sun, most of them waving placards up and down. They were marching in an orderly way—chanting "No arms to South Africa. No arms to South Africa," "Apartheid stinks, apartheid stinks," and "South Africa kills." Mary pulled Jerry into the march. An organizer of the march, a young black man Mary's age, shouted, "Let's march on, brothers and sisters, to the racist regime's illegal consulate!" Everyone shouted, "Down with the killers" and "Down with racism."

And a line was formed, snakelike, which began marching. Jerry and Mary marched and Jerry found himself beginning to shout, to feel good. It was genuine, short of desperation and strength. At the South African consulate the police, dozens of them, formed a protective fence of human uniforms, flesh, guns. One of the demonstrators threw himself against a policeman in an effort to enter the building. He was clubbed and laid out on the sidewalk where two policemen carried him away. The organizer turned to the group and spoke. "We don't want any violence. Just march, brothers and sisters."

Mary was excited. As if she had suddenly come home to a place where she belonged. It reminded her of the sixties, the injustice was something she felt so strongly about. She had been in peace marches and protests against munitions factories in California. Nobody seemed to care about South Africa. Nobody seemed to care about Chile. Nobody seemed to care about the military government in Brazil. The atrocities in South Africa. The class war. The poverty. The separated facilities which made humans into species treated less well than people's horses in the United States. Treachery. Defeat. Humiliation. All of these things were personal to Mary.

Back at his suite Jerry collapsed on one of the couches and ordered some Perrier. Mary was high from the demonstration. When the room service arrived they toasted each other with Perrier.

"Here's to your first demonstration. Let's hope it won't be your last."

"Here's to my getting my head together."

"How did you feel?"

"It's better than bullshit theatre. I felt as if I were participating instead of just looking on. I'm glad there was no violence."

"I've had my head knocked in plenty of times. I've been arrested, beaten up, spit on just for speaking up about what's decent."

"I love you, Mary. You're genuine. You're fanatic, but you're genuine. I watched you at the demonstration. It's where you come into your own. It's not a cause. It's real. It's even fun. It's your real life. It's where you live."

"Everyone has their own meaning. The question is to connect with it. I've connected with mine. I may be young but I know what my life is about. I've always known. Somebody asked me the other day at the storefront, 'What would you do if you could do anything?' I answered, 'I'm already doing it.' "

"I wish I felt the same way."

"You would if you were political. I don't relate to nonpolitical people. I don't know what they're about."

"Then how do you feel about me?"

"Mixed up. I love you. You're a secret artist. You write. You deal in good art. You don't mean anyone harm. I relate to that. But other things freak me out."

"What?"

"Who is Ursule to you? Why did you run back to her?"

"She was a very gentle and generous person in my life at one time. I was in love with her! So was the whole world. You could fill Shea Stadium with the men and women who were in love with Ursule Hirsch, the actress. When I fell in love with her I began writing. She brought out of me a new person, a secret person

I didn't even know that I had inside me. 'Possibly my writing will last as long as a sixty-nine Ford. Certainly not as long as a Volkswagen.' José Emilio Pacheco, a Latin American poet, wrote that. That's the way I feel. I became a lover. With Ursule I felt like a pubescent tiger. We loved. And parted. I thought we could love again. There are no words left now. Only memories."

"And telegrams, cables. And perhaps you'll go back to her again. Oh, she'll need you one of these days. And perhaps you'll go back. But I'm not jealous. I see jealousy as an illness. If we have a tight friendship nobody can interfere with that."

"I keep translating what you say into my own thoughts. It's almost as if you speak a foreign language and when you speak I have to make the words come out into something I understand. It's not that I'm older than you. It's just that at my age I'm in a different place. I often feel wiped out, as if I've done every-thing and fucked everyone. Jogging is the only activity that means anything to me because it's a kind of race against myself—and it makes me feel as if I've accomplished something."

"I don't want to chip away at you—but aren't you ready to make some changes in your life?"

"What? Drop out? Where to? A guy I know just moved to Hong Kong to be where the action is. He has gurus all over the world."

"Somewhere you have to find the part of you that is lost."

"I keep translating myself to the world. It's as if I have to constantly translate the private part of me into the public part of me. Into words that are not mine. I feel like a ghost who lives in a limbo between two worlds.

"And it's more than that, Mary. It's the feeling of being jaded, fucked out, the feeling that there is nothing *new* that bothers me. I want to always have something to look forward to. That's why, I suppose, we invented the idea of romance."

"If you're political you don't really need romance. Passion. Yes. Friendship and genitals touching one on one. Sex being the definitive translation—one person coming into another's flesh—inside the mouth, the holes—getting inside another language, another body."

"I feel my life changing. I feel myself wanting more than what I've always had. A part of it is anger, Mary. Anger at having wasted my own time, wasting what I do. You know what I feel like when I'm making a deal—buying—selling a picture? That I'd rather be somewhere else. Fishing. Or chopping wood. Or in another environment. It's only that selling doesn't nourish me anymore. It once did. After all I'm not creating paintings. I'm selling them. I'm *doing* something out of anxiety, because I'm *missing* something. And still I feel that I have enough money—what am I doing it for?"

"I understand. A certain purposelessness. The western con. You were brought up to think you *want* all those houses and cars and things."

"You know the best time I've ever had in my life?"

"No."

"Spending a hot summer in New York with you. Every summer of my life I've had to *go* somewhere. *Escape.* Go to Italy. Or to France. Or the Hamptons. It was a crime to be caught in New York in the summer. Now I've gone with you to that store-front—I feel I don't have to run anyplace. Now when I'm with you, just being contented is growing to be a habit. I feel myself in a continuum. I don't have to watch the clock the way I did with Lillian. Or feel attentive to alarms.

"I feel alive every moment. God damn it, there's so much to see, explore. Understand. Investigate. I want to shout, like Jimmy Hendrix, 'Hurrah, I wake from yesterday.'

"I want to go back to living—to writing. There's something ticking away in me like a small clock that wonders what it's doing and won't give up. At night, when I lie in bed, that clock goes off inside my head, ticking away."

Jerry poured himself another drink. This time he added scotch to the Perrier. She could see the wrinkles under his eyes. "He must be tired of the youth game," she thought.

As if he heard her he began to think of age. To talk about what grew inside his mind like a turnip. He couldn't see himself going through another season of art dealing. The thought of flying to London for more auctions at Sotheby's and Christie's, more selling trips to Madrid and

Paris, all of this now seemed to be "too much for him." Just as some men have heart attacks and later have to adjust their ways of being to their new physical condition, have to slow down, rest, consider ways to undo their habits—Jerry Hess felt as if something quite the opposite had happened. It was a health attack, a quickening of activities, a new surge of energy that had happened to him. He wanted to do more, to be more, to enlarge his life. His life no longer seemed relevant to buying murals for a library or private museum. Art exhibitions, the buying and selling of paintings, now he was ready to find another part of himself. But the problem was—what was the right *change* to make?

Jerry had heard stories of the menopausal person—man or woman—who, suddenly in the middle of the life game, took up the great escape as a way of life. The Human Potential Movement was held up, as if by stilts, by middle-aged folks who suddenly sensed the imminent surge within them and sought out new ways to live.

Was he now to become a human potential candidate? Was it now his business to search out "thirty-six ways to make life your hobby"?

"Those boobs have no class, alas!" Mary said.

"I'm not suggesting that I go to the Altered States of Consciousness Induction Center," Jerry remarked.

"Stay away from astrology," his analyst said.

"Avoid bioenergetics," said Jerry, Jr.

"Chanting is a way to blow your mind," Friedman once said.

"Analyze dreams," said the analyst.

"Go on a fast," said Mary. "Reach a new altered state of consciousness."

Gestalt therapy?

Hare Krishna?

Humanistic psychology?

I Ching?

Should he browse around the International Transcendental Meditation Society? ("At last a group of learned men have found a meditation discipline ideally suited for the American way of life. Maharishi Mahesh Yogi's way requires no effort at all. All the meditator has to do is utter a sacred syllable—a mantra designed especially for him—over and over. No concentration required. No physical or mental control.")

Should he turn to natural foods? ("Who says they're good for you?" asked his mother. She was talking to him again.)

What about nude research? ("The human body. Everybody has one. But for some reason we spend boundless energy devising new means to cover it up, hide it, enhance it. The nude encounter, once only a tenuous speculation, then the experimental power play of ill-trained leaders, is now being given careful, quiet, serious research.") Was therapy in the buff for him?

Was psychodrama?

Was Rolfing?

Should he choose a guru?

Subud, Arica, Gurdjieff, Ouspensky, Sufis, Zen, women's liberation—or perhaps men's liberation? Should he join the Women's Action Alliance?

Practice Zen studies?

Jerry Hess knew that he wanted to help others. If you wanted to cure the pain inside of you, the emptiness, loneliness, frustration—the best gimmick was to cure the pain of other people (he reasoned). He'd become a new sort of healer—one who worked with kids. The kids could teach *him*.

The marathon.

The run for hope (the idea took shape).

It would be for ghetto kids. It would be for him also. He had seen all the little kids in Harlem, with no place to go. He could lead the children out of the wilderness and make them go deeper into themselves by jogging. When he ran he felt clear, open, hollowed out, unmuddled. As if he put jet fuel in a go-cart. He'd have a run for kids.

The day of the children's marathon was warm and sunny. A day in the fall. Jerry had gotten the mayor to block off a section of Central Park. With his salesman's ability Jerry had sold the media to cover the race. "Kids like coverage. They want to be part of the action, just like adults."

Kids were jogging out of their homes, running toward the reservoir. They had been preparing for the race. Thousands of kids came running in New York. Each one was given a number for the Young Runners' Marathon. Jerry, Mary, and Liza were directing the event. Jerry, Jr., was handling the media. Madame Solovieff had been given the honor of waving the flag. Florynce Kennedy, the black activist, was announcing the event. The marathon began. Kids running.

They were clattering, panting, sweating, and laughing. They were tall kids and short ones, fat kids and skinny, kids with families, orphans, kids who played guitars, kids who were lost, kids who came jumping out of their thin ghetto beds, kids from all the districts of Manhattan. From Confucius Plaza there were Chinese kids and from the Upper West Side there were Puerto Ricans. From all over the city, from the Upper East Side kids were wearing the best jogging shorts, pretty girls and homely girls, fat girls with fat smiles, girls round as globes, ripe as oranges, boys who were fearless and brazen. Jerry looked at them all and thought how he loved children. The child in him, the brazen child in him came spilling out.

75.

It wasn't just Jerry who was changing. Mary was changing too. In the back of her mind was the desire to get more work, even take a job, so she wouldn't have to ever feel strapped. She found herself looking for a job at *Women's Fur Weekly*. Someone told her they needed someone and she found herself wandering through the Garment District. Shades of her mother. Years ago her mother had been a model, walking through the same streets. No. *Women's Fur Weekly* was more than she could cope with. The pelts of dead animals; writing about the "fur" industry. Cookbooks were one thing. Furs were another. She remembered reading about a "Meat Ball" given in the stockyards of Chicago where all the guests dressed up in white aprons and straw hats and danced under the dead carcasses of animals who were moved around on pulleys while their guts fell down on the floor and the blood dripped. The fur industry was not for her. She didn't have a pelt mentality. Then what was for her? To work for a union publication? Or to get an advance on a book? In the heat of New York she went around talking to editors trying to get work. At night she would meet with Jerry. He was excited about the marathon. He was animated now instead of the passive person she had known.

"I've taken all my paintings and put them in the warehouse. I'm giving up that ridiculous pretentious suite at the Towers starting next month. I'm renting a loft."

"Lofty thought?" Mary asked.

"It's either a loft or move out of the city altogether."

"To New Jersey? Be a hipster in Fenway, New Jersey?"

"Don't make fun of me. I'm thinking of moving away. Starting a whole new life. New friends. No more dancing at discos. Lunches at Doubles. Flying to Paris to visit Beaubourg. No more weekends buying at Versailles or catching the horses at Deauville, no more bullshit. Maybe I'll write my memoirs."

"Hadrian did it. I don't see why you can't."

"Would you leave New York with me?"

"I'm based here. But I'd visit."

"I love you, Mary. I do. Since I've known you I feel free. As if there's anything in the world I could do. Live in a loft! Run with kids! Dance without feeling guilty about tomorrow morning!"

Jerry was able to feel closer to Mary than he had ever to anyone. He became affectionate, held her, spent long hours talking to her. At night when they came together in bed, there was a new energy running between them. "I want to love, I want to love, I want to love," ran through Jerry's mind. It was almost as if he had always wanted to be a lover—to feel close to someone, but outside of Ursule he had never been able to feel that way. And had Ursule returned his feelings? He always suspected that she was toying with him, using him, and giving what his mother called "lip service" to her love. She was always removed, above fucking for love. She was a great lover—but her heart belonged to Stanislavski.

Mary was different. Her generation didn't make a big thing out of fucking. She could jump out of her clothes, get into bed, feel comfortable in the nude. She was an innocent. When she passionately held his cock in her mothering mouth, which suckled and excited, she did so with ultimate innocence. What excited him was the "ritual" of their lovemaking. The candles. Her beautiful body. He knew every part of that body, the way a blind man memorizes a street corner. He ran through the memory of her body in his mind. Her pink cheeks and high cheekbones, her thick and sensual lips, her long neck, her full, perfect breasts, down her stomach to the pubic hairs, her curls, her cunt, her muscled thighs, her long, long legs: all of her was perfection. She was a masterpiece. He ran his hands over her body, feeling the texture of her skin. When they made love she kept her eyes wide open, just like a child. He could see her eyes staring at him as he made love to her. The eyes of a child, wondering!

For Jerry to make love to Mary was to experience an excitement that was more than the excitement and rush of blood that comes with sex. There was a "rightness" to his being with her. An "authenticity" that he found it difficult to explain. It was almost as if a fusion of poles, of opposites, came together, a different kind of fleshy synthesis. In bed, nuzzling in her hair, licking at her ears, tonguing her lips, her legs, her thighs, watching her excite and become filled with heat, he wondered at the mystery which made them close. It was part fleshy miracle—just when he had thought he never wanted to really get "involved" (a Lillian word) this young girl had brought new blood to his body and mind. He felt the excitement in his bones. In his balls. When she excited him it was as if he were climbing higher and higher into a wordless excitement, a ladder which took him high into a blood-filled energy where he knew that just before the explosion he was experiencing ecstasy.

He thought of Ralph Waldo Emerson's "Nothing can give you peace but yourself" and the other saying of Emerson's that meant so much to him: "Nothing will ever succeed without enthusiasm." It was for the enthusiasm that he caught from Mary—actually caught the way one catches a virus—it was for that that Jerry Hess felt grateful.

Lillian's life had changed also.

She had fallen in with a group of young men from South

America who were all good-looking, all friends of Sergio's. They all holed up together in a big suite at the Delmonico. The big decision at night was Studio 54 or Xenon's or Barnam's, the new disco which just opened up. Lillian found herself on the dance floor with Sergio, who put two big rubber balloons under his shirt so that they looked like huge bosoms as he discodanced with her. She hoped he didn't look like a transvestite. She hoped she didn't either. At night, after the dancing, she would go home to the apartment at the Dakota and go over the men she had met that evening. There was Phil, in public relations. Fat. Nice. There was his lover. Sleazy. There was Juan from Caracas who was flying home and complained about taxes. There was Nino, a filmmaker from Chile who reported on the ugliness of the new regime. There was Lee Burbos, a slick dark-haired gay playboy who specialized in rich women. She saw some of her friends on the dance floor who were desperately trying to "keep up." What an assortment of people there were at Xenon's. Under the multicolored lights, it looked like a circus. A blond barker kept the undesirables out. Most of the dancers were gay or trying to be young. The lights flashed on and off. "I've spent my whole life studying law, bringing up a child, so I could end up a go-go dancer with no one to take me home," she thought wearily. She missed Jerry. But she knew better than to call him. That fucking bitch Mary always answered the phone and had told him to tell her not to phone. Someday she was going to get even with her. She knew she was getting old. Losing her looks. It wasn't easy. She was tired of dancing. She wanted to go home and read.

Jerry gave up his accountants. The lawyers. The investors. The middlemen. Jerry gave up the analyst. The dermatologist, proctologist, ophthalmologist, periodontist, the quacks of New York City. ("So long, quacks!")

292

In the town of Redville, Vermont, a man drove up in an old Volkswagen and began looking for property. A girl was at his side. The real estate agent showed them a cabin which had no plumbing, only an outhouse, and three acres of land. Jerry liked it. Mary said it looked "daffy and workable," and Jerry bought it outright for cash. A new era had begun.

76.

Yes, it was the season of dancing elegants, dancing elephants, discodancing and politics. It was the hot season in New York City and everyone (the world of Jerry Hess was a world of everyone who was anyone), yes, everyone was invited via blue-and-white invitation from the Biddles to attend at the home of the Lehmans' a disco cocktail party to raise money for the new political hopeful, Woody Woodward. It was a summer night's dance, for a *purpose*. The Long Island Expressway was covered with elephant cars crawling slowly in the grey desert of smog and fallout, a long parade of motorized elephants wending their way to the sea.

In the late afternoon Lillian sent the large grey limousine to pick up Sergio. Sergio, dressed in his white suit, emerged from his high-rise building on York Avenue, cool, elegant, hair slicked down for the party. His dark South American good looks did not betray his annoyance with Lillian. His tolerance for her loneliness, her bitterness, her "alienation" was beginning to wane. Behind his smile, his perfect white teeth, his tan and his well-combed beard, he was plotting how to trade in Lillian for a less boring divorcée. He had just returned from Ischia, where he had lain in the hot blazing sun with naked South American and French boys, the beautiful people, the bisexuals who travel the world in search of pleasure paid for by credit cards and dinero taken out of soft maroon Cartier wallets with golden tips. Ah, Dinero! Dinero! On the way to the party Lillian sat in the back seat complaining, as usual, about Jerry.

"He just dropped out, Sergio. Do you believe it? He's what you would call a classic dropout."

"I believe it, darling," said Sergio, looking out of the window of the grey limousine, thinking how ugly the expressway was, suddenly wondering why he wasn't still in Ischia. Little questions went through his mind. How much did he make last year? What was his salary? His bonuses? His interest? His dividends? He took a little census of his life while Lillian, hand on his thigh, continued her lament.

"You see, Jerry worked all his life to be successful. That's why he married me. I'm sure of it. He never *loved* me, but he never really knew how to love anyone."

"I know, my darling."

"But now he's decided he can live on very little. He's given up his business—can you imagine?—not one client left, and he writes to our son that he's testing his capabilities."

"You must have done very well in the settlement."

"We finally settled out of court. But I'm taking him back to court this month. I want *everything*. It's a way of making up for the humiliation I felt. Financial strength isn't everything, of course."

"Of course not, darling."

"But he's gone up to the hills to live *permanently*."

"Maybe he's getting in touch with himself. The most important thing in life is to know how to *enjoy*."

The car moved slowly in the safari toward the sea. Lillian

296

relaxed and poured herself a scotch from the bar in the back of the car. What was the point of talking about Jerry?

The party took place under a huge blue-and-white tent erected on the lawn of the Lehmans' house. The house itself, enormous, stately, and grey, was locked so that no visitors could ramble through the rooms. Bars, a disco machine, a wooden dance floor, and slides attempted to turn the party into a disco event. Sergio hated these parties that Lillian dragged him to. He noticed, not without arrogance, how a fat man with great lack of grace twirled on the floor. He wore oxfords, high socks, red Bermuda shorts, and a sweat shirt. His paunch stood out. He could hardly dance. His partner, a woman in a white dress, was immaculate. She was South American and tried to keep up with him.

It was embarrassing for Lillian. The Scharffs were at the party, waiting in line for the buffet. So were the Deans, the Blooms, and so many of her dearest friends. Surrounded by torches they stood on the line waiting for the roast chicken and their wilted salad. The talk was soft but the gossip shot through the line about Jerry Hess.

"Just left. Lock, stock, and barrel."

"Vermont? Jerry Hess? In Vermont? And what about his paintings?"

"Not selling paintings?"

"With a young girl? I heard about her. She's supposed to be a Commie. But very pretty."

The disco music blared over the guests, most of them in white. No one could understand why Jerry Hess had deserted them. It was taken as a personal offense.

The political candidate, Woody Woodward, crossed the lawn. He was an attractive man and might well be the next president of the U.S. He was serious, concerned, wealthy, uncorruptible. Everyone liked Woody.

Note was taken of Lillian at the party. Of course everyone

felt sorry for her. She was condemned to escorts. The Lehmans took her under their wing.

"One day I saw your ex, my darling, running in the park with his paramour. He didn't look very well."

"I know," said Lillian. "She's an opportunist."

"You're well out of it," Mrs. Lehman said sympathetically. Her dimpled fingers clutched a paper plate upon which a servant was loading macaroni salad. "I hear that he's completely given up his life in New York and started a new one somewhere in the hills. Well, if the shoe fits. I guarantee you she will betray him."

Lillian looked around for Sergio.

She saw him talking in the corner with Jim Wertheim, a tall florid boy with golden chains around his neck. They were laughing a little too loud. "Damn that little pisspot," she thought.

"Hello, *Beauty*," said Grinda Levenwald.

"My God, I haven't seen you in years," Lillian said.

Grinda was an heiress in her late thirties whose bosoms were always on display. She had a sweet voice and a bitchy personality. Under the honey, the queen bee was easily annoyed. But tonight she was looking better than usual. She dragged a judge from the Appellate Court on her arm. The judge had freckles and a drinking problem. Grinda introduced him to Lillian and Lillian pretended she had not met him several times before. Grinda was no longer wearing her bosoms out the way people wear jewelry.

"How's your photography?" Lillian asked.

"I've stopped working in my darkroom," Grinda said. "I'm now trying to write a play. If that doesn't work I'm going to law school."

"It's boring," Lillian said.

"I know, darling, but I've to got to do something serious. I'm taking the boards the next time they're given. There's a course at NYU that prepares you for the test. If I pass them, I know I can go to Columbia Law School because my father is on the board. It's a moment to choose a new life."

"I know what you mean."

Lillian looked at Grinda and wondered what she would be like ten years from now. She had once been married to a passionate doctor and had spent her life giving dinner parties and complaining to her guests about "the flower arrangements. They just didn't turn out right." Then she had dabbled in politics, writing, flying airplanes, sailing. Lillian's thoughts switched to Jerry in his shack in Vermont. From the letters he had sent to Jerry, Jr., she tried to piece together what his life was like. Was he wearing shorts? Reading Rimbaud as he used to in East Hampton?

He was a snapshot now that existed somewhere else in time, a snapshot that was beginning to fade. He would be sorry that he ran off with that bitch. The joys of the bucolic life would make him miserable, she thought, as she danced on the wooden discotheque floor with Sergio. She hoped he was having a rotten time with his cracked wheat, oatmeal, raisins, brown sugar, honey, and vegetables. She hoped they both choked on their warm ash cakes. Surviving in New York City as a divorced woman must be just as difficult as surviving in the woods. As she danced with Sergio she looked at him with disgust. His tan skin, his chains, his tiny ass, his tight pants, his smile, his musical voice, all of this was beginning to get on her nerves. She excused herself and went over to the bar.

Hell was going to a political party in Bridgehampton and having to be asked about Jerry. Lillian looked up at the stars. She had always had hysterical faith in her marriage to Jerry. She had once a magical interpretation of the world. As if it were ordered and it would all turn out perfectly. She wondered how long it would take her to feel really *divorced* from him. She was like a chicken with its head chopped off that still kept jumping around.

The party was going on in the darkness.

The large flares sent their flames of kerosene light up to the sky. The disco music continued.

The widows with capped teeth and wedgies danced into the early morning. Lillian looked around for Sergio. He was on the disco board with a skinny South American woman who had left her husband, a Chinese shipping lord, sitting alone at one of the tables.

After the dance Sergio came and asked her to dance. "Shall we stay at your house in East Hampton?"

"No thank you, darling, I think we should drive back to New York. I have a lot of work to do tomorrow."

"As you wish, my darling."

They walked over the enormous bright-green lawn, hearing the music in the darkness. Behind them, the party continued. The politician, a perfect gentleman, mingled with the guests, dancing or talking about concerts, theatre, and the latest movies. Lillian remembered how Jerry Hess hated those outdoor parties. He had attended them always. He never spoke a word. Now he was saved from them. She missed him terribly.

77.

Acres of land. Two typewriters. A library in the town. A little bookshop in the town. And time.

At first it was difficult to get used to the silence. Mary would be reading in the sunny room which they had made into a library reading room. There was a large bed covered with a white Greek blanket, a portable FM radio, and no electricity. Jerry started a garden in back of the house. There was a well and they were able to pump water from it. For Jerry it was paradise. The first time he was away from technology long enough to really hear the wind, the air. It was almost as if the senses that he lived with for so long—the hearing, the eyesight, the taste, the touch—came alive for the first time. He heard birdsong. He went jogging in the mountains.

Mary. She could be who she really was. A child catching birds in the sun. Her mother was writing desperate letters from California: "What are you doing in Vermont? Are you still working on your career?" How could she make her mother finally understand? Her grandmother dreamed that she would be a judge, a lawyer, a senator. The old woman with Irish tea inside her hands—always embroidering—or knitting—the old woman with great Irish hands, always holding on to tea.

She thought of her mother and grandmother. She was the continuation of that long line of strong Irish women, she was their "future," their little seismograph whose business it was to explore the beauty and meaning and confusion of living. She was all that. But in dreams she often imagined herself to be *more* than that, different from that. Her mother had been a romantic who never made any adjustment to the real world, a mystic who constantly listened to the sad music that was inside of people and believed in "miracles." Her grandmother's inner history had been a history of stage poetics—a world of domestic settings—like so many women she had been given the stagehand's job to adjust the setting, the lights, costumes, the music of life. Mary had never recovered from the wounds and desolation of childhood. She had seen the sadness in her mother and grandmother, the lack of spunk, and had wanted to throttle them. How dare they piss away their lives? How dare they watch the elders, the men, the people of power go marching on beyond them, doing a soft-shoe and shuffle, while all they were able to do was to pull the curtain, or adjust the light, or deliver the props on time? It was her father and grandfather who had done the "acting" in life, they were the great hams who took center stage. Was she, Mary, to be another prop-girl?

It had been clear to Mary ever since she could remember that she had a galactic destiny, and had to explode. She was the fierce fiery girl who had to break open the earth—she felt that she was going to burst like some great stellar explosion. Who was she, anyway? She was the girl with the solar energy. The girl who hung out with cultural crazies. She thought of the friends she had made in New York City—they were not the "nice" people her mother thought she was associating with. She hadn't even told good old Madame Solovieff of her friends, guys from the SDS, the extreme feminists who adopted her for their street demonstrations. Often, in the city, she had felt as if she were really a female Beowulf—she dreamed that she had a corona of rattlesnakes around her head and antlers around her breasts. That was it! She was a female warrior, a throwback to the Vulcans, the Amazons with their ancient strength. She was the girl with the nitrogen energy, she lived always in a seizure of energy—as if she were always about to explode.

Jerry understood her.

In many ways he wasn't like her, didn't have her energy or her guts or even her joy and innocence—he didn't have her dreams to blow up the world—he was not Promethean, wanting to scatter sparks of fire. When she told him that the Meyerband gang were hanging out in Vermont and that she wanted to interview them he said she should "take a holiday from radical acts." But he loved her. She knew this.

They both were now in their "earthworks" period. He saw Mary trying to come to grips with a transitory period of her life. She was in between the Mary she had once been and the Mary she would be. He knew he could not hold her down, away from the world for long. She was too restless, too kinetic, too vital. She had lived the life of a radical lion tamer, a snake charmer, a roaring street troubadour, she had lived in the way that music-hall artists live—by intuition, on the edge. "The only reality is the translating of one's life into rhythms," he said, and tried to teach her to really listen to the long-legged fly, to really see tiger lily and the changes of color in the autumn. Their days were filled with earth lessons. Morning, up early. Pumping water. Study.

Writing. Gardening. And running. It was a life where they both tried to learn increased self-control. She as a journalist, keeping diaries and learning the craft of writing. Jerry, who had never really seen the country, now was involved in the exhilaration of a life change. Here he could think. He could look at nature bursting its colors and understand the child's infectious wonder.

Jerry felt free. He was rid of investments, rid of the "job" of selling pictures. What had once given him a rush—the game of power—being in charge, what had made him gay and ebullient— the sale, the pitch, the soft-shoe of the salesman and then the run to the bank—all of this was gone. His new life took on new attire. Jeans. Sneakers. Old shirts. He saw his hands changing. From chopping wood and planting in the garden his hands had blisters. He grew a beard. He learned how to survive on very little. He learned to listen to himself growing, the way one listens to one's own pulse. All of his life he had wanted to be a writer— but he had never given himself the days he needed to learn his craft. Now he could write all morning, all afternoon, all evening. No phones. No phonies. He opened his senses. The smell of new warm milk, the smell of honey, the touch of the hairy caterpillar, the feel of the earth under bare feet, the chill of night and the moon, the first bean-shoot, the wasp cutting a morsel of rare meat with its scissorlike mandible—his senses were sharpened to these things and he felt as if he were living for the first time. He wasn't wishing. He was doing. Not dreaming of change. Living change.

And so it was that they started off on a run in the woods, Mary and Jerry, in the cold frosty morning that got warmer as the sun came up until they were both really hot. Running they decided to run without clothes and threw everything into a heap which they put near a tree to claim on the way back. There was no one around for miles and they could easily run without clothes. Civilized things seemed far behind as they ran naked, in a new rhythm; children running into the sun. Mary ran faster than Jerry, he tried to keep up with her. He realized that she was the solar woman, the strength, the crystallization of strength and youth and energy. He tried to keep up with her. She was leading him but it didn't matter. They ran together like Indians, through the grass and the fern and the woods. He felt as if he was running in a sphere, in global harmony. History was a compensation, politics was fact, but here it was possible to outrun everything he had ever known. He felt suddenly clarified. Green everywhere. Green turning yellow. Turning orange. Fall leaves. Running through the leaves, naked as children.

78.

When Ursule heard that Jerry had "gone off his rocker" she was deeply disturbed. She wanted to send him a telegram, but he was beyond the country of Telex or cable. He was somewhere in the woods, she heard. On a hunch she called Jerry, Jr., at Deerfield and he told her where Jerry was living. When she arrived in New York she immediately hired a limousine and mapped out the route. After spending a day at the vet's with her Labradors, she put on her version of a "country suit" and set off for the country. Ursule was setting off on a holy mission. She was Joan of Arc out to save the Dauphin. She wore her diamonds turned around on her fingers.

The ride wasn't comfortable.

Ursule never went into the country without keeping a limousine waiting. As she drove past Bennington, Vermont, and the old inns, the cheese stores, the barns, the country-bumpkin stores (created for tourists) she imagined that Jerry had been driven to all of this by that hysterical liberal madwoman. She would reach Jerry and bring him back to his senses.

Jerry sat on the front lawn, dreaming and reading while Mary was off in town buying a week's supply of vegetables, and saw something that seemed like a mirage. He did not believe what he saw and thought he was dreaming. But it was real. Ursule, in a yellow Lincoln Continental limousine driven by a black driver, pulled up in front of his home. She looked at him from behind the plate glass of the window the way a fish stares out of a tropical aquarium. She was horrified. She got out of the car. She made her entrance over the grass.

It was surreal.

"Darling, you've gone out of your mind!" she screamed, walking slowly over the stones to the hick who sat on the grass and looked at her with amazement. Blue skies. Green grass. A mad woman.

"Ursule," was all he could say.

As she walked toward him, her stockings caught in nettles. The chauffeur parked the limousine discreetly under an elm. Her low seductive voice could barely be heard as the wind swept over the trees, showering down leaves on her shoulders and in her hair. She was weirdly unsettling. She was playing Queen Lear. She was playing the mad Lady Macbeth. This scene was her great triumph.

"Watch out for the wasps," he said, finally.

"Jerry, this is *not you*. What happened to your paintings? You put a lifetime into collecting great art? And your son? And your life?"

"This is my life now. My son is grown-up. I plan to have him visit."

"But it's so isolated here. Uncivilized."

"Compared to Beverly Hills?"

"Who is there to talk to?"

"Mary's here."

"Where is she? I intend to smack her."

"She's buying vegetables in town. She'll be back."

"Why did you come?"

"I felt I needed to get free. To be clarified. To dream. To live out a secret life. And to write."

"This sounds like nonsense. Hallucinations."

She behaved now like a deposed monarch who had suddenly found her son and intended to put him back on the throne. He noticed her heavy makeup and her jewels. Her bosom was visible from the tweed suit. She was as seductive as always. But the country was obviously irritating to her.

"I have always depended on you, Jerry, to stand for something in life. Life is never easy. There is always a play within a play. But it is our joy, our responsibility, for the rest of humanity, to find meaning in our life. To find poetry. I don't want realism. I want magic! I try to give magic in the theatre, magic to my audiences, my students. I don't misrepresent life to them. I tell the truth of art. I tell what ought to be the truth. And if that's sinful let me be damned for it. Don't stay here, Jerry. Come back with me, darling."

"Stop playing Blanche duBois. Stop playing all those people. Ursule—I can't leave here now."

"There is more to life than grass and fields and caterpillars, darling. Dostoevski said it's just as hard to take up the pen as it is to take up the wheelbarrow."

"Oh, I'm tired of the bourgeois crap that's been laid on me. I'm tired of the myth of romance. The myth of success. I'm tired of looking for all the *power* only to find out that underneath all their masks everyone else is just as fed up with all the shit as I am."

Ursule sat down on the lawn next to him. She had her hand on her breast.

"Darling." She held out her hand to his face.

"I've loved you," he said simply.

"I've loved you too. I've seen you bloom like a great flower into the man that you are. I've loved being with you."

"It's the past."

"Leave this slut. Get out of here. It's ugly. It's uncivilized. Is that what your whole life has led to? A shack with an outhouse?

Come back with me. I'll live with you, Jerry darling. We will start all over again. I've just found a fabulous apartment at the River-house. That's my surprise. I'm moving back to New York, Jerry. I'm letting one of my assistants run the school in Los Angeles. We can live in the Riverhouse. I will start directing. You can write plays. We will work together."

The Labs started barking from the limousine.

"Ursule. This is the life I want now. Everything is always in the state of change. If I do leave I will certainly let you know. But right now I must stay."

"Come back with me, Jerry." She was coaxing him now, seductively. "Pretty please?" She began to pout.

Finally she got on her feet. Her hair blew in the wind. She took a deep breath. She towered over him.

"I remember things as they used to be. I remember the moon in the evening as we sat at the Gritti in Venice. It was a clear moon that was cold and slippery. We sat. Holding hands in the garden."

She provoked memories to excite him. They only made him feel lonely for Mary. Ursule could no longer seduce him. Realizing how futile her trip was, she rose and walked majestically across the grass. The car turned around slowly. Entering the car, she waved to him and then, almost like a young girl, put her hands up to her mouth and called to him out the window. "You know where to find meeeeee."

God, he was glad she left. Ursule didn't belong in Vermont.

Mary returned with a basket of ripe vegetables. She began slicing radishes, washing lettuce. Jerry helped her. They set the table for dinner. Then they sat out on the porch. Jerry dreaming on the porch. Mary painfully thinking of how hard it is to love someone.

"You want to leave, don't you?"

Mary thought, "No. Not exactly. It's Eden here. It's paradise. Butterflies. Sun. Leaves. Cold water and soap. Clean pieces of paper. I feel like the hermit of childhood stories. I've found the rainbow at the end of the pot or whatever it is. I think my true vocation is to explode. To be active. To burst into who I am. I've stripped myself down to be like the trees, a naked sponge. I have a different heartbeat from you. Sometimes when I hear mules braying as I walk down the rode on my hike into nowhere, I look at the mules and wish they could tell me the news. And then at midnight I look up at the stars and think the news is all in me. 'Be quiet, Mary,' I say to myself, calming myself down for sleep."

"There's beauty here, Jerry," she said. "I'll try and calm myself down and keep you company for a while. I know that I'll leave you one day. I can't say when. When I do, I hope it won't leave you feeling lost and lonely and make you sad."

"After the ulcerous rigor of my other lives, I can't anymore. I'm happy to stay put. I feel young and green and safe with myself here. Right now I'm home free."

"Me too," she said.

It was their only wedding.

79.

Mary was restless.

This was not the way "transformations" were supposed to happen.

"What did you think this was going to be? A Christmas pageant? Where the Virgin Mary and Joseph trek off to a barn in the woods?"

He didn't like it when Mary was a hard bitch. It reminded him too much of what he was frightened of. They were not ships that passed in the night. They were ships that were shipwrecked. They were ships that were bound to wreck each other. Sink each other.

It was evening. The fire was slapping away in the fireplace, making loud fire-flicking noises that sounded so much like the sea. He wondered how much fucking she could stand before she became bored. He loved her lying on the bed, her legs spread wide, the dark curls opened to him, her moisture in his mouth.

Then he loved her. But he could see that instead of falling on the plump pillows into sleep, while the firelight cast its shadow on the bare cabin walls, and the moon hung like a shiny white button in the window of the sky, Mary antagonized him by getting up, putting on her jeans, and writing notes for an organization that she belonged to in New York, an organization that she corresponded with religiously. She turned to him in the firelight.

"Do you know what the record shows so far about U.S. policy in Angola?"

"As you go through life, brother, no matter what your goal, keep your eye upon Angola and not upon the hole."

"What's that?" she asked, confused.

"The motto of the Mayflower Donut House."

"Seriously. Can you listen to me for one moment? Do you realize that the CIA started a secret war in Angola in 1975? That Congress was later told our aim was to counter communist intervention? However, John Stockwell, former chief of the CIA Angola Task Force, has recently revealed that our real purpose was to prevent a nationalist movement we didn't like from taking power. *We*, we *Americans*, initiated the war together with South Africa. How do you like that for asshole buddies? The CIA falsely accused the Soviet Union and Cuba of intervention in order to justify our involvement."

"Horseshit. What do you mean *falsely accused*? Didn't you see that cover of *Newsweek* that showed Cuban artillery and soldiers riding into Africa?"

"And didn't *you* see the tiny insert that said the cover photo was a mistake and it was actually a photograph of a military parade in Cuba?"

"Does everything have to be clandestine? Does everything have to be another Vietnam? Mary, what's bothering you?"

"I'm tired of being cooped up in this chicken coop. I'm not a chicken."

"Well. Now we're hearing a little honesty."

"I love you, Jerry. This has been relaxing and good meditative time for me. But when I go to town, and get the newspapers, and read about Rhodesia, Namibia, read about Bolivia, read about the Clamshell Coalition in New Hampshire—I want to get up and go where the action is."

"I understand. I didn't think I could keep you down on the farm forever. But I thought—hell, a few months would be good for you."

"I'm sorry, Jerry. You're right. I'll try harder to love the hay and the chickadees and you smoking a pipe. But my private opinion is that Thoreau was a neurotic who hid out because he didn't know what else to do with his life. It's great up here if you're a chipmunk. But even our making love doesn't keep me satisfied. Even Gandhi got tired of contemplating his navel."

"So go on a march like Gandhi."

"It's just that I'm thinking of sneaking away two days to go up to New Hampshire. They are marching against nuclear plants and I'd love to put on a knapsack and join them."

"Go ahead. Who am I to hold back nuclear nonproliferation?"

"Why don't you come with me?"

"Sorry. I don't have a nuclear personality."

"Would you really be miserable when and if I go? Because if you are, I'll just stay here and examine mushrooms. Or read."

He went over and kissed the nape of her neck. She was so lovely when she was cross. And it might be good for them to be away from each other for two or three days.

"I want you to go," he lied.

He was jealous of Africa. Jealous of fallout. Jealous of anything that took her away from him. But to show that jealousy meant to lose her.

"Go," he said.

"Thank you," she said to him in a soft voice. "I appreciate your understanding. I'll let them march without me. I'll stand it. I want to stay here with you. Sometimes I think having someone you love, actively, is just as political as marching. But why is love so hard?"

"I feel close to you, Mary."

"I feel close to you too, Jerry."

"I'm tired."

"I'm tired."

"Do you want to go running in the morning?"

"I do."

"Let's sleep."

Hugging her, he began to feel what a mistake Vermont had been. He could not admit this to Mary but he realized that he was beginning to hate the country and as the days grew damper and colder he wished he had gone to a tropical island instead of Vermont. He hated his pipe. His checkered lumber jacket itched his neck. He realized, with terror, that the country was boring. The blazing leaves were falling off the trees. Winter! He was due to spend a cold winter in the misery of his new life. He hadn't expected it to be so fucking *quiet*. He felt like Adam with Eve. He knew how much Adam must have longed for someone else besides Eve to talk with. He would have talked with a snake. He understood Eve. She didn't want an apple. She just wanted someone to talk to in Eden besides Adam. A cold sweat poured over him as he thought of an eternity in Vermont. Eden was hell.

As Mary slept he allowed his mind to go back over the things he missed. To begin with he missed having a home. A log cabin might have been fine for Abraham Lincoln as a boy, but Jerry Hess frankly missed the comfort of a shower. Oddly, he found that he missed not looking at paintings. He had been able to give up the paintings and put them in the warehouse, put some of them into Manhattan Storage, some in a bank vault. That was easy. But now he looked for them in his dreams. He missed Madison Avenue of Saturday afternoons. Not that he missed the bullshit of selling paintings. He could live without that forever. But could he live without the city? His mind went back to Paris. He thought of the boulevards, the Sixteenth Arrondisement. Greedily he let his mind create the rue de Lille slowly, the way a child creates a map, thrilled to be putting together the pieces. He thought of Rome. He had lived there for a year with Lillian before she had opened her own office. Jerry, Jr., had been ten. He had gone to the American School and he, Jerry, had enjoyed what it meant to be lost in Italy. The Italian music. The trattorias. The speeding out to Frigene in his Lancia. The sun on his back. The smell of garlic and wine. The vitality of the men in the cafés whom he sat and talked with. The mad drivers. The women whose tight dresses always excited him as they walked down the streets. The sound of the language. He missed the simple words of "*Ciao, bambino,*"; he missed "*Buon giorno*"—no one would ever say "*Buon giorno*" to him in Vermont. God, he missed Venice. He missed the Cipriani and Giudecca. The gondoliers. The smell of seaweed. The polished large marble floors of the palazzi that looked out on the sea. The palms. The palms that lined the marble floors. The dances. The film festival. The Biennale. He missed walking with Lillian through the corridors of paintings. What was Vermont doing to his mind? He now even missed Lillian. He remembered Lillian dressing the baby in his overalls, he remembered carrying the crib, the portable crib, into a restaurant in New York. Why were memories so painful? How could he forget that they fought like boxers? Now that he was apart from Lillian, the ghost of the Lillian he had loved came floating over the green fields of Vermont to haunt him. He tried to put these thoughts out of his mind.

During the day, as he scribbled in his notebook he tried to make sense out of what he was feeling. He realized that he had depended on women and not on himself. What remained now was to find out if he could live alone. Could he have the guts to live without them? He watched as the leaves fell from the trees. He would have given anything to see the leaves of the yellow pages of a Manhattan phone book. First he abandoned Lillian. Then he abandoned Ursule. Now he was ready to abandon Mary. What did he want at the end of all this abandonment? What did it matter? As long as he got the hell out of Vermont. He remembered as a child he had fallen in love with a brochure about a boys' camp. He had begged and cried until his parents sent him to the camp. When he arrived there, he hated it. The food. The bunks. It had said in the brochure "square dancing with girls" and there was no square dancing with girls. He had been conned. He hadn't learned what every child had learned—that things are not what the brochures say they are. Was it memory that conned him? The memory of Vermont? He realized, sadly, that he had made a decision to change his life. But the real change had taken place inside of him and had nothing to do with geography. The real change was that he was free of being a peddler. The real change was that he no longer had to act out being a husband. Or a father. That he was greatly relieved of his burdens.

The next morning he went into town. He bought the papers and read, greedily as a starved person, about what was happening in New York. He read the art section, the theatre section. God, he missed movies! He saw what co-op apartments were selling for. The real estate page even smelled good. The book section took his breath away. He read the *Times* from cover to cover. Mary was smart. He knew if she saw him devouring the *Times* the way a buzzard devours a body she would be on to him. He decided to buy a copy of the *Farmer's Almanac*.

In town he had a beer.
In the saloon he was hoping to find country people whom he could talk to. Instead there were teenagers with acne about his son's age playing the jukebox. And truck drivers who were privately encased in their own jargon. He felt like someone's ill-bred uncle. He didn't fool those dudes about being a Vermonter, for God's sake. He had on the right canvas boots, the faded denims, the heavy shirt and pipe of a city slicker. He looked as if he had been dressed for a commercial by Abercrombie & Fitch. Down to his Hoffritz pocket knife he was wrong. It wasn't that he looked wrong. He felt wrong. He had overdone it. Something had gone wrong in his mind. He had responded to it. But he had gone too far. It wasn't the "geography" of Vermont he wanted. It was the sense of saying to the world, "Look. I've changed." On a

whim he went over to the phone booth. Feeling like a covert spy, a sneak, a stoolie, he telephoned Lillian. He heard the phone ringing at the Dakota. He actually heard the phone ringing on beloved Central Park West. Lillian answered. It was just about the time she would be getting ready to go to the office. He could see her standing there in her pink Hanae Mori dress. Oh, dear Lillian. Why have I wronged you? Why was I such a monster to you? Why did I insult your Danish sense of fairness and ask you for more than you were able to stand? What was so awful about the face cream you wore in the morning? What was so bad about feeling *comfortable*, eating sardines with you in the kitchen and drinking black beer? What was so bad about sitting with you in the living room, reading *the news*?

"Yes?"

"It's me."

"Jerry?"

"Don't you know my voice by now?"

"I didn't expect you to call. Of all people."

"How's our son?"

"He's fine."

"I'm calling to make sure that you're all right."

"I'm fine. The divorce was difficult and humiliating. But I've gotten over it. I feel free and have adjusted to a single life much sooner than I thought."

"I'm sorry for what I've done to you. That's the real reason I'm calling. And also, as I think over things, I realize that you were very good to me and gave me a great deal for nearly twenty years. The last few years weren't good, but it was probably just as much my fault as it was yours. In fact, it was my fault."

"Let's not open old cases. I haven't committed hara-kiri. Our son is fine. And you love Vermont. Maple sugar and all."

"Stop being sarcastic. I hate Vermont."

"That doesn't surprise me."

"Why not?"

"You were never a country boy, Jerry. Your idea of the country was a shooting box in Scotland, a private box at Deauville, a tennis court on Long Island. I don't see you mixing with ants and hicks."

"I'm planning to move back to New York," he said, for once amazed at his own decisions.

"Do you want me to help you find an apartment?"

"Could you? Oh, no. I couldn't impose that on you."

"Since when are you afraid of imposing on me?" She laughed.

It was marvelous to hear Lillian laugh. The only time Mary laughed was when an airline terminal blew up in Japan or another capitalist was kidnapped and his ear shipped home to Milano.

"Can we have lunch together when I return?"

"Of course."

"It's good of you to be such a friend, Lillian."

"It's hard to be mean to Santa Claus. I'm living in the lap of luxury that you wanted. As a matter of fact I've put the apartment on the market. Now is a good time to sell. And a bad time to buy. I'm thinking of renting a small apartment near NYU, where I'm going to be teaching. I thought it would be nice to live in the Village."

"Remember when we had lunch at the Jumble Shop?"

"How could I forget?"

"Lillian . . ."

"What?"

"Oh, never mind."

"All right. This phone call is costing a lot of money. See you soon, Jerry."

She hung up.

He was holding the phone in his hand. It was hard and plastic and filled with wires that ran into some unknown valley until it reached where he used to live by digital imperatives. But it had brought him into another decision. He was leaving Vermont. He was leaving Vermont! He ordered a double Dewars on the rocks. They didn't have a twist of lemon. It didn't matter. His days of baking bread were almost over.

When he entered the doorway he saw Mary. "What's wrong?" she asked, looking at his leg.

"Can't you see my leg is swelling up and swollen? I'm not standing on one leg because I like to hop."

"Oh, my God. What happened to you?"

"I was running home. As I ran I tripped over a rock. I think I've broken my foot and also my leg."

"Your metatarsal is swelling up. I better just sit you down here and I'll get a doctor."

"Where?"

"There must be a doctor somewhere around here. I'm sure I can find help. Just relax."

He leaned on her until she got him to a chair. She fixed him up with some bourbon, lifted his leg so that it was raised and didn't hurt so much. Then she went out on a search for a doctor. A few hours later she returned with an ancient-looking man in an old beat-up suit. He carried a beat-up black leather bag. He introduced himself as Doctor Hanks. "Bone injury you have there, boy," after a brief examination he declared. (To Doctor Hanks everyone was a boy.)

"Do you think it's serious?"

Doctor Hanks: "Anklebone's broken. Needs fixing up."

Jerry: "What happens now?"

Doctor: "It's not serious. Needs a small cast. You'll have to drive into town with me, boy."

Jerry sat with his foot in a cast.

"I remember an opera I once saw with Lillian in Cologne. It was written by Nicholas Nabokov, the composer and cousin of the novelist. It was a modern opera where a man sang with his foot in a cast. A great opera. The only thing is—how the hell can someone sing with his leg in a cast?"

"You don't have to be depressed just because your foot is broken."

"I'm not depressed."

"You are."

321

"Look, Mary, I know when I'm depressed and when I'm not."

"Jerry, we are not the Hansel and Gretel at the end of the wood that we thought we would be. What am I doing wrong?"

"Darling Mary. You're not doing anything wrong. I've been writing you so many long love letters in my mind. But they all end with good-bye."

"Good-bye?"

"I think finally now I want to be alone."

"Is it time to split?"

"I think so," Jerry said. He was sorry he had said that. The one thing he knew he did not want to be was cruel to Mary. "You have been my muse."

"But a muse isn't a wife."

"I don't know what a muse is, to tell you the truth. I just know that you have a long way to go in your path toward what you want, and I just don't see myself following in your footsteps. Or you following in mine."

Mary made it easy for him. She packed her clothes in a big wicker basket and didn't cry or even seem surprised. "I'll see you later," she said.

"Where are you off to?" How sudden it all was.

"Life," she said in a cheerful voice.

"Thank you for not paying me back with meanness."

"Why should I be mean? I know that everything ends. And begins again. It's not as if you're leaving my life forever. We both need space. I'm really not as sad as I thought I'd be."

"That's because you're young."

She bent over to kiss him. "I'll be thinking of you. And I'll call you. Where will you be?"

"Probably at the Stanhope as soon as I'm able to drive."

"I'm taking the bus."

"Where to?"

"Probably to New Hampshire for a while. Then back to California. Then I don't know."

When she left he felt a terrible emptiness. As if a bubble had broken inside of him.

80.

Before it snowed, Jerry left Vermont.

All he could think of on the drive back to New York was how happy he was to be leaving nature. It had been a contest of nerves. Vermont had won. Well, he had learned something. As he drove the car toward the city he thought of how nice it would be to have a massage. To go to a barber and have a really good shave and then the luxury of a face massage.

When he arrived at the Stanhope he checked in. It didn't matter that they only had a small room. He went up to his room, whistling for the sheer joy of being in New York. Then he hung up his clothes. Then went to the front desk. He told the manager of the hotel to take all messages. (He had told Jerry, Jr., and Lillian and his parents that he was arriving.)

"I'm going to be at the barbershop on Eighty-third and York Avenue," he said to the manager. "I'll be back later this evening."

For Jerry Hess, the barbershop was one of the great offerings of civilized existence. It was an escape, and the place where he could be made to feel whole. Tired, he entered the barbershop and was happy to see the barber who had taken care of him for so many years. He loved the oils. The table he lay on. The steam. It was the one place in the world he could just disappear. No one to disturb him. He could relax. Pull his life together. As the barber covered him with towels he could relax under the steam and totally undergo the process of total relaxation. Under the towels he could think. What would be his next move? Teaching? That made sense. He certainly didn't want to go back to selling art. Writing? He couldn't do that all the time. Then he heard the phone ring. It jangled his nerves. "Mr. Hess?" he heard the barber say. Goddamn it, he knew who it was. Ursule had wangled where he was out of the clerk. First she found out from Jerry, Jr., when he was coming to New York. Then she had probably called the desk clerk and been put through to the manager. "But this is a very important call, darling. This is an emergency," he could hear her saying to the manager. "Of course he wants me to call him. He's *waiting* for this call." Ursule always had an emergency. Under the towels he groaned. Was there no escape? He reached out his arm under the towels to take the phone.

"Jerry, I've got to talk to you. It's an *emergency*." (It was *always* an emergency.)

"What is it?" (He said this cheerfully. He was damned if he would let her know she was ruining his tranquillity.)

"When are you coming to see me?"

"Very soon," he lied. "I'll call you later."

Back to the blessed towel. He would never let her seduce him again. A man under a hot towel, thinking, is a powerful force in the universe. He made a list of things he would do. He would rent a small apartment. He would jog around Central Park every morning. He would court Lillian. What would Lillian be like now? And why the hell wasn't she home? He would take Jerry, Jr., skiing this winter. He would buy an apron and take up cooking. He would tell everyone the good things about them. He would appreciate his life. His new good life.

81.

But it was not so easy. Later that evening he learned that Lillian did not want to be courted.

"For God's sake, Lillian, I decided under a towel I wanted to go back to you. I love you. And I think we can both have a different kind of marriage if we compromise."

"Marriage is out of the question."

"All right. Then let's see each other."

"I do need you, Jerry. And I've missed you. But we can't turn our backs on our own history."

"All right. Let's remember our history."

"Shall we play Ulysses and Penelope? I knew you would come back if I waited long enough."

"Let's not speak. Let's just sit like raccoons. Or better yet, let me just ask for pardon."

The following morning he resumed his jogging. As he ran, Jerry thought how tired he was of being manipulated under the guise of love. Was it love? Or a power play that he had to run away from to save his life? Wasn't that what women were teaching men? Hadn't he finally woken up to the only lesson of the twentieth century concerning relationships: *Don't be afraid*? And as he ran, he thought: of a cartoon which had stayed in his brain like a warning from a mystical world, the world of symbolic dreams where he often lived, the world of shrikes. The cartoon was of two dogs. One dog said to the other, "Who do you love most in the world?" The other dog replied, "My master."

"But he cut off your balls."

"That's what people do with people!" Jerry thought. He was tired of the slave/master syndrome. He was responsible for his own balls now.

END

Printed in the USA
CPSIA information can be obtained
at www.ICGtesting.com
JSHW022208140824
68134JS00018B/925